Jak's hand was red and swollen

The slash was dark, puffy and angry looking. It had stopped bleeding, but now it oozed a clear fluid. Mildred sniffed, then wrinkled her nose.

"Sweet-sour stink. Either those little bastards have some kind of venom in them, or their feces are more virulent than I first thought."

J.B. squatted over one of the corpses, probing it with the tip of his flensing knife. "Fangs seem solid, not like a rattler's, if that helps. I don't see any poison sac in its mouth or throat, either."

"Thanks, John. Whatever the cause, I have to radically revise my prognosis."

"What do you mean?" Krysty asked.

Mildred glanced up. "Judging by how fast it's progressing, instead of a day or two, Jak might have six to eight hours—if he's lucky."

**Other titles in the
Deathlands saga:**

JAMES AXLER

DEATH LANDS®

Downrigger Drift

A GOLD EAGLE BOOK FROM
W🌐RLDWIDE®

TORONTO • NEW YORK • LONDON
AMSTERDAM • PARIS • SYDNEY • HAMBURG
STOCKHOLM • ATHENS • TOKYO • MILAN
MADRID • WARSAW • BUDAPEST • AUCKLAND

Recycling programs
for this product may
not exist in your area.

First edition January 2011

ISBN-13: 978-0-373-62606-9

DOWNRIGGER DRIFT

Printed in U.S.A.

Nothing could be worse than the fear that one has given up too soon, and left one unexpended effort which might have saved the world.
—Jane Addams
(1860–1935)

THE DEATHLANDS SAGA

This world is their legacy, a world born in the violent nuclear spasm of 2001 that was the bitter outcome of a struggle for global dominance.

There is no real escape from this shockscape where life always hangs in the balance, vulnerable to newly demonic nature, barbarism, lawlessness.

But they are the warrior survivalists, and they endure—in the way of the lion, the hawk and the tiger, true to nature's heart despite its ruination.

Ryan Cawdor: The privileged son of an East Coast baron. Acquainted with betrayal from a tender age, he is a master of the hard realities.

Krysty Wroth: Harmony ville's own Titian-haired beauty, a woman with the strength of tempered steel. Her premonitions and Gaia powers have been fostered by her Mother Sonja.

J. B. Dix, the Armorer: Weapons master and Ryan's close ally, he, too, honed his skills traversing the Deathlands with the legendary Trader.

Doctor Theophilus Tanner: Torn from his family and a gentler life in 1896, Doc has been thrown into a future he couldn't have imagined.

Dr. Mildred Wyeth: Her father was killed by the Ku Klux Klan, but her fate is not much lighter. Restored from predark cryogenic suspension, she brings twentieth-century healing skills to a nightmare.

Jak Lauren: A true child of the wastelands, reared on adversity, loss and danger, the albino teenager is a fierce fighter and loyal friend.

Dean Cawdor: Ryan's young son by Sharona accepts the only world he knows, and yet he is the seedling bearing the promise of tomorrow.

In a world where all was lost, they are humanity's last hope....

Chapter One

Ryan Cawdor clawed his way up from black uncon-
sciousness one slow second at a time. His single blue
eye fluttered, then opened to take in the familiar-yet-
different ceiling of yet another mat-trans unit, his arms
and legs sprawled out around him. Wisps of the ever-
present white mist that accompanied the matter transfer function swirled around his face, dissipating into
nothingness as his wits returned.

As jumps went, this one hadn't been as bad as
many—at least, not for him. The dark nightmares that
could accompany each body-wrenching trip had been
faint for once. Ryan dimly recalled a journey through a
forest, and a strange sensation that he couldn't place for
a moment, recognizing it as peace and quiet only after
a bit of pondering. That feeling vanished as quickly as
it had come when he raised his head, only to lower it
again as a pounding wave of nausea crashed through
his skull. It was the one usual reaction to a jump. This
time it felt like someone had stuck a stiletto into his ear
and given his brains a good stirring.

"Mebbe not *that* used to it." His tongue was dry and
thick in his mouth, and an attempt to hawk up saliva left
him coughing hot, fetid air. "Fireblasted whitecoats." He
was never sure what was worse, relying on the unknown
technology of the mat-trans to instantly transport him
and his companions to an undetermined location in the

blink of an eye, or wondering each time he entered one of the smooth-walled chambers if this was the time it would malfunction and scatter their molecules across the entire universe.

Slowly drawing in his arms, Ryan's right hand spidered to his waist, where he felt the comforting grip of his holstered SIG-Sauer P-226 blaster under his fingers. Glancing left, he spotted the long outline of his Steyr SSG-70 sniper rifle on the floor next to him. Without rising, he reached for the weapon's smooth walnut stock with his other hand, drawing it close.

The queasiness in his head abating, Ryan risked lifting his head again. The armaglass walls of the gateway chamber were a color he hadn't seen before, and slumped around the chamber were his five traveling companions, all in various states of consciousness.

The first person his eyes fell on stared owlishly back at him through a pair of wire-framed glasses as he sat on the floor with his legs straight out in front of him. Wiry and short, with close-cropped hair and an intense gaze, J. B. Dix knew more about weapons, vehicles and munitions than anyone else living in Deathlands. Whether it was five different ways of taking out a mutie from a hundred yards away or setting a booby trap to ambush a convoy, the man known as the Armorer could handle either task with ease.

Adjusting the battered fedora that only left his head when he was asleep, the sallow man's left eye dropped in what might have been a wink. "Gettin' old."

Ryan pushed himself up on his elbows, the rifle still in his hand. He wasn't sure if the other man was referring to the situation or his general condition, but at the moment, he gave the only answer that made sense. "Yeah."

The next person he saw was a woman, stretched out on the floor as if she might have been napping, her hair a luxuriant blaze of red that cascaded across her neck and shoulders. Apparently the jump had gone well for her, too, for instead of curling tightly around her neck, her semi-sentient tresses flowed loose, framing a face with high cheekbones, full lips, and eyes, currently closed, that were a brilliant emerald.

Ryan had had his share of lovers over the years, but none of them held a candle to Krysty Wroth. Beautiful, intelligent and lethal, she was his partner in every way imaginable.

He would chill for her.

He would die for her.

In the Deathlands, it was as simple as that.

Her long lashes opened, and she grinned at him, looking like a cat that had gotten the best of the cream. "Hello, lover. Nice sight to wake up to."

"You're not so bad yourself. How do you feel?"

"All right. This one wasn't too bad, thank Gaia."

"Yeah, 'bout time one of these damn things worked without trying to turn us inside out."

A loud snort from next to her made both Krysty and Ryan glance over, each tensing to burst into action if necessary. But the man who'd made the noise simply smacked his lips, moaned softly and rolled over again, revealing a lined face surrounded by limp, gray-white hair. A small trickle of blood leaked from his patrician nose to drip on the floor as he snored, the bass sound rumbling off the walls.

Ryan rubbed his stubbled chin as he contemplated the enigma wrapped in a riddle wrapped in a mystery that was Theophilus Algernon Tanner. A man born out of time, he was a unique specimen, as he had lived in the far-off past of the nineteenth century, way before skydark, when he had been time-trawled into the twentieth century, and then dumped into Deathlands without so much as a by-your-leave. The mental and physical strain of repeated jumps had left Doc's mind more than unbalanced. On a good day, he could be a fount of information about history and times past. On a bad day, he rambled about things that made no sense to anyone, had imaginary conversations with people long dead, and acted a senile old fool.

J.B. had cautiously risen to his feet, stretching the kinks out of his back. "Doc awake?"

"Not yet. Give him a minute. Looks like it went hard for him."

Blinking a few times, J.B. scanned the rest of the group with a glance. "Looks like Jak soiled himself."

"Shut the fuck up, J.B." The fifth member of their group pushed himself into a sitting position, his ruby-red eyes glittering from underneath a mane of frost-white hair hanging to his shoulders. He swept vomit from his chin with the back of a pale hand and spit on the floor. "Feel fine."

J.B. smiled. "Equal parts piss and vinegar, as usual."

Jak Lauren's only response was a raised middle finger, drawing chuckles from both men. An albino from the deep swamps of what had once been the state of Louisiana a century earlier, the teenager had been with the group through many of their adventures across the Deathlands. At one point he'd settled down with a wife and child in the Southwest, but when they had been killed, he'd rejoined the group. Though shorter than J.B. and skinnier than Doc, Jak was one of the best hand-to-hand knife chillers Ryan had ever known.

Carefully wiping a drying crust of puke from his

jacket, Jak checked to make sure his .357 Magnum Colt Python was secure on his belt, and also the placement of his several leaf-bladed throwing knives hidden about his person.

"Oh, my aching brain. Sweet Jesus, will these damned jumps ever get any better?" The last member of their group was also stirring, raising brown hands to her forehead and holding it as she curled into a tight, sitting ball.

Ryan and J.B. exchanged glances, and the Armorer walked over, kneeling by her side.

"You okay, Mildred?"

"Yeah, yeah. It's nothing I haven't been through too many times before." Mildred Wyeth raised her head, looking at the rest of them through squinted eyes. "Headache's going away. Just give me a moment. Someday we gotta find a redoubt with a pharmacy that hasn't been picked clean. What I wouldn't give for an industrial-strength aspirin right now."

"Settle for ammo—gettin' lower than I like," was J.B.'s matter-of-fact reply.

She looked at him with a rueful smile. "That is one of the differences between you and me, John. I just want to cure what ails me, and you're intent on keeping yourself well-armed."

"Both keep you from harm, don't they?"

Mildred's expression suddenly turned to a grimace of pain. "That they do, when you can find either."

"Best way to do that is to start lookin' now, isn't it?" Ryan's gaze flicked to the door that would lead them to the rest of the complex. The redoubts scattered throughout what was left of America and the rest of the world could hold great and terrible treasures. Often containing weapons, vehicles and equipment, some also contained darker things, like the time-trawling equipment that had brought Doc to the future—or the cryogenic equipment that had held Mildred in perfect hibernation until she had been awoken by Ryan and his crew. A skilled physician, she knew much about the cryo-chambers, having worked on their development before being put in one herself, and was also the best pistol shot in the group, even surpassing Ryan and J.B. She had even won a medal in the last ever Olympics, back when it was considered a hobby, not a way of life.

Ryan rolled to his feet in a single smooth motion and extended a hand to Krysty. "We better rouse Doc. It's time we find out where we are."

"Never fear, my dear Ryan, I am fully awakened, cognizant of my surroundings, and more or less in full command of my mental and physical faculties, such as they are."

With the help of his lion's-head ebony swordstick, Doc rose to his feet, knees popping with the effort, and dusted off his ancient frock coat before favoring them all with a broad smile. "Let us sally forth and investigate whatever new labyrinth we find ourselves inhabiting this day."

"Awake sure. Mouth already runnin'." Jak shook his head, then glanced at the walls. "Color different."

The walls of the mat-trans chambers were a bewildering variety of colors that seemed to have no rhyme or reason to them, from black to silver and every shade in between.

"Triple red, people. Let's see what we can see." A broad variety of weapons appeared in everyone's hands. J.B. readied his ever-present mini-Uzi, flicking off the safety with his thumb. He had taken up a position to one side, ready to catch anyone—or anything—outside in a lethal cross fire.

Although the self-sustaining redoubts had been built in secret and carefully hidden from the world more than a century earlier, the companions knew all too well that time had a way of revealing the concealed. The walls were sometimes breached. Until they knew for sure, the only way to go was slow, steady and ready to shoot anything that moved outside.

"Everyone set?" Ryan kept his blaster up and ready as he reached for the lever that would open the gateway door.

Chapter Two

The door hissed open, and Ryan immediately felt a breath of warm air waft over him. Blaster leading the way, he edged out past the left side of the mat-trans wall and into the anteroom, scanning for the slightest hint of movement. On reflex he checked the small rad counter clipped to the lapel of his jacket, but it edged up into the green.

"Seems clean—no leaks. Not much else either."

The control room was empty, filled with blinking banks of comp consoles with plain chairs in front of them. The walls were dull gray, and as bare as stone.

J.B. was already moving to the right, the muzzle of his submachine gun tracking in a forty-five-degree arc in front of him, ready to spray chattering death in an instant. He reached the sliding door that would take them farther into the redoubt. "Green clear." He wiped at his forehead. "Warm."

Krysty and Jak came in next, still carrying their side-arms. Mildred and Doc brought up the rear, all looking for any sign of where they might have ended up this time.

Doc's gaze wandered around the barren room. "Besides what hope the flight of future days may bring, what chance, what change worth waiting—"

"Shut it, Doc."

"My apologies, dear friend, it was my hope that a bit

of doggerel might enhance the otherwise drab quarters
we currently find ourselves in."

"That was John Milton, wasn't it, Doc?" Mildred
looked wistful for a moment. "*Paradise Lost* indeed."

"Let the future take care of itself and let's all con-
centrate mighty hard on the here and now." Frowning,
Ryan crossed the room to the door, blaster held down
at his side.

"If anything happened here, it was long ago and far
away," J.B. opined. "Let's get the hell out."

"Hopefully the rest of the place is as well-preserved,"
Krysty said, opening one of the small drawers next to a
station, only to find it empty. "Been dreaming of a hot
shower lately."

Mildred nodded. "You and me both, sister."

"Best not be running your bath water just yet, ladies.
J.B., on me." Ryan waited for his friend to reach the
other side of the steel door before punching numbers
on the keypad, and readied himself again as it cycled
open.

"Phew!"

"Stink dead dog shit!" Jak commented.

"What sort of odorous miasma is assaulting us,
friends?"

Ryan thought Doc's question was the winner. The
corridor beyond was filled with a stench that nearly
made him gag—a heavy, clammy, stomach-churning
reek so overpowering it was almost tangible, pouring
into his nose and mouth to settle into his lungs as if it
would never leave.

J.B.'s nose twitched once as he took in the sight ahead
of them. "Black dust, what the hell is that?" Fluorescent
lights had flickered on down the hallway when the door
opened, revealing what had once been a plain, concrete-

walled, tiled corridor. Now, however, the floor and walls were caked with several inches of a green-black, viscous substance, piled in clumps in the corners, and stretching as far as the eye could see. Overhead, a triple row of olive-drab pipes ran down the tunnel before snaking off deeper into the complex walls.

"Krysty, do you sense anything?"

The flame-haired woman came up behind him, swallowing hard. She frowned as she tried to fathom what might have made this hallway a communal toilet. "Nothing really dangerous—some kind of rats crapping down here for a few years—mostly just disgusting."

Ryan resisted the powerful urge to cover his nose as he edged into the filthy hallway. "Right in one."

J.B. stepped into the corridor, his booted feet breaking through the top crust and squishing into the muck. "Got something here, Ryan. Cover me."

Fighting the urge to vomit, Ryan watched for movement as the Armorer scraped crusted gunk off the wall. Meanwhile, Doc and Mildred looked on in horrified fascination.

"Upon my soul, I would swear that I have breathed in this very stench before. Indeed, it is almost familiar, which is not something I admit to lightly, my friends."

Jak's assessment was more succinct. "Stinks! Go back?"

"Let's see what J.B.'s found first." Ryan saw absolutely no signs of life in the tunnel, but if there wasn't, what had made this incredible mess?

"Got a map of the floor here. We're under a place once called Fort McCoy. Military base, looks like. Could be weapons, ammo topside."

"And quarters, maybe even with running water." Mildred's voice lilted with faint hope.

"Mebbe something better than jerky," Jak chimed in.

J.B. peered closely at the map. "According to this, the elevator's at the far end. Other levels look promising."

Ryan looked at the expectant faces around him. "Sure as hellfire anything's better than this. All right, let's try for the elevator. Wrap your nose and mouth if you can, and don't fall, because I'm not giving you a hand up." Gritting his teeth, he stepped into the ankle-deep waste.

Krysty sighed as her blue Western-tooled cowboy boots with the chiseled silver falcons on the sides disappeared into the dark muck. "Better be a shower, or at least a hose to wash down with."

"One thing I am always assured of is that you people take me to the most elegant of places." Doc stabbed his swordstick into the feces, but was stopped by Mildred.

The black woman offered Doc her arm. "Shall we?"

"It would be my pleasure to escort you across this sea of excrement, my dear." Mildred kept a tight grip on Doc's arm and caught Ryan's approving nod with a slight one of her own. While he had moments of grace, Doc also wasn't the spryest of men, and the extra support would keep him upright on the slippery floor.

Behind them, Jak prodded the odd couple. "Move. Nose 'bout fall off."

Looking for all the world like two best friends out for an evening stroll, the two advanced into the putrid sludge, breaking through the crust and releasing pungent bursts of stink with every step.

J.B. had explored the wall next to the map and found the door's number pad. "Think I'll close the door. Don't need shit dirtying up the place."

Mildred sneezed and threw her arm up over her mouth and nose. "I don't know if I can take much more of this."

"Just keep moving and try not to think about it." Ryan swallowed hard and did his best to follow his own advice. It was harder than it appeared, for each time his boot sank into the waste, it picked up a bit more gunk, until it felt like his feet were encased in twenty pounds of shit. They still had twenty yards to go, and Ryan was laboring for each step.

"Hold up. Gotta clean some of this off. Everyone else should do the same."

"Ryan," Krysty said quietly, "we've got company."

Flicking off a handful of sticky crap off his fingers, Ryan wiped them off as best as he could on the wall, and looked around, not seeing anything. "Where from?"

"Around. Hard to say. Mebbe in the walls. Lots of movement, though."

"Don't like that. All right, people, let's keep moving." Ryan continued slogging forward, trudging through the sludge. The elevator doors beckoned, now only a few yards away.

"Ryan!" Mildred's voice was controlled but tight. "Movement behind us!"

He whirled, seeing Jak already turned to the rear. "J.B., get up there and get those doors open. What have you got, Jak?"

"Dunno. Ugly fuckers, though." The teen's .357 Magnum blaster was out and tracking something, but there were too many people between for Ryan to see.

Putting his hand on Krysty's shoulder, Ryan pressed her forward. "Make sure Doc and Mildred get to the doors."

"Dozen, mebbe more," Jak called out. "Shoot?"

"Careful Ryan," Mildred said as he passed. "Gunfire in an enclosed space like this will damage our eardrums. We could go deaf from the sound waves."

Ryan held up his SIG-Sauer blaster with its built-in silencer. Sometimes it worked, sometimes it didn't. "Got just the thing for that." At the teen's shoulder now, he got his first look at the creatures inhabiting this part of the complex.

Jak's succinct description of the mutie animals—a hideous crossbreed of pig and rat—didn't even begin to do them justice. About eighteen inches long, each had a low-slung body covered in wet, dung-slicked fur. Their front legs ended in sharp claws, but as they moved, Ryan saw their back legs were porcine, right down to a pair of pointed hooves. Their faces combined the ugliest features of both species, with large, black eyes over a flat, porcine nose and a mouth filled with sharp, gnawing teeth, capped by a double pair of up-thrusting tusks about two inches long. The noise they made as they appeared out of the muck was a cross between squeal and a snort, a high-pitched sound that grated on Ryan's ears. The small pack seemed more curious than anything, although he didn't like how close a few were getting.

Jak had a throwing blade raised in one hand, his Magnum blaster in the other. "Take out?"

"Let me." Ryan braced his SIG-Sauer in his hand and squeezed off two shots, the silencer reducing the shots to a muffled cough. The 9 mm bullets tore into the nearest mutie and sent it writhing into the slime, its scream of agony cut off by the second round.

Although the two pig-rats nearest to the body immediately tore into the carcass of their former brethren, the rest of the muties did something unexpected.

As one, all eight or nine of them fell silent, sat up

on their hind legs and stared at Ryan with unblinking black eyes. They were joined by a half-dozen more, all of whom watched the interlopers with the same inscrutable expression. Feeling a prickle of unease between his shoulder blades, Ryan tried to keep his eye on all of them at once, an impossible task, he soon learned.

"Ryan—" the albino began.

"Yeah, time to go." Keeping his pistol trained on the growing mob, Ryan took a careful step backward, then another. "Take one out, blade only."

Jak's hand flicked and it was as if one of the larger muties suddenly sprouted a steel horn from its side, the blade carving deep into its vitals. Again, a pair of its fellows set upon the wounded monster, but the rest, now at least two dozen strong, all kept their eyes on the two humans. As if receiving some kind of silent signal, they all tensed at the exact same time.

The pig-rat at the head of the pack threw its head back and squealed, a bone-chilling sound that reverberated through the corridor. A moment after, the rest of the colony followed suit, the resulting noise so loud Ryan could barely think.

He and Jak had the exact same thought at the exact same second: "Run!"

Turning, they tore through the muck in great leaps, only a step or two ahead of the flowing mutie tide swarming after them. Jak ran so fast he appeared to be skimming the top of the crust, his feet touching so lightly he didn't break through. Ryan, on the other hand, didn't have that luxury, and had to power his way through the shit with each step. He knew one slip meant certain death, as the horde would be upon him before he could rise. The furious chitter-squealing of the pig-rats thundered in his ears, drowning out the shouts of encouragement from the rest of the group, who had reached the safe haven of the elevator. Seeing Krysty's face taut with fear as she held her hand out to him spurred Ryan to even greater speed.

Jak had pulled ahead and slipped through the doors with ease. Ryan was a couple of yards behind, and right after to him were the muties, so close he thought he could feel their grotesque fangs snapping at his heels. Four yards to go…three…two…

With a final great bound, Ryan soared through the air and into the small room. "Close the bastard door!"

J.B. was already slapping at the button, and the doors began to slide shut. But before they could seal completely, the vanguard of the swarm was upon them.

Chapter Three

"Holy shit!"

"Watch the blasters! Ricochets will chill one of us!"

"Kill the fucks!"

The small room exploded into furious action as the six friends saw what was coming at them.

Ryan hit the back wall with his forearms up and whirled to find a half dozen of the creatures streaking through the gap before the door closed. Doc was already on the offensive, his gleaming rapier drawn from its cane scabbard as he moved to protect Mildred, who had no melee weapon. He immediately drew first blood, skewering one of the beasts as it lunged at him, its fanged mouth gaping and ready to rend his flesh. The long blade pierced its throat and sank deep into its vitals. Even as the mutie died, its paws and legs scrabbled for purchase, still trying to reach the old man.

"Riposte and finis, you hideous fiend," Doc calmly said as the pig-rat stopped struggling. Pushing aside the carcass with the toe of his boot, he moved to help the others.

Another of the beasts was also down and dying, one of Jak's knives protruding from its eye. Krysty had met the charge when Ryan had sailed by, lashing out with a booted foot and punting one of the swine back into the corridor, where it was lost in a brown-furred sea of gnashing fangs.

J.B. had drawn his flensing knife, held point-down, ready to slash or stab, weaving a deadly pattern of steel in the air as he faced off with one. Instead of rushing in, it crouched low to the ground, needle-sharp tusks glistened in the white light as it sidled around, looking for the opportunity to strike.

The Armorer bided his time, feinted left, and when the mutie fell for it, lashed out with his foot, slamming the toe into the beast's ribs, and sending it crashing into the wall with a dull thud. Even as the repulsive creature regained its feet, J.B. planted his blade in the top of its skull, the point razoring through to pierce its jaw, bursting through skin and muscle. The pig-rat squealed once, horribly, as it died.

Whether it was because of his bone-white hair or his already having chilled two of the muties, Jak had attracted a pair of the creatures, squaring off against them with a blade in each hand. They both leaped for him at once, one low, one high, teeth bared to carve into the albino's flesh.

Jak met their attack head-on, blades blurring as he defended himself. The high one he took out with a slash across the throat, dark red blood spattering as the flying corpse crashed into the wall. The low one he also stabbed, right through the stomach. Writhing on the blade, the beast lashed out with its fang-filled maw, ripping a bloody furrow in Jak's hand.

"Son of a—!" Whipping the convulsing body off his blade, Jak stomped its skull, crushing it into the floor. "Bastard bit me!"

Ryan didn't have time to help him, however, as the

last pig-rat left was coming straight at him, its maw wide open, shrieking with bloodthirsty rage as it lunged.

Heeding Mildred's warning, Ryan had already dropped his SIG-Sauer and drawn his panga, bringing it out and around in a ferocious sweeping blow. The mutie met cold steel and was knocked sideways by the force of the blow, its head, the black eyes already dulling, separating from its body, which lurched forward before collapsing to the floor.

Blade ready, Ryan looked around for more, but saw only lifeless rodent bodies, filling the elevator with their loathsome stink. "Everyone all right?"

"Jak got tagged." Mildred was bent over the youth's hand. "It's fairly shallow, but those things live and breed in shit 24/7, and we don't have anything to wash the wound. We'll need to find antibiotics in the next day or so, to make sure he doesn't have blood poisoning."

"Here, use this." J.B. passed her a canteen, which Mildred immediately dumped over Jak's injury, before binding it with a strip torn from his faded T-shirt. She pulled it tight, then blew out a breath.

"It'll do for now. How about we all get topside. I don't know about y'all, but I think I've spent enough time underground for the time being."

"Ace on the line with that, Mildred." After cleaning his blade on his pants leg and sheathing it, Ryan strode to the elevator's controls, kicking a mutie carcass out of the way as he went. He leaned over to examine the buttons, noting a small slot with two lights above it.

"J.B., you have any problems getting in?"

The Armorer shook his head. "Doors opened slick as sh— Well, slick enough, anyway."

Ryan jabbed a button with his thumb, but nothing happened except the two lights above the slot came on, blinking red. He hit the other buttons in order, but there was no movement, only the same blink of twin red lights.

J.B. joined him at the panel. "Broken?"

"Don't think so, looks like sec is still running. Think we need a key card or something to get it moving."

"Shit." The Armorer looked around, at the rest of the walls, ceiling and floor. "No access hatch. Hope no one ever got trapped in here."

"You mean like us?" Mildred asked.

"Jury-rig a work-around?" Ryan asked, staring at the smooth steel panel.

J.B. tapped the metal with the hilt of his knife. "Don't have the tools to get through this. There's no screws or seams. Could go through the buttons, but short this panel out, and we're stuck. Got a bit of plastique left, but the concussion'll likely scramble our brains besides destroying its guts." One corner of his mouth quirked up in what might have been the ghost of a grin. "I think we aren't going anywhere for the moment, unless you aim to take another walk outside."

"You—" Ryan started to reply when Krysty held up her hand.

"Shh! Hear that?"

Everyone fell silent, straining to pick up what the flame-haired woman was hearing. Then the sound came through the thick doors—the frenzied squeals of the pig-rats outside, accompanied by the thud of dozens of bodies hitting the elevator doors, the pack slamming into the barrier in their frenzy to get at the group.

"Dark night!" J.B. said, taking off his glasses and polishing them on his shirtsleeve. "They sound bastard hungry."

"They sound goddamn insane, is what they sound

like," Mildred replied. "Well, what's the story, morning glory?"

Ryan frowned at the woman for a moment until he realized she wasn't insulting him. The term had to be more of her strange twentieth century slang. He shrugged. "Not sure just yet. We don't seem to be able to go up, and you know what's outside, so the mat-trans is out for the time being, as well."

"So, we're just going to hole up here a while and wait them out?" Mildred asked.

Ryan picked the cleanest corner of the floor he saw and sat down. "Yup. They should give up in an hour or two. Mutie bastards'll be off looking for their next meal soon enough."

"Mildred, my dear?" Doc's sonorous voice cut across the discussion. "I think you might want to have a look at Jak. Our snow-headed companion appears a bit under the weather, even to my less-than-trained eye."

All five heads swiveled toward the albino youth, who was huddled in another corner of the elevator, his shoulders shaking. "Don't worry me. Fine." He fixed them all with his chilling, red-eyed stare for a moment before his eyes rolled back in his head as he slid down the wall, crumpling in an untidy heap on the floor.

Ryan pushed himself to his feet. "Thought you said he'd be all right for now, Mildred?"

"He should be, damn it." Frowning, the doctor trotted to Jak and felt his forehead, then grabbed his wrist.

The boy stirred weakly under her ministrations. "Lemme 'lone. All right. Just cold. So cold..."

"He's got a fever and is burning up. His pulse is also racing." Mildred took the bandage off his wound. "Jesus H. Christ!"

Jak's hand was red and swollen, and the slash was

dark, puffy and angry looking. It had stopped bleeding, but now oozed a clear fluid. Mildred sniffed, then pulled back, wrinkling her nose. "Sweet-sour stink. Either those little bastards have some kind of venom in them, or their feces is more virulent than I thought."

J.B. squatted by one of the grisly corpses, probing it carefully with the tip of his flensing knife. "Fangs seem solid, not like a rattler's, if that helps. Don't see any kind of obvious poison sac in the mouth or throat either."

"Thanks, John. Whatever the cause, I have to radically revise my prognosis for him."

"What do you mean?" Krysty asked.

Mildred glanced up, her brow knotted. "Judging by how fast it's progressing, instead of a day or two, Jak might have six to eight hours—if he's lucky."

Chapter Four

"Hey, Doc, lend me your coat, please?"

"My pleasure, dear lady." Shrugging out of his frock coat, Doc presented it to Mildred with a slight bow. "It does not look good for young Jak, does it?"

"No, it sure as hell doesn't," Ryan answered. He turned back to the panel, which still silently mocked him with its obstinate refusal to work. "Our clock just started ticking a whole lot faster. Either we figure out a way back to the mat-trans, or we get this hunk-of-junk steel box moving."

"Got four choices." J.B. pointed at the double doors, then at the elevator floor as he leaned against the wall, his dusty brown fedora tilted up. "Over, under, around or through."

Even under the circumstances, Ryan couldn't help smiling at the phrase, one of the Trader's favorite aphorisms. "Yeah. Let's try up first. C'mon, I'll boost you."

Ryan squatted, and J.B. nimbly climbed on his shoulders. When the tall man straightened, the Armorer reached the elevator roof with ease. For the next several minutes, he looked for any kind of hidden hatch, lever or emergency controls but came up empty. As he was finishing his sweep, he jerked his hands away from the ceiling. "What the—?"

"You got something?"

"Felt something. Wait a sec…." J.B. gently placed his hands back on the plastic grilled ceiling tiles. "Black dust!"

Mildred looked up from tending Jak. "What's going on, John?"

Ryan glanced up to see J.B. staring down at them with wide eyes. "I can hear them jumping on the roof. There's gotta be more of those rad-blasted pig-rats." He slid off Ryan's shoulders to the floor. "Stirred up one hell of a rat's nest."

They all listened, and once again, heard the squeals and thumps of rodent bodies hitting the ceiling, followed by the click-click of their hooves as the muties clattered around on the roof of the elevator.

Ryan shook his head. "What the fuck—fireblasted muties takin' this personal?"

"Either that, or we smell better than whatever they been eating recently." J.B. shrugged, as phlegmatic as ever.

"Rats chew on just about anything," Mildred said with a shudder. "Think they'll gnaw through the cable?"

"If they do, all the more reason to get the hell out of here. Let's take a look at the floor."

Two minutes later, the thin industrial carpeting had been torn up, revealing more of the same smooth metal. Drawing his knife, J.B. pressed the point into the steel as hard as he dared without risking the blade, but didn't even make an impression. "No-go that way."

"Right. That leaves the hallway." Ryan turned to face the doors.

"Lover." Krysty placed a hand on his arm. "You can't be serious. You wouldn't make it ten steps."

Glancing at her, Ryan took her hand in his own callused one, squeezing for a moment before letting it fall.

"Got no plans to take the last train to the coast just yet."

J.B. joined him, the sallow man scratching his forehead. "What are you thinking?"

Ryan flashed him a tight grin. "Over. The way I remember it, those three pipes ran the entire length of the corridor."

"Leap up, grab them and scoot. Crazy enough that it might work. How do we open the doors and get out without being overrun?"

"That's the tricky part. Doc?"

"At your service, good sir."

"Got any rounds left for that scattergun barrel of yours?"

"I believe I can find a few at the bottom of my capacious pockets."

Ryan nodded at J.B., who had already picked up on his plan and had unslung the M-4000 shotgun and was checking the load.

"Ryan, you aren't serious about this?" Mildred asked, rising from beside Jak.

The dark-haired man turned to face her. "Look into my eye and tell me I'm joking."

She frowned. "The blasts in this enclosed space could permanently deafen us all."

"Better alive and deaf than hearing and eaten alive. If you want to help, figure out a way to protect our hearing as best you can." Ryan shrugged off his rifle, leaning it against the corner of the elevator, and made sure there were no loose pieces of cloth on his garments that might provide a convenient rope for the mutie horde outside. "Make sure everything's secured, J.B."

"I'm on it."

Mildred shook her head, then looked around. "You two are both nuts."

Ryan saw red for a second. "Fireblast, Mildred! If you aren't helping, you're hindering! Now get useful, or get the hell out of the way!"

Mildred's face tightened, but Ryan didn't give an inch, pinning her under his icy glare. Finally she turned away. "We need cloth, cotton wadding, anything to shield our eardrums."

"How about that carpet we tore up?" Krysty borrowed J.B.'s knife and began cutting it into long strips.

Mildred felt it, then nodded. "Got just enough padding to do the trick. Make them narrower if you can. The more we can cram into our ears, the better."

J.B. glanced over at their work. "At least it'll muffle the noise of those little bastards slamming into the door."

"I'll get Jak ready." Krysty moved to the motionless albino teen, plugging his ears and covering his head with Doc's coat.

Doc had finally fished out a round for the shotgun barrel of his LeMat, and now stood with the pistol ready in both hands. J.B. had his shotgun ready, his gaze on Ryan. "Who's going?"

Ryan smiled. "You and me, of course. I need your devious mind in case the cards are locked up or hidden somewhere."

J.B. sighed. "Hip-deep in the shit, as usual."

"Where else?"

Doc pressed his ear against the door. "Is there any chance that waiting a bit might make the cretins leave us in peace and seek more suitable prey?"

"They might, but if Jak's getting worse—"

"Which he is," Mildred broke in from the corner.

Ryan glanced over to see the kid convulse and vomit a thin stream of pale bile onto the floor.

"We've got to move now. I think this is our best bet. Hellfire, it's the only one we got. All right, let's go over the plan."

Ryan scooped up the unconscious Jak and moved him to the other side of the elevator, sweeping mutie corpses out of the way with his boot. "Krysty, you're on the door. We give the signal, you hit the button. As soon as J.B. and I are out, close it triple-quick."

"You just don't let it hit your ass on the way out." She smiled, but it vanished from her face as quickly as it had appeared. Her vibrant crimson hair was tucked up tight at her nape, revealing how she felt about this whole idea.

"Doc and J.B., you're the firepower. Soon as the door opens wide enough, you both let fly with everything you got. Doc, hold your blaster at this angle." Ryan adjusted the man's hands to get maximum spread of the shotgun pellets.

The old man nodded, his limp, white mane flying around his shoulders. "Never fear, Ryan, I shall endeavor to send as many of the feral scum to hell as possible."

J.B. didn't say a word, only removed his beloved fedora and handed it to Mildred who, not having anywhere better to set it, perched it on her own head, where it sat incongruously over her beaded plaits.

"That's the spirit, Doc, but just fire the one round, don't switch to the cylinder. Mildred, you hang back and grab J.B.'s M-4000 when he's empty. You know how to reload it, right?"

Wordlessly, she accepted the round magazine from J.B. and nodded, handing him a wad of carpet strips in exchange. "I got it."

"Way I figure it, in less than five seconds, you two shoot, then we scoot. You seal that door tight after us."

Krysty's full lips were pressed tight with concern. "Assuming you find the card, how do you expect to get back inside?"

"We'll just knock on the door, and you'll do the same thing again." Ryan looked at all of them. "Ready?"

Everyone nodded. Doc took a tighter grip on his LeMat, carpet strips sprouting out of his ears. J.B. braced the M-4000 shotgun against his hip, ready to spray the corridor. Krysty was poised at the door controls, her face pale. Mildred stood in the middle of the elevator, ready to grab J.B.'s weapon. Ryan folded up a strip and inserted into his left ear, then did the same with his right, feeling the noise inside the elevator fade away into a dull buzz.

Ryan paused for a moment, removing the carpet from his ear. "Hey, hear that? They've stopped."

Everyone cautiously removed one of their earplugs to listen. It was now ominously silent.

J.B. frowned. "What you think that means? They get tired and left?"

Doc cleared his throat. "More likely, John Barrymore, they are regrouping to plan another method of attack. I recall a fascinating study on the common rat that proved the rodents possessed the ability of metacognition, previously found only in humans and some primates—"

"Skip the lecture, Doc. What the hell are you talking about?"

With a sigh, the old man stared pointedly at Ryan. "My point, my impatient companion, is that rats are one of the few animals who think about thinking—on an instinctual, primal level they are able to analyze their own thought processes. Beating themselves against the door was not working, so they are now trying to find another way into the elevator. The more salient point is that these mutated animals are probably more intelligent than you are giving them credit for. A dangerous assumption indeed."

"Mebbe so, but we're about to give them the surprise of their lives. Let's see what your supermuties do when we charge straight into them," the one-eyed man replied.

Ryan inserted his wedge of carpet earplug again. "Let's do it."

Chapter Five

On Ryan's nod, Krysty stabbed the door button. There was a pause, and Ryan thought the whole plan might go to hell before it even began if the doors didn't open.

He felt a tremor shiver through the floor and made sure J.B. and Doc were both ready. He was more worried about Doc. J.B. could be wakened from a sound sleep and be alert and ready to chill in less than three seconds. Sometimes Doc was the exact opposite, snoring through events that would rouse an entire ville. But now he looked more than ready, his eyes alight as he waited to unleash blood and thunder.

Ryan's breath hissed through clenched teeth as he waited for the doors to open. His hands itched for a weapon, and he was acutely aware of the oddity of not leading this assault by example. But neither his handblaster nor longblaster was suited for the job, and he needed to get into the corridor and on the pipes triple-quick so J.B. could follow before being mobbed by the surviving muties.

After what seemed like an hour, but was probably just a few seconds, the double doors separated with a squeal, pulling apart to reveal the boiling, furious mutant mass outside. Ryan was counting on a moment's surprise as the pig-rats took in this new development, and he was well rewarded. As one, the churning crowd all looked up at the suddenly disappearing barrier in front of them.

But as the muties took in this new development, Ryan's breath caught in his throat as he stared out at what they were up against.

The hallway was completely buried in squirming, wriggling pig-rats, crawling on and over one another in their single-minded desire to get to the end of the hallway and the live food trapped there. They were at least five or six deep in the hallway, a living carpet of gray-brown fur, dotted every few inches by a pair of large, black eyes and thousands upon thousands of needle-sharp teeth.

For a millisecond, everything came to a halt. The mutie rodent host stared up at them, and Ryan and company stared back.

The moment was broken by the soft chime of the elevator announcing to all that the doors had opened.

"Now!" he shouted.

Primed and ready, Doc unleashed his shotgun round first. The concussion slammed through Ryan's head like a wall of bricks had fallen on him. The cluster of lead balls smashed into the first group of rats, already crouching to leap at them. The pellets ripping away limbs, tearing through faces, pulverizing bodies, disintegrating the point guard in a welter of blood, bone and brains.

A heartbeat later, J.B. opened up with the M-4000. With each shell containing dozens of razor-sharp steel fléchettes, he laid down a curtain of metal moving at a thousand feet per second, obliterating anything in its way.

The next wave, already running toward the door, was pulped where they stood, their remains bursting apart to splatter comrades behind them. Encountering little resistance, the fléchette wave continued into the next line, each tiny dart carving into another furry body, and another behind that.

For a moment, Ryan thought he knew what the sound of the bombs going off during skydark sounded like. The Smith & Wesson's awesome roar reverberated through his head like the pounding hooves of Death's hellhorses. His plugged ears trembled in agony, and his skull felt like it had been stove in by a sledgehammer.

But the gambit worked. For a few precious seconds, the pig-rats' onslaught was broken as they retreated before the impenetrable steel veil of death sweeping through them.

J.B.'s shotgun clicked on an empty chamber, the over-powering roar echoing off the walls to beat through Ryan's head one last time before fading away. He glanced around to see similar expressions of shock and awe on the rest of his companions' faces.

"Let's go!" Ryan said, his voice sounding muffled and far away, even to him. Stepping into the corridor, he saw the multitude already massing for another run. Turning to face the group, he leaped up and clamped both hands around the pipe on the left, using the wall to climb up until he could wrap his legs around it as well, and shimmying forward as fast as he could. He felt the strain on the pipes as J.B. followed suit, then the crack of a blaster from the elevator.

"Shut it!" he yelled back, but immediately stopped as the effort unbalanced him, nearly causing him to lose his grip on the cold metal.

"They got the doors closed," J.B. grunted behind him. "Move, move, move!"

Clinging to the pipe, Ryan began inching down the corridor, aware of the fanged, clawed death that awaited below if he slipped. Left hand, right hand, left foot, right foot. Inch-by-inch, foot-by-foot, he made his way along. Once he brushed the middle pipe, only to draw back in surprise.

"J.B., the middle pipe's bastard hot. Watch it."

"Got it."

Below, the pig-rats went absolutely crazy. The squealing and gnashing of their teeth was deafening now, and Ryan sensed movement below him, closer than he would have liked.

"Hold up." Twisting his head, Ryan looked down just in time to see one of the muties launch itself at his face, its claws outstretched to rip the skin from his cheeks, dripping fangs bared and ready to feast on his eyes, nose, and tongue.

"Shit!" Unable to move, Ryan pressed himself against the pipe, staring as the beast grew larger in his vision. But about a foot away from him, it reached the apex of its jump and fell away into the writhing mass below. "Fireblast!"

"What happened?"

"Mutie nearly chewed my face!"

"Get you?"

Even though he'd seen it fall before striking, Ryan took a second to check. "No!"

"Then get moving!"

"Just a sec!" Making sure his left grip was secure, Ryan drew his SIG-Sauer, thumbed off the safety, pointed down and fired three times. The pained squeals of the wounded pig-rats ended quickly as they were torn apart by their ravenous, uncaring brethren.

"Little free with the ammo, aren't you?"

"If what Doc said was true about how these bastards think, I want them to know if they try for me, they pay the final price." Holstering his blaster, Ryan crept forward mechanically, his leaden arms and legs clamped on to the pipe, his fingers growing more numb with each yard gained.

After what seemed like an eternity, Ryan saw the pipes bend at a right angle and vanish into the wall a couple of yards away. Carefully hanging his head down, he saw the doors to the mat-trans anteroom just beyond them. Turning his head sideways and looking out of the corner of his eye, he watched the pig-rats tumble and swirl over and around one another, with the occasional one making a futile leap at him, only to fall back into the teeming mass.

It was at that moment Ryan realized the fault in his plan. "Son of a bitch!"

"Yeah?" There was an odd tone in J.B. voice that Ryan couldn't place, but he had more pressing things to worry about at the moment.

"How in hell are we getting' through the bastard door without bringing half the muties in with us?"

"I thought it might come up, so I made us a little door knocker," J.B. replied. "Wedge yourself between the pipe and the wall, eye closed, mouth open."

Ryan knew what was coming, and scrambled to brace himself into the narrow space between the cold gray wall and the colder green pipe. Forcing his body into the crevice, he secured himself firmly enough so that he could also cover his left ear, which would suffer the most from what was about to go down.

"Ready?" J.B. called.

"Ready."

"Fire in the hole!"

Ryan squeezed his eye shut and opened his mouth to equalize the coming shock wave. A few seconds passed before another thunderclap erupted in the corridor, and he felt an invisible force press against him for a moment, right before his entire left side was splattered with sticky wetness.

"Go!"

Without looking, Ryan dropped his legs from the pipe, trusting J.B.'s skill to have cleared a path. Even before his feet had touched the ground, his SIG-Sauer filled his fist, ready to chill anything that might still come at him.

The immediate space in front of the doors looked like a small bomb had gone off, which was exactly what had happened. J.B.'s small wad of plastique explosive had cleared an area about two yards wide of pig-rats, shit and everything else, blowing it out in a neat, smoking circle. The rest of the horde milled about in confusion, some stunned by the blast, some confused by the noise, all unwilling to approach for the moment.

Whirling, Ryan tapped in the keypad code, praying that the barrier wouldn't choose that most inopportune time to malfunction. The portal silently opened, and he rushed inside, J.B. hot on his heels. Stabbing the reverse code into the keypad, he endured the agonizing wait as the doors cycled closed again. Leaning against the wall, Ryan closed his eye and let out a long, shuddering breath. Too close.

A low, sibilant sound brought him out of his respite. Ryan opened his eye to see J.B.'s lips twitch in the slight chuckle that passed for his laughter. "What the fuck's so funny?"

"Nothing, 'cept your left side looks like you marinated in rat guts and dried shit."

Ryan glanced down to see exactly what J.B. had described coating his left boot, pants leg, shirtsleeve, and even his face. Wiping the disgusting mess away, he looked up at the Armorer, who was oddly untouched. "How the hell'd you stay so clean?"

"Got higher on the pipe. Also helped that I wasn't point man." J.B. wiped his mouth with the back of his hand. "Dark night, but you're smellin' worse by the second."

Ryan stared at him for a moment, then the corner of his mouth quirked up in a slight grin. "You had that booby ready before we left, didn't you?"

J.B. ran a hand through his hair. "I was prepared to take as many of those fuckers on the last train with me if I had to." He strolled deeper into the room. "Let's look around."

For the next ten minutes, the two men methodically searched the room, leaving no wall, comp station, or desk console untouched. Neither one discussed the possibility of what would happen if they couldn't find an access card to unlock the elevator.

"Fireblast," Ryan grunted after bending down to check the underside of the last desk. "Too much to ask for them to place the cards in a neat little box in the wall with a sign on it?"

"We could rig up a harness to get Jak over here, use the mat-trans again."

"Too hard to move him that way. Besides, do you really think Doc could hang upside down and hand-over-hand it all the way down here like we did?" Ryan didn't even mention Krysty, and as he stared back at J.B., he knew he didn't have to mention Mildred either. "Nope, all of us are gettin' out, one way or another. We've just got to figure out which way to go."

J.B. sat in one of the dusty chairs and propped his feet up on the desk. "I'm open to suggestions."

Ryan whirled, his ears straining. "What did you say?"

J.B. shrugged. "I said—"

Ryan held up his hand. "No, it wasn't that, not exactly. I heard something else when you sat down, a noise, beep of some kind."

The smaller man swung his legs off the desk, then his eyes widened as he saw the top of the flat console. "Look at this."

Ryan walked over and was as surprised as his friend. The formerly blank, black surface had lit up under the pressure of the J.B.'s feet, and now showed long, horizontal rectangle, a nine-digit numeric touchpad, each button containing a row of three letters and a number. A single directive was next to it, followed by a small, blinking line: Enter Passcode:

Chapter Six

Instinctively, Ryan edged back a bit, J.B. right beside him. Although he didn't fear anything living on this hell-blasted planet—after all, if it breathed, he could chill it—the soulless machines created by the predark whitecoats were something else entirely. Often just one breath away from a malfunction, they had to be handled with extreme care just to keep them running.

Ryan had seen plenty of comps shut down in showers of bright sparks or go what passed for crazy when touched. In the back of his mind, he feared one of these days the incomprehensible machines controlling the mat-trans would malfunction and tear them apart molecule by molecule. If that ever happened, he hoped he'd already be unconscious before it started.

Shaking away the thought, he returned to the here and now, staring at the glowing countertop.

J.B. rubbed his chin as he studied the machine. "Never saw anything like this before. What do you think?"

Part of Ryan wanted to have nothing to do with the strange console, but he also understood it might be the way to fix that elevator—if they could make it work. "Guess we should enter something."

"No shit. What'd you have in mind?"

That question was worth all the jack in the world, or at least the way out of this nightmare tunnel, which would be just as good. What would the passcode be?

What word or numeric string would be the magic key to unlock this thing's secrets?

Tentatively Ryan reached toward the console, his fingers hovering above it. "If each button represents a letter…"

His index finger stabbed the button with the letter *c*.

A small, black dot appeared in the rectangle.

Ryan slowly tapped out the rest of his guess, one button at a time: e-r-b-e-r-u-s.

Nothing happened. Ryan noticed the lowermost right button on the pad, marked enter, was flashing.

"Mebbe this'll do it."

He pressed the flashing button.

The entire screen flashed bright red, startling both of them. New letters appeared on the screen: Invalid Passcode Please Try Again

"At least it's polite." J.B. noted.

"Yeah, but not enough to let us in easy. You got any ideas?"

"How about the entire program name, you know, Project Cerberus."

"Yeah, that might work." More confidently, Ryan pressed the buttons to spell out the word, then pressed the enter button again.

The screen flashed red again, and the warning appeared again, with more writing: Invalid Passcode Please Try Again Warning: Third Failed Attempt Will Result In Activation Of Security Procedures/Automatic Lockdown Mode.

J.B.'s face darkened. "I don't like that."

"It probably doesn't mean anything. It might just try to summon long-dead guards."

"Or it might gas us and the others in the elevator. Or

seal all the doors and pump all the air out till we black out and die."

The Armorer's bleak scenarios stopped Ryan's finger as it was about to touch the surface again. He took a step back and racked his brain, trying to do the impossible— think like a whitecoat.

The majority of the men and women claiming to be scientists that Ryan had encountered during his travels often had a few things in common. They were highly intelligent and inbred, often living sequestered from the rest of the population in hidden laboratory redoubts. They were usually very dedicated to their work, whatever it might be, often bordering on passion—or mania.

And they were often crazier than shithouse rats.

"The code would be most likely be something simple, easy to enter, easy to remember. Something you could punch in almost without thinking—"

His breath caught in his throat. "Could it be that bastard easy?" he whispered. No sooner did he think it than his fingers stabbed the buttons—3-5-2

The general access code to open the doors of the redoubts.

"Here goes nothing…."

Tensing, Ryan pressed the enter button.

Chapter Seven

For a moment, nothing happened.

Then the screen flashed a brilliant, deep blue and a new menu appeared.

> Access Granted
> Welcome To Fort McCoy Redoubt Main Menu
> 1) Operations
> 2) Programs
> 3) Security
> 4) Maintenance
> 5) Matter Transfer/Enter Passcode To Access

"Looks like number five is out." J.B. noted.

"Yeah." Ryan ground his teeth in frustration. In every base they'd jumped to, he had always been on the lookout for more information on the mat-trans units. How they worked, and more importantly, how a person could control where they jumped.

He'd come close a few times. Once, in an abandoned space station high above the planet, he'd had to leave a file full of documents behind just as the station comp began its self-destruct sequence. Another time, in the desert of what had been New Mex, he'd run into Major Drake Burroughs, from predark, who knew how to direct the jumps, sending a squad after Ryan and his companions when they escaped captivity. Someday,

Ryan wanted to go back there and find out exactly what Burroughs knew. But that was another day...

Right now he still needed to figure out what to do about the elevator. They'd been lucky enough getting into the general system—trying to guess the passcode to access the mat-trans info would be like firing a bullet into the air blindfolded and still expecting to hit your target.

Wiping his forehead, which was now damp with sweat, Ryan ran his finger down the choices. "Security's probably passcoded as well—they never trust anyone. Mebbe maintenance?"

"Good as any."

Ryan hit number four, leading to yet another menu:

Maintenance Menu
1)   General
2)   Area
3)   Room
4)   Matter Transfer/Enter Passcode To Access
5)   Other

Ryan sighed. "Feels like we're wading two steps forward in shit, only to slip one step back."

"Already done that today. Keep going. I think you're almost there. Try number five. Mebbe we can tell it to unlock the sec code on the elevator."

Ryan pressed the button. This made the console change again. Now a keyboard appeared, along with the usual horizontal rectangle, and a command: Enter Maintenance Task

Ryan looked at J.B. again, who shrugged. "Don't look at me. You're the one talking to it."

"Some help you are." Holding his breath, Ryan stabbed keys: Repair Matter Transfer Elevator.

The screen flashed, and more text appeared: System Diagnostic Running Matter Transfer Elevator Operating Normally. Last Inspection Of Matter Transfer Elevator Performed On 9/10/2000. Elevator Inspection Overdue. Do You Wish To Send Elevator To Maintenance Level For Visual Inspection?

Ryan grinned. "That sounds about as good as anything we can expect. Maintenance level's got to be near the surface."

"Makes as much sense as anything else we've seen so far."

Ryan entered yes. A line of text appeared, with an entry rectangle underneath: Please Set Time For Elevator Inspection.

Ryan's smile dropped off his face. "Nuke shit. How do we do this?"

"Hey, check the lower right-hand corner—some sort of timer."

Ryan glanced down, and sure enough, there were numbers there: 13:37:10. As he watched, the last pair counted up to sixty, then the next pair to the left added one, and the rightmost pair started counting up from one again.

"Looks like that's the clock. Ten minutes should be enough to get out of here and back to the elevator, right?"

"I'd say so."

Ryan entered the time: 13:48:00, and hit Enter.

All of the earlier text disappeared, replaced by four lines: Countdown To Matter Transfer Elevator Inspection: 00:09:59 Please Ensure That All Personnel Are Clear Of Elevator Before It Departs.

Ryan slapped J.B.'s shoulder. "Time to go."

The other man held up a finger-sized lump of plastique. "Ready. Hope we find some more of this soon. It's my last detonator."

"We'll know soon enough." Ryan trotted back to the access door.

"It's a four-second fuse, so when the doors open wide enough, I toss it, wait for the boom and we go."

"Three...two...one—" Ryan stabbed the keypad.

The door cycled open again, and as soon as the crack was wide enough, J.B. pitched the explosive into the corridor, calling "fire in the hole!"

Both men spun away, covering their ears and opening their mouths again. Seconds later, the C-4 detonated, sending a spray of pig-rat parts into the formerly spotless mat-trans control room.

Ryan peeked out to see yet another, deeper puddle of mutie pieces, blood and feces in front of the door. The pig-rats milled and scurried beyond, unwilling to approach at first, but fast losing their fear as they began scurrying closer.

"Go!" Ryan stepped out and leaped for the pipe again, his fingers already aching as they gripped it. Swinging his feet up, he pushed along it to make room for J.B., who keyed the door closed before jumping up just as a pair of muties sprang at his legs.

"Dark night!" J.B. lashed out wildly, catching one of the creatures in the face with his boot, and sending it crashing into the wall, where it fell back into the rodent army. The other one, however, latched on to his pant leg with its sharp claws and sank its tusks into his leg.

"Nuking hell!" Hanging on with one hand, J.B. drew his flensing knife with the other and stabbed the beast in the neck, blood spurting over his fingers and wrist.

Sawing with the blade, he severed its head from its body, which fell away, leaving the jaws still locked on his thigh. Hammering at it with the butt of his dagger, grunting with each blow, J.B. broke the mutie's jaw after several blows. Inserting his blade between the pig-rat's open lips, he pried it off and flipped it away.

Meanwhile, Ryan hadn't been a passive observer during the pitched battle. As soon as he heard J.B. curse, he'd looked over, seen the problem and acted. Drawing his SIG-Sauer, he'd raised the blaster over his head and fired several rounds into the swirling, squealing vermin below, ensuring that their attention was on their wounded and dying brethren. The hammer of his blaster had just clicked on an empty chamber when J.B. had finished removing the gruesome head of his attacker.

"You okay?"

"Yeah—for now." J.B.'s face was flushed with the exertion of killing the mutie while hanging on the pipe, but he nodded. "Move out."

"Give me a sec." As fast as he dared, Ryan slung his forearm over the pipe to hold himself up, ejected the empty mag from his blaster, tucking it into his pocket, and replaced it with a full one—his last. Holstering his weapon, he reached up to secure his hold on the pipe with his free hand. "Ready."

An ominous groan echoed through the tunnel, and the pipe Ryan and J.B. clung to dropped an inch, then another before shuddering to a halt.

Chapter Eight

"Pipe's breaking! We've got to move!" Ryan began, hand-over-handing it as quickly as he could, sensitive to each shudder and jar as he clambered along the metal tube. He thought about telling J.B. to put some more space between them, but dismissed the idea. Every second they spent here was more stress on the pipe, and if it gave way, there was only one place to end up—straight down into the hundreds of slavering maws of the muties below.

So Ryan kept moving, trying to crawl as lightly as possible, if such a thing could be done while hanging from a pipe with his two-hundred-odd pounds pulling on it every time he braced a hand or foot. With every yard he gained, the pipe swayed and creaked ominously, and Ryan half expected that each time he reached up to grab the slick metal, it would be his last. The horde below was erupting into a frenzy, the pandemonium overwhelming, even to their carpet-stuffed ears. As he pushed forward, Ryan swore he felt something brush his back more than once.

"Ryan...hold up...need to rest..." J.B.'s voice, already weak, drifted to him above the shrieking of the muties.

"No, J.B., keep moving! We're almost there. If you stop, you drop!"

"Gettin' tired..."

"Keep moving." Dipping his head, he saw the elevator doors about ten yards away. "We're almost there!"

"All right…"

Although his fingers felt like numb pieces of wood, Ryan kept bulling forward. Stretch, grab, pull, stretch, grab, pull. Once more, and he was at the door. Drawing his blaster, Ryan hammered on the door with the butt.

"Clear the entrance, we're back! Open the doors!"

The muties were screaming so loud now that Ryan couldn't hear if anyone replied from inside. He was about to beat on the doors again when the pipe dropped another six inches with a shriek of rending metal.

"J.B.! Get on top!" Reaching around, Ryan threw a leg over and pulled himself up on top, just as he felt something scrabble through his hair, followed by the click of teeth snapping near his ear. "Fireblast!" The moment he was secure, Ryan brushed a hand through his hair, making sure nothing was about to tear into his scalp.

"Ryan…can't make it…up…"

The weak shout made Ryan whirl to see J.B.'s hands slipping. Throwing himself forward, he stretched out full-length, his hands reaching out to grab the other man's wrists. The pipe screamed at the impact of his body, but still held, even under their combined weight. He grabbed J.B.'s arms a moment before he would have fallen to the floor.

"You aren't leaving this place without me, you hear?" Ryan gritted between clenched teeth. His hands and arms, already sore and unfeeling from the trip to the mat-trans control room and back, radiated pure agony as he held J.B. in place. "On three, I'm going to lift you, and you're going to grab this pipe with both hands and hold on with everything you got, you understand?"

"All right… Don't have to yell…"

Ryan braced himself for was he was about to do. "One…two…three!" He heaved up with every ounce of strength he possessed, muscles cracking under the strain. One inch, two, three…

Straining until he thought his arms were going to tear out of their sockets, Ryan pulled J.B.'s arms up until he could get them wrapped back around the pipe, then he grabbed the scruff of the other man's battered jacket and, with the last of his strength, hauled the man up so he was half on, half off the pipe.

A feral chitter from J.B.'s knees made Ryan slowly raise his head. There, with its front claws dug deep into the other man's left leg, squatted a pig-rat easily two feet long, drool oozing from its two-inch tusks.

"Ryan, what—"

"Don't…move…" Ryan stared at the mutie only three feet away from him, pinning it with his hardest stare. The beast gave as good as it received, its large, black eyes gazing back into his, as if it knew it would have to fight to keep this meal.

Not taking his eye off the abomination, Ryan's hand slowly crept toward the handle of his panga. The pig-rat tensed in anticipation, hindquarters lowering to J.B.'s stained, bloody pants as it prepared to spring.

Their eyes locked one last time, and Ryan moved the millisecond he saw the pig-rat jump.

As the brute pushed off, Ryan drew the heavy blade and brought it around in a short, vicious arc. The flat of the machete smacked into the rodent's head right before it would have sank its teeth into Ryan's face. The blow sent the creature hurtling away, falling with a startled shriek into the ravenous crowd below.

"Thanks…fucker clawed me bad…"

Ryan nodded, unable to speak, and more so because he had no idea what to say. It didn't seem like Krysty or the others had heard him inside, and the pipe was about to break loose at any moment, sending them down to a very short, one-way trip to be a feast for the rad-blasted muties below.

He shifted his weight to lessen the strain, but his movement only caused the pipe to groan again and drop a few more inches. With his free hand, he drew his blaster and cocked the hammer.

"This is it. I'll break the pipe free, hope to crush a shitload of them underneath. When it drops, make for the door. We might be able to get inside before they bring us down. I'll be shooting the whole way, so you just run. Don't stop for anything, and that includes me."

J.B. raised his head, and Ryan was startled to see his friend's face flushed a bright, mottled red. "Be…right… behind you…"

"All right, here we go." Ryan turned to face the elevator, about to throw his entire weight upon the pipe to send it crashing to the floor, when the metal doors below began to slide open.

Krysty was framed in the doorway, looking every inch like a flame-haired, avenging angel, only instead of a sword, she was holding something much better.

The S&W M-4000 shotgun was braced against her hip, ready to spew a hailstorm of metal death.

"Fire in the hole!" Ryan shouted, throwing himself back on the pipe, jamming his right ear into his shoulder and clapping his left hand over his left, just before the world split apart in explosions of thunder and flame.

His head aching and rattled from the weapon going off right under him, Ryan was dimly aware of strong hands pulling him from the pipe and helping him into the elevator. Other hands gripped him and helped him to a corner of the small room, where he sank to his knees. "J.B.—"

Krysty's face appeared in front of him through a pall of smoke, speaking slowly and distinctly. "We got him out—"

That was as far as she got before Ryan crushed her to him and kissed her long and hard for as long as he had air in his lungs. Her strong arms curled around his back was the best sensation he'd felt in a long time.

When they parted, he wasn't the only one breathless. "Nice to see you too, lover," she panted.

"Bastard good to be seen. The doors…"

"Are locked as tight as a drum, my good man." With a courtly flourish, Doc spun his ancient LeMat on his finger, nearly dropping it before steadying it with his other hand and dropping it back into his holster. "I dare-say your paramour was like a woman possessed. She swore she heard you outside the door, even when the rest of us could not through the ruckus of that hellspawn outside. At the last, she said she was going to open them, and would perforate with lead anyone who tried to impede her. Obviously she was right on the money and gave those impudent beasts the what for. While she went out and brought the two of you back, I stood guard with my trusty sidearm, and when she got J.B., I gave them something to think about with my second barrel while we closed the doors again."

"So, we're moving?"

"Most assuredly, my dear Ryan. However, I'm not sure you are going to like the particular direction we seem to be heading."

Doc's words made Ryan realize just what was off

about the movement of the elevator. It didn't have the stomach-lurching feel of ascension at all. Pushing off the wall to his feet, he stalked to the panel with the buttons, his face darkening as he saw which one was lit.

"Fireblast, Doc, why the hell'd you press the bottom one? We want to go up, not down!"

"Easy, Ryan." Krysty grabbed his arm, distracting him. "About fifteen minutes after you left, a recording came on telling us to clear the elevator as it was due to go to the maintenance level in ten minutes. We started counting down, and when it got to thirty seconds—well, I wasn't leaving without you."

"But as to where exactly we're going, we don't have a clue, other than the maintenance level," Mildred said from where she was bent over J.B., field-dressing his wounds as best she could. "Jesus, Ryan, where the hell did you two go—swimmin' through a sewer?"

"Yeah. We used a little plastique to clear the mat-trans comp room. J.B. got bit and clawed by a pair of them. How's he doing?"

"Not good. The exertion worked the infection into his bloodstream more quickly than Jak, so they're running neck and neck regarding who's worse off at the moment. We've got to get medicine into them, fast."

She didn't mention the unspoken truth: if there was any medicine to be had it was in the upper levels. Assuming they made it that far in the first place.

The elevator ground to a halt, and the disembodied voice spoke again, startling Ryan, who was hearing it for the first time.

"Maintenance level. This elevator will be inoperative until the proper visual inspection has been performed, and a supervisor has approved it. Thank you."

"Never met such polite machines," he muttered,

slinging the Steyr longblaster over his shoulder, his SIG-Sauer filling his right hand. "End of the line, people. Krysty, you got Jak. Mildred, help J.B. Keep your blasters out if you can manage it. I don't know what the hell we're going to find down here. Doc, you're on my left. Let's get the fuck out of this metal coffin."

Doc took his position at Ryan's left shoulder, levering back the trigger of his LeMat with a click. "Truer words were never spoken, my friend."

Ryan raised his SIG-Sauer and nodded at the old man. "Do it."

Chapter Nine

The elevator doors opened into impenetrable, pitch-blackness. The bright fluorescent light emanating from the elevator was quickly swallowed by the stygian dark outside.

"Guess the lights aren't on down here." Mildred said. She had J.B.'s left arm draped around her shoulders, holding it in place with her left, and her blaster in her right hand, ready to shoot. Krysty had done the same with the skinny, shivering Jak, careful to avoid the shards of razor sewn into his jacket.

"No, and it certainly doesn't smell any more pleasant than the festering pit we just left, does it?" Doc said, covering his mouth and nose.

Indeed, it didn't smell any better outside. In fact, the reek was much worse. It was warmer here than in the mat-trans corridor, and more humid, and the pervasive odors of rot and mold surrounded them. Although he didn't say it, Ryan was pretty sure of one of the components making up the miasma around them—rotting meat.

"Need a light." Bending to grab one of the carpet strips, he rubbed it in the filthy fur of a dead rat body, smearing it with feces and hair, then wrapped it around the blade of his panga. "Mildred, J.B.'s got a flint on him, find it."

"I'm not dead yet…" Ryan half turned to see the

Armorer holding out the small stone, a scowl creasing his eyebrows.

"Hell, never said you were, just figured you were takin' a little nap after our running around up there. Since you're awake, you can make yourself useful and carry the rest of that carpet. We're gonna need more fuel when this runs out."

J.B. accepted two handfuls of the thin strips, stuffing them in his pockets.

Kneeling, Ryan struck the flint against the steel of his knife, sending a shower of sparks into the makeshift torch, which flared into sullen light. He caught Krysty's worried stare and nodded, wordlessly telling her it would be all right, when in fact he had no idea whether any of them would survive the next few minutes. With Jak and J.B. incapacitated, their numbers were down by a third. That meant two of the best warriors in the group were out of action, and Ryan estimated their ability was more or less cut by half, particularly with two others carrying them along. Doc and Mildred were more than capable, he'd grant them that, but they simply weren't in the other two men's league. Krysty was another story, easily equal to any of the other men when it came to chilling, as she had demonstrated time after time. Her lethal performance in the hallway had proved that point yet again.

Rising, he raised the torch overhead to cast the maximum available light out in front of them. "All right, let's move out. Stay close and sing out if you see anything. You ready, Doc?"

The old man stared at the limp corpse of one of the rats with unfocused eyes. "Would that I had a piece of string to swing it on, that is a fine pastime for a young boy to while an afternoon away, is it not?"

"Ah, Doc..." Ryan toed the stiffening body with his boot. "You saying you used to swing these on a string?"

"Oh, yes, it was great fun for the boys to scare the girls with—that or a dead cat, you see."

"And they say the twenty-second century is uncivilized. Sometimes I think you boys don't have anything on the nineteenth." Mildred muttered.

At the moment, Ryan agreed with her. "Doc? Doc, snap out of it. We might be walking into trouble down here, and we need you in the here and now, understand?"

The white-haired man's eyes blinked once, twice, then he stared up at Ryan with his more-or-less usual gaze. "Beg pardon, dear sir, I was gamboling down the misty paths of memory lane for a moment." Doc hoisted the LeMat in front of his face. "It shall not happen again, I assure you."

"All right, let's go." Ryan's torch was already burning low, and the first order of business was to find a better light source, and quick.

His blaster extended into the room, Ryan took a step out, then another. The stench hit him like a physical blow, almost overpowering in its intensity. Beside him, Doc exited the elevator, and immediately turned to be quietly sick in the corner.

The floor was alternately slick and dry, making footing treacherous. Bringing the torch down, Ryan saw more mutie shit covering the floor as in the hallway, just not as deep here. The lumps were larger, however, some the size of a child's fist, which sparked a faint alarm in Ryan's mind. "Go slow, everyone. We don't need any twisted or broken ankles here."

"Yeah, we got enough problems already," Mildred replied.

"Well, here is some news of import that may cheer us." Doc darted off into the darkness, only to return a moment later wheeling something in front of him on squealing, crusted wheels. "I found a chair."

"Great, Doc, great." Ryan grimaced as he stared at the ancient piece of furniture, which looked as if it would fall apart if he breathed on it, much less sat down. It was also covered with feces, which Doc busily brushed off. "What in the hell are we supposed to do with it?"

The old man's expression turned sly, as if only he knew the answer to a great riddle. With effort, he wrenched off one of the metal arms in a squeal of rusted metal and held it up. "Wrapped in your clever mixture of mutant shit and U.S. government-approved carpet—supplied by the lowest bidder, of course—I believe this would make a more than adequate torch, would it not?"

"He's got you there, Ryan," Krysty said.

"Guess he does." Shaking the guttering remains of his first torch off the panga, Ryan cleaned and sheathed it before breaking off the other chair arm. In two minutes he had fashioned a pair of torches, one of which he passed to Doc. "You found them, you get to carry one."

"Its lustrous gleam blazes like the bejeweled flame that lit the brazier whenst mankind came together to celebrate the first Olympiad in Athens, shining out like a shaft of gold when all around is dark—or is that a stream of bat's piss? In either event, I will guard it with my very life."

"I'd settle for finding a light of some kind, electric

or otherwise—" Ryan began to reply before Krysty's urgent whisper cut him off.

"We're not alone."

Everyone froze, and Ryan lifted his torch higher to try to spot what might be coming at them from the dark. "How many?"

"A lot, all around us—and they're bigger than the ones in the hallway."

Now Ryan heard the skittering of many feet; the peculiar rustle-clack of the pig-rats as they approached. A shadowed form remained just out of the yellow circle of torchlight, and Ryan's breath hitched in his throat for a second—it was as large as a medium dog. He brought up his blaster, but with a flash of a naked, pink tail as big around as his thumb, it vanished into the gloom.

"What's the plan?" Krysty asked.

"Give me J.B.'s Uzi." Holstering his SIG-Sauer, Ryan accepted the submachine gun, unfolded the stock and snugged it into his shoulder to brace when he fired. "All right, we follow the wall until we come to another exit. They can't surround us then. Keep your blasters out and shoot anything inside the light. Above all, keep moving. There must be another way out of here. Let's move."

Keeping his back to the wall, and the torch in front of him, Ryan led the way, searching for the corner that would take them deeper into the cavernous room. The patter of many paws and hooves grew louder now, as if they were being shadowed by a veritable mob of the hideous beasts.

Ryan stopped short when he saw what he was about to walk into. The muties had been crapping down here for so long they had created piles of feces as high as Ryan's head. He couldn't even see the wall beyond in the dimming light. "Far as we go this way, people. Follow me."

A flash of greasy, gray fur appeared in the torchlight, and Ryan squeezed the trigger of the Uzi, sending a single bullet into the pig-rat's skull, the noise of the shot drowning out the scurrying of the stalking rodents for a few moments. It skidded to a stop at his feet, a mottled pink and back tongue lolling out as it spasmed and died. Even lying on its side, the creature's body rose almost to Ryan's knee.

"Good lord!" Mildred said. "They grow them big down here."

"Keep moving. That shot scared them off, but they'll be back, and probably a lot more next time." Ryan set the pace, but was distracted by Doc, who stepped ahead of him to peer at a pile of shit, torch held high.

"Doc, we've got to keep moving."

"Is it? It is! Give me a minute or two, my dear Ryan, and I will have the answer to your prayers in hand shortly." Dropping his torch on the ground, Doc plunged his hands into a pile of shit, flinging fist-sized lumps aside with an expression of demented glee on his face.

"Ryan!" Mildred's urgent hiss swiveled his head around to see a pair of the large pig-rats creeping in behind them. Stepping in front of the women, Ryan aimed and fired two careful shots that took the muties down, but they were quickly replaced by more. Ryan waved the torch, which seemed to keep them at bay, but the brutes only retreated far enough to be outside the immediate reach of the blazing brand. Lifting the torch overhead again, Ryan saw they were encircled by a double ring of the beasts, with dozens of claws scraping the floor as they approached. Finding the fire selector on the Uzi with his thumb, Ryan flicked it to full-auto and prepared to send a burst into the front line.

"Whatever you're doing, Doc, you better do it fast!" The pig-rats were only a couple yards away now, grunting, snuffling and drooling in their desire to tear into fresh meat. Tightening his grip on the submachine gun, Ryan squeezed off a burst. The 9 mm rounds punched through a trio of muties, sending them squealing away to be set upon by their comrades.

The crack of Krysty's and Mildred's blasters also joined the fray, but Ryan saw it was hopeless—there were just too many of the vermin. He triggered short bursts until the Uzi clicked empty, then handed it to Mildred and drew his SIG-Sauer intent on making the nearest mutie's attempt to steal a bite a fatal decision.

He had just drawn a bead on the closest one, which was hungrily eyeing his leg, when a two-foot-long tongue of flame shot past him and into the mutie's face, searing it to a crisp as he watched in stunned amazement.

Chapter Ten

The pack of pig-rats halted its advance upon seeing the face of their comrade immolated right next to them. The burn victim screamed in agony and staggered away, its eyes heated to milky-white blindness. One of the others snapped at its foreleg, and when it turned to face that threat, another snuck in from behind and went for its underbelly. In seconds, the wounded one was down and dead, feasted upon by a half dozen of its fellows.

Ryan turned from the grisly sight—now nicely illuminated—back to Doc, who now held a curious apparatus. It looked to be a pipe about two feet long, bent at a sixty-degree angle, with a two-foot-long tongue of blue-orange flame erupting from a small nozzle. The other end was attached to a pair of large, steel cylinders by stiff rubber tubes. Above the odor of feces, Ryan now detected the faint scent of what smelled like burned garlic.

Doc's face had lit up like a boy's on Christmas morning. "MAPP gas welding torch—liquefied petroleum gas mixed with methylacetylene-propadiene. If I can get a hand with the fuel tank—" he waved at the pair of tall cylinders with a pair of gauges at the top "—we should be able to stroll out of here like walking out of church on a sunny Sunday afternoon."

"Then let's go. Neither Jak nor J.B. are getting any better while we stand around gawking!" Mildred said.

"Doc, look out!" Ryan aimed his blaster past the old man, who spun at the same time and adjusted a knob on the handle of the device, sending a five-foot burst of flame at the encroaching group of rats trying to ambush him. The searing fire drove them back, and Doc advanced into the group, wielding the pipe like a demented conductor, swinging it back and forth, singeing hair and mutie skin as he cleared a path through the pack surrounding them.

"Ryan, help me move the containers!" he snapped. "Everyone else stay close!"

Ryan kept his SIG-Sauer ready as he grabbed the handle sticking up above the pair of tanks. Upon a closer look, he saw that they were fastened to an upright, mobile cart, the rubber wheels jammed solid with fecal matter. Tipping the handle toward him, Ryan tried forcing them to move, but neither one budged an inch.

"Hold up, Doc!" Ryan tugged on the handle, breaking the cart loose from where it had stood for the past hundred years, and dragging it out before Doc could damage the hoses connecting the flaming wand to its fuel source. "Okay, stay close to the wall! Everyone, follow us!"

The muties snarled and shrieked their displeasure, but none were bold enough to risk the fire to attack the norm keeping them at bay. Guided by the wall on his left, Doc steadily drove through the crowd. Ryan was torn between keeping up with the old man and watching their back, but Krysty and Mildred seemed to be doing fine in that regard, the two women teaming up to protect their own flanks and guard each other. Pig-rats snapped and whined, but the occasional well-placed shot kept any rear force from becoming too organized or large.

Slowly, they forged deeper into the room, which Ryan

was beginning to think had no end, but seemed to go on forever, with the group surrounded by darkness and muties, only held at bay by Doc's improvised flamer. Always, the pig-rats probed their defenses, looking for a weak spot to swarm in for the kill. And time after time, wave after wave, Doc, Ryan and the others fended them off with fire and lead.

After what might have been the sixth or seventh assault, Doc, his narrow chest heaving like a bellows, pointed with the blazing torch. "Ryan, I see something ahead. It looks like a wall. It might be the way out!"

"Go! Go!"

Doc increased the spray on his torch, sending a stream of fire arcing out, scattering scorched muties out of his path. Ryan and the others increased their pace as well, pulses quickening as they realized they might be close to leaving this hellhole.

Then, as quickly as he had spoken, Doc stumbled to a stop, the torch drooping in his hand. "Holy mother of God…"

Ryan skidded to a halt beside him, the cart almost banging his shins before lurching to a stop. "Doc, what the hell, why you stopping now?"

In answer, the other man simply raised his arm and pointed.

At first, Ryan couldn't make out what was ahead, but then they advanced into the light and his blaster rose instinctively, even though he knew it probably didn't have a chance in hell of putting this new enemy down.

From around the wall lumbered huge, furry shapes, their front claws scraping through the muck, and their rear hooves clattering on the floor. Each of these muties, six in all, stood as tall as Ryan on their four legs. One of them yawned, exposing teeth as long as his hand, capped by a double pair of tusks the length of his forearm. Ryan knew that if they wanted, each one of these abominations could lunge forward and bite his head off, or disembowel him with one swipe of their three-inch claws.

Mildred, her eyes wide, was bringing up her blaster to target one of the huge beasts, but J.B. got his hand up first and managed to clamp his fingers around hers.

"No! No shooting, you hear?" he whispered.

"But we can take them out right now, before they kill us," she hissed back.

"If they'd wanted us dead, we'd be on the floor, guts around our ankles," Ryan said, his low voice carrying to everyone in the group. "No one makes a move until I do, got it?"

Mildred nodded. Ryan didn't have to check the rest; he knew what the answer would be.

He did, however, steal a glance at Doc, who was staring as if entranced—but not at the six horse-sized mutants. "Is it not amazing, my dear Ryan? That life, in all of its blind and infinite wisdom, somehow finds a way to continue, to forge forward, despite all of our pathetic attempts to shape or control or destroy it?"

"Hey, Doc, right now that life you're so all-fired moony over is about to swallow us whole, so why don't we try to get by them as quick as possible? If I can get the shotgun, it might even—"

Doc shook his head, his gray-white hair flapping around his shoulders. "No, Ryan. Look closely at what lies ahead of us, and tell me if you think we have any chance of escaping this room alive."

The old man's words were spoken with perfect, chilling clarity, and the look on his face was anything but

insane, if Ryan was any judge. He looked back at the
huge pig-rats, none of which had made a move toward
them yet.

None of them…Ryan glanced around to see that the
rest of the pig-rats had also retreated to a safe distance,
many of them sitting on their haunches and regarding
the party, as if they were an audience, watching some
sort of macabre play.

He peered closer at what he first thought was a wall,
only to realize the torch light was playing tricks on his
eyes. It had to have been, for the barrier curved away
at the top, and was covered in thick, matted gray fur,
liberally caked with shit. And even stranger, it pulsed
in and out rhythmically, almost as if…

"Fireblast…" Ryan breathed as he realized exactly
what was lying in front of them. At that exact same
moment, the wall of flesh and fur undulated and rippled.
From the top he saw a massive paw, longer than he was
tall, tipped with curved, short-swordlike talons at the
end, descend toward the floor. He stared in mingled
revulsion and awe as the leviathan—for there was no
better word for it—continued to turn over.

The queen of the mutie pig-rat horde was an appalling
vision straight out of a nightmare, brought to breathing,
quivering life. Easily twenty feet tall lying down, she
had to be at least three times as long from her twitching nose to her huge, naked pink tail, a bloated rodent
mountain at the center of her filthy empire. Completing
her turn, which Ryan figured she didn't do very often,
brought a double row of her engorged teats into view. As
he looked on in horrified fascination, a dozen mewling,
blind, four-foot-long infants swarmed over her, seeking
out the swollen glands, which oozed a thick, greenish-

white liquid from their tips. The next generation eagerly suckled at her chest, climbing over each other in their eagerness to get at the life-giving fluid.

The face of the mother was just as large as the rest of her, with huge, black eyes swimming in a puffy face swollen with layers of fat. Her teeth were the hugest Ryan had ever seen, jutting from a mouth so cavernous that if she yawned, he figured he might be able to walk inside if he stooped a bit. She regarding them with a penetrating stare, however, appearing anything but a mindless rodent. Her gaze seemed particularly drawn to the flaming torch, hanging almost forgotten in Doc's hand, and she twisted her head away, although her eyes never left the flickering flame.

That seemed important to Ryan, but damned if he knew exactly how at the moment. A straight-up fight was impossible—it would only result in their immediate deaths, even if he managed to get the shotgun off J.B. and firing. The torch itself was good on the smaller animals, but the huge rats would simply devour them before they could be burned to death. He didn't doubt that a bite from those massive jaws could easily sever a limb.

"Ryan!" The urgent whisper made him glance back at Krysty, whose normally calm face was furrowed in concentration. "Be careful. Do not underestimate her. She knows…things. She—thinks like us…."

Krysty's words scared Ryan even more, but at the same time, the glimmer of a plan was forming in the back of his consciousness. He just needed another moment to put it together….

One of the guards swung its head over to his leader, as if seeking permission for whatever he was about to do.

The queen's eyes flicked toward him, then back to the group, and the huge pig-rat started forward, saliva dripping from his jaws, his killing intent more than clear.

Chapter Eleven

The silent exchange gave Ryan an idea.

"Wait!" His command shattered the stillness, even checking the guard mutie, who stopped and cocked its head, regarding him in what Ryan could have sworn was puzzlement.

"Doc, you said these things were smart, right?"

"Verily, they exhibit intelligent behavior beyond any rodents I've ever seen. The queen structure is most fascinating, almost like a collective hive. It would also explain the simultaneous reaction of the first group we encountered."

"Good, then they should understand what I'm doing. Give me the torch." Ryan grabbed the weapon from the old man. "Stand back. If this works, we're going to have to move fast. If not, everyone take as many of the fuckers down as you can before they get you."

Moving slowly, Ryan held the welding torch up so all of his rapt audience saw it. He twisted the knob, releasing a spurt of blue-orange flame into the air, which got everyone's attention. Two of the giant pig-rats hissed angrily at the sight, but a short bark from the queen silenced them.

Next, Ryan brought the pair of tanks forward so they were in plain view to everybody. Slowly pulling his blaster out, he carefully ejected the magazine, keeping them both in his hand as did so. Using his thumb, he

flicked a bullet onto the ground, angling it with his toe
so that it pointed at the nearest pile of shit.

"Everyone stand back." Making sure the colony of
muties was still watching, Ryan leaned over, keeping his
eye on them as he did so, and carefully applied the flame
to the casing, making sure the bullet still faced away
from the group. Seconds passed, then a minute, then,
with an explosive pop the cordite in the shell ignited,
sending a burst of flame up as the lead corkscrewed into
the dung heap.

Stepping back to the pair of fuel canisters, Ryan
began bringing the blazing torch closer to them. The
queen's eyes went from the blackened casing to the
four-foot-tall containers, and she suddenly screeched
in alarm. The guards tensed to spring, but another howl
from her froze them where they stood, poised to leap
on the group.

Having reloaded his blaster while the muties were
distracted by the bullet, Ryan's weapon was back up
in a flash, pointing at the queen's head, which felt like
threatening a mutie grizzly with a flyswatter. But the
torch, coming ever nearer to the valves that regulated the
flow of oxygen and fuel, was Ryan's ace in the hole.

Now he just had to make sure the bluff he was running didn't turn into a dead man's hand.

Doc, as if noticing what Ryan was doing for the first
time, said mildly, "I wouldn't do that if I were you, my
dear man. The explosion would kill us all."

"That's what I'm counting on, Doc, and that she real-
izes it, too."

Doc's eyes widened in sudden comprehension. "My
dear Ryan, you are one of the most low-down, con-
niving, sneakiest men I have ever had the privilege to
meet."

"Just trying to make sure we all don't get our faces— or any other parts—chewed off. And don't start slapping my back in congratulations just yet. If you haven't noticed, we still aren't out of here." Ryan grabbed the handle of the tank cart. "All right, we're going. Don't make any moves unless they do first—then chill anyone who does."

Holstering his blaster, Ryan started hauling the cart toward the rear end of the queen, keeping the torch near the fuel tanks and his head as far from her giant behind as possible. The huge pig-rat nearest to him growled low in its throat, its long, pink tail, as thick as Ryan's thigh, whipping back and forth. For a moment, Ryan thought he'd have to draw and take the big bastard down, but a gigantic, hairy leg swept over and clouted the guard in the head, making him stagger away.

Ryan glanced up at the queen, who regarded him with cold, malice-filled eyes as she nodded slightly. Stepping around the stunned guard, he motioned the rest of the group forward with his head. Up close he saw the pups still gulping down the noxious fluid, which smelled even worse than it looked.

The queen shifted again, rolling back over with an effort. Ryan couldn't blame her. In her place, he wouldn't have trusted himself either. The procession was oddly silent, only the irritated squeaks of the young as they scrambled around again for the milk, the thick, sibilant breathing of the rats as they watched the humans leave and the hiss of the lit torch breaking the silence. Ryan felt more than heard the pack of medium pig-rats pacing them, flowing around the queen's head to follow the group.

A sudden shot caught Ryan off guard, and he stumbled, catching himself before dropping either the torch or the tank. Before the echo died away, he heard something slither down a pile, and looked to his left to see a medium pig rat with a bloody hole where its right eye had been roll to a stop from the nearest pile of dung.

The guards had tensed again, ready to leap, but a shrill hiss from their queen stopped them.

Ryan looked back to see Mildred with her blaster still extended, pointing at the top of the nearest pile. "Saw it tensed to leap and took the shot."

Ryan nodded, then turned back to the queen, his expression hard. "Doc, put your blaster up here, pointed right at the valves."

"Ryan, I—"

"Do it right now."

Doc hastened to comply, setting the heavy barrel of the LeMat so its muzzle was aimed squarely at the two valves on top.

"Cock the hammer."

"Really, Ryan—"

"Cock it! I won't say it another time."

His thumb trembling only slightly, Doc hauled back the hammer until it caught on the sear. Ryan's stony gaze pinned the queen, who had raised her large forepaws in the classic 'I surrender' pose, which would have been funny if his life and those of his companions weren't on the line at that particular second.

"Glad to see you get my point." Drawing back his foot, Ryan kicked the carcass of the dead pig-rat over to her. "Any more of this shit happens, and we all go up." For emphasis, he brought the torch right up to the tanks, close enough for the flame to kiss the curved metal surface. Even the guards shifted uneasily at that, and the queen waved her front paws in unfeigned terror, chittering as she attempted to placate him.

"Ryan, I think I see the true wall a few yards distant," Doc said.

"Well, then, let's get the hell over to it." Hauling the tank cart into motion again, Ryan forged ahead, straining his eye to see the end of the room. After a few more yards, he held the torch just high enough to see the real wall perhaps another five yards away, the flat, gray plane rising to the ceiling out of the piles of crap.

"Son of a bitch—where's the bastard elevator?"

Doc pointed to their left along the wall. "We have to follow it to the other door and pray it isn't also covered in feces."

Ryan had taken a single step when a new noise caught his attention—the slight sputter of the torch. He looked at it in time to see the flame waver a bit before regaining its bright, steady flare.

"Hey, Doc?"

The old man was intently scanning the tops of the dung heaps. "Yes, Ryan?"

"The torch just sputtered on me."

"Oh dear." Doc glanced back just in time to see it happen again. "I suggest all of us redouble our efforts to find the elevator door before that tank runs out of fuel."

"Everyone else, search the wall. I'm going to make sure our friends here don't get any more bright ideas." Ryan lugged the tanks and cart a few more yards, then set it up on its end, keeping the torch close to the tanks and, drawing his SIG-Sauer with his now free hand, turned to face his attentive audience.

The pig-rats had followed their every move, the medium-sized ones closest now, dozens of them arrayed in a gray-brown carpet that stretched out into the darkness. Interspersed among them were the half dozen giant muties, each one looking as if it wanted to bound over and rip Ryan's head off. And behind them was the bloated queen, still suckling her young as she stared at the group of humans with unblinking eyes.

Ryan kept the torch near the tanks, but the flame sputtered again, flickering once, then again before regaining its constant glow. One of the guard pig-rats edged forward, and Ryan swung his blaster to point at its head, which remained perfectly still when it saw the muzzle line up on its face.

"How we coming back there?" he asked over his shoulder.

"Doc, over here! I found it!" Mildred, with her sharp eyes, had spotted the floor markers of the elevator above the piles of crap. "Oh God! There's shit all over the front."

"Don't just stand there like a stupe, clear it!" Ryan was trying to keep his eye on three of the huge pig-rats, who all seemed to be moving in perfect concert at him; one from the left, one from the right, and the largest one coming straight up the center. Ryan triggered a shot in front of the massive one's foot, maiming a small pig-rat near it, but the horse-sized beast simply crushed the wounded one into the ground with its next step, leaving the remains to be fought over by his smaller comrades. Ryan raised his blaster, sighting down the barrel at the middle one, but held his fire, sensing that if he took this one out, the others would be feasting on his guts in the next two seconds, blazing torch or no blazing torch.

Setting down their burdens, Krysty and Mildred joined Doc in attacking the large pile of mutie shit blocking the elevator doors. With muttered curses, they shoveled double handfuls of it out of the way, flinging it aside until a pathway began to take shape.

"Don't keep cleanin'—as soon as one of you can hit the door button, do it!"

As he said that, the torch sputtered again, spitting out several brief bursts of flame before the fuel flow continued. As one, the entire mass of muties surged forward, then stopped as the flame reasserted itself. Ryan threw a glare at the queen, but she seemed content to watch from her position behind the front lines, observing her soldiers advance on the group's seemingly hopeless position.

"Get over, Mildred. Doc and I'll keep working on this." Krysty kicked at the pile with her booted foot, dislodging large chunks of feces and sweeping them out of the way. At the same time, Mildred tensed and leaped up over the two-foot-high pile to the door. She slipped upon landing, but caught herself and slapped the door button. "Nothing's happening. Wait, I got a green light! It's coming down!"

"About fucking time something went right in here." Ryan shook the torch to keep it going, but maintaining the flame was getting harder and harder. Get Jak and J.B. to the doors!"

Sensing a presence beside him, Ryan turned just enough to see Krysty at his side, the M-4000 leveled on her hip. "What are you doing?"

"Sure as hell not leaving you behind to face them alone." Bracing the shotgun, she fired a single round at the nearest small rat, pulping its head and dropping it where it stood. The shotgun's echoing boom made the entire mutie army pause, the larger ones peering at the remains of their companion before lifting their heads to stare at the flame-haired woman and the lethal black cannon she wielded.

"You certainly know how to get their attention."

"Learned from the best." Krysty swept the M-4000's round muzzle back and forth, and Ryan was gratified to see the beasts shy away from it, even the larger ones.

The next thing he heard was one of the sweeter sounds in his lifetime—the soft yet distinct chime of the elevator announcing its arrival.

"Ryan, Krysty, we've got Jak and J.B. inside," Mildred called to them. "Let's go!"

"Okay, you head in, I'll be right behind you." Ryan waited until Krysty was over the hill of crap before taking a cautious step backward, then another, until he felt his foot sink into the pile of dried mutie shit.

"One more thing." With all his strength, Ryan shoved the fuel tanks out into the mass of pig-rats, sending dozens of the smaller ones scattering as the heavy steel cylinders toppled over, hitting the floor with a muffled clank.

"Ryan, what are you doing! Come on!"

The huge muties sniffed the tanks delicately, avoiding the still burning torch, now guttering among the layers of filth on the floor. One lifted a massive leg and released a thick stream of urine onto the nearest cylinder.

"Just leaving them something to remember me by." Raising his blaster, Ryan sighted on the top gauge and squeezed the trigger once, blowing it clean off. Whirling, he turned and leaped into the elevator, accompanied by a loud hissing—the sound of pressurized fuel escaping.

"Close the doors!" Krysty stabbed the button, and Ryan rolled J.B.'s unconscious body to one side. The medium rats were already rushing the shrinking opening, but there was Doc in their way, LeMat raised.

"See you in hell, *mes amis*." Triggering his scattergun

barrel made Ryan's ears pound one last time, but also stopped the first wave of muties.

Just then the tanks exploded, lit by the last dying gasp of the torch. As he dragged Doc down and turned away, Ryan saw an expanding fireball consume the two large muties, along with at least a dozen of the small ones. The flames bloomed outward, coming straight at them...

And then the elevator doors slid shut, cutting them off from the inferno outside. Ryan sat with a thump, letting out a sigh and slumping against the wall, quietly exulting in the elevator's perceptible rising. Catching Krysty's eye, he mustered a tired smile.

"Bet you could really use that shower right about now."

She sniffed. "Look who's talking. You aren't exactly a Deathlands daisy yourself."

Ryan looked down at his clothes, covered in dirt, dung and blood. "Phew. I haven't stunk this bad in weeks—and that's saying something. Which button did you push?"

"The one marked one, of course."

"At least we're going up. That's the best damned thing I've seen in a long time." Mildred spoke without looking up, still bent over to check on the two still forms.

Ryan shifted over near her. "How are they doing?"

"Hard to say. Jak's in shock but that's just his body trying to protect itself the best way it can. J.B.'s better, but he's going down fast. If we don't get help for both of them soon..."

"Least we're out of that hellhole. Anything's got to be better than that."

The elevator dinged again as the cage came to a stop.

Ryan rose to his feet, blaster out, and turned to face the doors.

"Once more unto the breach, dear friends, once more." Doc's voice was low, and Ryan stole a glance at him, his eye widening in surprise. The old man looked exhausted, his already pale skin turned ashen, his thin lips two bloodless lines across his face.

"Doc, mebbe you should sit this one out."

"My dear Ryan, I am in blood, stepped in so far that should I wade no more, returning were as tedious as go o'er. Let us acquit this ghastly place and retire to climes more accommodating, shall we?" The old man attempted a smile, but it came across more as a baring of his uncommonly even, white teeth instead, unnerving enough that Ryan found himself easing back a bit.

"Krysty, keep an eye on him," he muttered from the corner of his mouth, then slapped the button that opened a door for what seemed like the tenth time that day.

Chapter Twelve

The very first thing everyone noticed was the air—clean, calm and a bit sterile, like many of the other redoubts they'd been in.

The doors opened onto a plain, drab-green hallway that stretched off into the distance. Its floor was pristine, light-green tile. More fluorescent lights flickered on as Ryan stepped out, scanning all around for the barest sight of the muties. Only when he was sure there was none around did he wave everyone else out.

"Ryan, there's a map here, too." Mildred, still supporting a limp J.B., peered at the wall next to the elevator. "Main level—barracks, cafeteria, infirmary. This way!"

"Mildred, hold up! Fireblast!" Ryan paused only to pull Jak from Krysty's tired arms and hoist the albino teen over his shoulder. "Come on!"

They set off in a ragged procession, following the determined black woman, who set a grueling pace as she half carried, half dragged the unconscious J.B. through the maze of corridors. After a few minutes, they found her in what was obviously an infirmary ward, setting J.B. on one of the clean beds.

"Put Jak right next to him. This room looks good. Let's just hope I can find what I need." Mildred was off again, darting through a side door, and Ryan heard her joyous whoop. "Yes!" He heard sounds of boxes being opened and rummaging, then she came back pushing a long metal pole on wheels ahead of her, her arms filled with supplies.

"Wheel this over between both beds. We've got to start each of them on intravenous antibiotics. Thank God for vacuum sealing. Even after who knows how long, these should still be good."

Mildred snagged a small cart from a corner and dumped her treasures onto it—needles and surgical tubing, all sealed in plastic, and two empty, clear plastic bags, along with several small, sealed plastic pouches.

"Let's see, ciprofloxacin, daptomycin, and vancomycin ought to do the trick to start." Selecting three packets, she was about to open them when she paused, staring at her crusted, filthy hands. "Damn, let's see if there's any water in the place."

Running to the large sink in the next room, she whooped again. "Everyone, come here. You'll want to wash up!" Ryan and the others trooped into the small room to find Mildred standing at a large metal sink, rolling up her sleeves while the faucet spurted dark brown liquid that gradually faded to yellow, then clear. On a shelf under the sink were several wrapped bars of soap. Grabbing one, Mildred unwrapped it and vigorously scrubbed her fingers, hands and forearms. "Unless you enjoy the feel of rat shit on your hands, you might as well join me."

She rinsed off, then headed back into the main room, leaving the water running for the rest of them.

Krysty was next, luxuriating in the hot soapy water. Ryan watched her with a grin on his face. Noticing him, she arched an eyebrow. "What's so funny?"

"If they've got running water here, I bet they've got showers somewhere else in the complex."

"That would be heavenly." Krysty rinsed off and moved over for Ryan to clean up. "Let's see if Mildred needs any help, then mebbe later we can poke around, see what we turn up."

"Works for me." Ryan sluiced the last of the crap off his hands, glad to see the bits swirl down the drain, then joined Krysty in the main room.

"Doc—" Ryan began, wanting to let him know about the sink.

"Shh!" Mildred nodded toward the curtain that now divided the room in two. "He's in the next bed out cold. I think our little journey took more out of him than he'd admit."

Krysty walked over to where Mildred was busy measuring out various powders from the sealed packets. "Do you need any help?"

"Yes, as a matter of fact." She held up a small bottle of rubbing alcohol and cotton pads. "If you could clean Jak's left arm and J.B.'s right—the palm side, about four inches above the wrist—with this, that would be great. Get Jak's coat off first."

Krysty set to it immediately, leaving Ryan feeling like a bit of a third wheel as the old saying went, although he'd never figured out what it meant. But for the moment he was content to remain quiet and watch the two women work. As usual, he admired the calm, measured way Mildred handled the situation, as skilled in attempting to save lives as she could be in taking them.

"All right, Krysty, I'm going to show you how to blend the antibiotics into the lactated Ringer's bag. Once that's done, we can insert the needles, hang these two, and make up another batch for the next six hours."

"All right, what do I do first?"

Mildred instructed her on creating the solution in a hypodermic syringe, then squirting that into an empty Ringer's bag, and finally using more tubing to transfer the vacuum-packed saline solution into the plastic bag, which would be hung on the pole. When they were both ready, Mildred had Krysty wrap another length of tubing around Jak's skinny arm, pulling it tight until a vein rose, light blue against his white skin.

"There you are." Deftly inserting the needle, she made sure the flow was correct before hanging the bag and adjusting the drip. "I'd say 200 cc's an hour should be a good start. Now let's do J.B."

A few minutes later, both bags were suspended from the rack, steadily dripping their infection-fighting mixture into the two men. "How will you know if it's working?" Ryan asked.

Mildred cleared away the torn packaging and other garbage left over from their work as she replied. "The first few hours are going to be the most crucial. I don't want to start them on something else until I see if this works. They should do the job. I chose the medicines that would be most effective for this type of infection. The problem with that is if it doesn't, they might get worse, but we won't know one way or the other for a while. Now, let's clean and dress those wounds. With any luck, we got the antibiotics into them before any gangrene could start."

They dressed Jak's hand wound first, washing it out with alcohol, then wrapping it in gauze and a clean bandage. J.B.'s legs were a filthy mess of dirt, encrusted feces and dried blood. Ryan's gaze rose to Mildred as they worked, but she was just as efficient as ever, cutting away the torn and dirty cloth of his pants with scissors, then cleaning and dressing the multiple bite and claw wounds on his thighs and shins.

When they had finished, Mildred straightened and arched her back, pressing on it with both hands. "That's about all we can do for them at the moment. I'm going to create another four bags of antibiotics for when these run out, and then we'll just have to wait and see."

Krysty rinsed her hands in the basin they had filled, and was gently tying her hair back with a strip of cloth. "I'll help. Four hands will make half the work."

"Thanks. Ryan, would you mind keeping an eye on these three while we make these up in the next room? Watch J.B. and Jak for any kind of allergic reaction— hives, difficulty breathing, convulsions if it's a severe case, and I hope it won't be. And check on Doc every once in a while. After that trek, he seemed to be more off than usual, if you get my meaning."

"Yeah." Normally Ryan wasn't all that keen on following orders, but he also knew when he was out of his depth, and although he could dress a wound with the best of them, this was one of those times. A wheeled chair had been left in the corner, and Ryan walked over to it, shoved it next to the beds and sat down, finding it surprisingly comfortable. Either that, or he was more tired than he thought.

Muttered voices and the clatter of instruments could be heard in the next room as the women busied themselves creating the next round of antibiotics. Pushing himself over, Ryan peered first at Jak's face, then J.B.'s. Both looked about the same as always. The kid's chalk-white skin was covered in a slight sheen of sweat, and his chest rose and fell rapidly. On the other hand, the Armorer looked as if he had just lain down for forty winks, his breathing even and slow, and his skin cool and dry to the touch. Ryan couldn't tell if that was good or bad, but decided to ask Mildred when she came back out.

The woman were in the small room for about fifteen minutes, just long enough for Ryan to traverse the room a few times on the wheeled chair, including checking the entrance twice for signs of muties, finding none. He had just returned to the space between the two beds when Mildred and Krysty returned, his lover empty-handed, Mildred carrying another of the empty plastic bags.

"Okay, that's done. The saline units are in the one working refrigerator unit back there. It should be chilled before using if it's going to sit around. How's our patients?"

"Not much change," Ryan said. "Jak's running a fever, but J.B. is as warm as he ever gets."

Mildred took another look at both of them, gently thumbing back an eyelid on each one to check the pupil dilation. "Both are still responding to light, so that's good. Jak's body is trying to burn the infection out. J.B.'s, I just don't know. I'd have thought he'd be doing the same."

She checked the nearby IV stand. "Come here, both of you, I'd like to run through the changing process in case I'm asleep when their bags empty."

She ran them both through the procedure, first showing, then having each one go through the motions with the empty bag until she was satisfied. "Why don't you two find someplace to get cleaned up? I'll take the first watch and come get you in a few hours."

Ryan and Krysty exchanged a covert glance, and he replied, "Sure. Anything we can bring back if we find it?"

"Real food would be a treat, although our recent luck

hasn't been great on that score." Mildred glanced back at the room, and the hint of a smile appeared on her face. "If you come across any clothes, I suppose J.B. would feel more comfortable with a new pair of pants nearby. Industrial-strength aspirin, too. I already checked here, but they didn't have anything that common."

"Right, we'll be back soon." Krysty slipped her hand into Ryan's as they let the double doors swing shut, leaving Mildred inside with the recovering members of their group.

Their boots clacked on the spotless floors as Ryan and Krysty spent the next twenty minutes exploring the level, finding a mix of good and bad. There wasn't a scrap of food in the place. Even the large kitchens were bare, although all the tools were still in place to handle the needs of several hundred people, including spices and other nonedible cooking supplies. When Ryan twisted a knob on the massive stove, he heard a clicking noise, followed by a ring of bright blue flames springing to life from the burner.

"Pots and pans and everything to hold anything you wish—and not a scrap of food. Not even self-heats."

Ryan closed a metal cabinet door, its slam echoing in the silence. "Yeah, but no sign of any break-in or internal theft either. It's like they got everything ready, but never dropped off the foodstuffs. Guess we'll have to head outside and try a bit of hunting."

The personal quarters made up for the culinary disappointment, however. The barracks section was as neat and clean as the rest of the place, and consisted of six large rooms, each of which could easily sleep sixty people or more in the rows of plain bunk beds. The rooms also had clothes, sheets and pillowcases, and towels, all sealed in vacuum bags. When Krysty carefully slit open one of the stiff white packages, the towel sprang into soft fluffiness in her hands as it absorbed the air around it. She brought it up to her face, inhaling the clean scent. "Now this is near close to heaven, far as I'm concerned."

Ryan had walked to the far end of the room to find a laundry room, complete with washers, dryers and single-serve packets of soap that had fossilized into solid, white, powdery lumps. But beyond that was something he knew would get Krysty's attention.

Stepping inside the long, tiled room, he walked to the first showerhead and turned the knob beneath, careful to stand out of the way as he did. There was a hissing gurgle from deep inside the pipes, then, with a rattle and a shake, more brown water gushed forth, fading to yellow for a minute before finally running clear.

"Tell me that's what I think it is." Krysty peeked around the entryway.

Ryan grinned back. "You got your wish."

An answering smile lit up her face. "We got a few minutes, don't we, before we head back?"

"We're here now. Might as well get cleaned up."

"Well, maybe not cleaned up right away. Come on."

Ryan didn't need any urging on that front. Leaving the water running, he came back out to find Krysty behind two open cabinet doors, hiding her shapely form. "You getting modest on me now?"

"Just humor me and shuck those filthy things. We'll probably burn them before we leave. I left a towel for you on the bed."

With a shrug, Ryan unlaced his dirty boots and pried them off his feet, then wriggled out of his pants and stripped off his shirt, grimacing at the stink when he was done. "Seems a shame to wrap this towel around my dirty self."

"We got lots more." Krysty closed the door, revealing herself to be also clad only in strategically placed white terrycloth. "Care to join me?"

With that she padded by on bare feet, heading for the shower. Krysty had a marvelous body, but he found that seeing only tantalizing glimpses of it—the curve and swell of the tops of her full breasts, the firm muscles of her lithe legs as she strode away from him, the crimson cascade of her hair as its swayed back and forth with each step—aroused him even more.

He picked up the towel, then tossed it back on the bed. "Won't need that for a while," he said, then strode after her into the warm fog of the shower room.

Chapter Thirteen

Refreshed in more ways than one, Ryan and Krysty walked out of the barracks, both dressed in new, well-fitting clothes.

"I'll say this, they knew how to make stuff that lasted back then." Krysty flexed and shifted, enjoying the feel of her new dark blue jumpsuit, the sleeves rolled up to her elbows, the zipper on the front down just enough to let the air in. After the shower, she had spent a good ten minutes carefully cleaning the muck off her boots, and now the chiseled falcons gleamed again. Her hair, now washed and treated with something called conditioner, flowed past her shoulders in a soft, dark red wave.

Ryan had taken advantage of the vast clothes stores they had found as well, changing his pants for a new set of olive fatigues with large cargo pockets on the sides, slitting the bottoms so he could pull them on and off over his boots. He also wore a new sleeveless black T-shirt that fit him almost like a second skin. His old, soiled boots had been falling apart, so Ryan had chosen the expedient route and selected a new pair of shiny black combat boots, flexing them with each step to break them in while they were safe. In the Deathlands, sore feet could be just as deadly as a bullet.

He also carried a selection of clothes for J.B. and Mildred, including a few towels in case she wanted to clean up more at the infirmary.

As they retraced their steps, Ryan was already thinking about what to do next. "Probably be here for a few days while the boys recover." His stomach rumbled, cutting him off in midsentence.

Krysty glanced at him sideways, a sly smile curling her lips. "Sounds like someone worked up an appetite."

"As I recall, I wasn't the only one," Ryan replied. "Although that does mean food's the first thing on the list, which means finding a way outside. Still got a few bullets for the rifle, so looks like that's up to me."

"Assuming we're able to go outside in the first place. We still have no idea where we are," Krysty mused. "Or if the nearby animals are even edible."

"Yeah, but let's take one thing at a time, okay? Once food's taken care of, then we search for ammunition. If this is a base, they should have that in good supply. Then, mebbe a vehicle, since I imagine none of us want to try to get back to the mat-trans."

Krysty shuddered. "Not in this lifetime, lover."

Ryan nodded. "That makes two of us, and I can't imagine the others feeling any different. I just hope we haven't ended up in the desert. If there isn't anything we can drive out of here, we may have to go back."

"Other than the lack of food, we're pretty comfortable here, so if it's inclement outside, we could hole up here for a while if need be."

"Until we start nibbling on our fingers and toes, no thanks. Let's see how Mildred's doing, and then you and I can go find an exit."

They arrived back at the infirmary to find Mildred struggling to stay awake while watching over her two charges. Neither one's condition seemed to have changed much, but the doctor was optimistic.

"They haven't gotten any worse, which is the best thing I could have hoped for. Means there's no allergic reaction. Now we just have to get enough into them to fight the infection itself."

"Why don't you get some rest, Mildred? We can watch them for a while," Krysty said.

The other woman turned to face them, a wry smile on her face. "Funny, you'd think that's exactly what I'd want to do, except every time I nod off, I keep imagining I hear those damn little rodent piggy mutie feet clattering around me, and I come awake, looking around thinking the little bastards're going for my ankles. Just before you came in, I almost drew my pistol, I was so sure they were in the room. Sometimes these redoubts are too quiet."

"Mebbe there's something here that would help you sleep?"

Mildred jabbed a finger at the two sleeping men. "I don't want to risk being doped if either of them starts having any problems. Nope, I'm in it for the long haul. If they make it into the second bag without a bad reaction, then I'll probably be able to sack out."

"Well, if you aren't going to rest, you might as well get cleaned up." Krysty offered the new clothes along with a bright white towel while she rattled off the directions to the living quarters. "And the showers work just fine."

Mildred pushed herself to her feet and took the bundle. "Now that I will take you up on. Hold down the fort here, and I'll be back in fifteen." She headed out the door and down the hall.

"We'll be here," Krysty said to her retreating back before turning to Ryan. "Or at least, I will be. You got that look in your eye like you want to check out the rest of the complex."

"That obvious, huh?" Ryan grinned. "Might not be the smartest move. Those damn muties might have found another way up here."

Krysty's eyebrow went up. "Think it was safe to let Mildred go off by herself?"

"Didn't see any sign of them in the parts we scouted. She should be all right. Other sections, however, might be another story…"

"But you're itching to take a look around anyway, aren't you?"

Ryan shrugged. "Mebbe. They seem all right, and with you here watching over them, shouldn't be any problem."

Krysty walked over to him, putting her arms around his neck. "You know the first rule of going into any new place—don't go anywhere alone."

Ryan resisted the urge to roll his eye. The rule was one of his own, established very early on, when they had first found the redoubts. "Yeah, yeah, but I didn't—you were with me, remember?"

"I certainly do, but we haven't been everywhere yet. However, it does seem like no one's been here in decades, so it should be safe." She leaned up on her tiptoes and kissed him, lingering there for a few seconds. "You just promise me that you'll come back at the first sign of anything strange."

"After that bastard trip through the basement, I'm not looking for any more trouble." Ryan kissed her again before heading to the door. "If I find the exit, depending on what's out there, I may poke my head out to try and see where we've ended up."

"Ryan…"

"Hey, if you want to eat salt and pepper soup in the kitchen, go ahead, but I'd much rather have something a bit more filling. Don't worry. I promise I won't go far." And before she could protest or caution him again, Ryan disappeared down the corridor.

KRYSTY'S CONCERNS were unfounded. In the next hour, all Ryan found were many more rooms, some filled, some empty, but no sign of life.

In many places, it was just like the barracks—equipment laid in, ready for people to take up residence or duty, but absolutely no sign of any inhabitation. One small room was filled with racks upon racks of thick, waterproofed canvas coats and rubber overshoes, in every size imaginable. Another large room, labeled Food Storage, held hope for Ryan, but when he opened the door, the dusty shelves were completely empty.

Using the posted wall maps as his guide, he made his way to yet another room, this one marked Ammunition. Holding his breath, Ryan opened the door and found himself standing before a wide array of wooden and metal boxes, all stamped with the familiar block printing consistent with the U.S. military of long ago.

Roaming up and down the aisles, he was delighted to find copious 9 mm bullets for his SIG-Sauer and J.B.'s Uzi, and took a few minutes to refill his own pistol's magazines. There were several thousand rounds of 7.62 mm for his Steyr sniper rifle, as well. He even found a few boxes of shotgun shells, and selected a mix of double-00 buckshot, rifled slugs and even a double-handful of the rare fléchette rounds for the M-4000. He also found 12-gauge shells for the lower barrel of Doc's LeMat, and a box of .357 shells for Jak's Magnum. The only caliber he came up short on was .38 caliber, leaving

Krysty's and Mildred's blasters still low on rounds. As he searched for them, he considered trying to have both women switch to a different weapon, particularly one that took the more common 9 mm bullets they often found in redoubts. However, after a futile search for any kind of weapons in the rest of the room, he resigned himself to leaving things as they were for the time being. Loading the needed ammunition into an olive-drab metal box, he left it by the door, intending to pick it up on the way back.

The last thing he wanted to check out before heading back was a broad passageway, wide enough to drive a medium war wag down, that appeared to be the entrance to the complex, complete with the usual vanadium steel door. The dull steel door itself looked as solid as the day it had been installed, keeping the elements at bay for more than a hundred years and looking as if it could do so for another thousand.

Drawing his blaster, Ryan thumbed back the hammer and readied it while he keyed in the code that would open the door. Several outside doors had a lever that allowed the door to be opened in increments. This one didn't. With a ponderous groan, the colossal door rose, revealing the outside for the first time.

The entrance was set in a recess in the ground, and the first thing Ryan saw was a profusion of dry, yellowed weeds that had grown up in the cracks between the concrete slabs serving as pavement leading to the door. The air that wafted in was hot and dry, carrying with it a puff of hot dust. Yellow sunlight illuminated the ground, and he caught of glimpse of a lavender sky overhead, punctuated by fleecy, lemon yellow clouds. Other than that, nothing moved nearby.

Blaster leading the way, Ryan checked the outside

keypad to make sure it still functioned before entering the code to close the door. Moving to the crumbling concrete wall holding up the earthen embankment, he edged out farther, checking above the redoubt entrance first in case an animal—or human—was waiting to pounce on the first thing to come out of the complex in a long, long time.

Nothing leaped onto him from the overhang. Other than the wind blowing a fine cloud of dust, the entrance was deserted. Ryan crept up the side of the slash in the ground until he could see the surrounding landscape.

At first glance, he thought they might be in the part of Deathlands formerly known as the Great Plains. The landscape looked similar, with rolling hills and grasslands turned a parched yellow and brown under the relentless sun. But as he scanned the landscape, he saw large patches of trees around, their leafy shade contrasting with the dry ground.

More interesting was the ruins of large buildings. The grasses, waist-high in places, surrounded the crumbled piles of concrete and rusted metal. Some off in the distance looked as if they might still be intact, and Ryan was about to take a walk over and investigate the nearest when a large animal stepped out from around the crumbling corner of a building about thirty yards away and stopped upon seeing the interloper in its domain.

For a moment, Ryan and the large beast just stared at each other. Large was a misnomer. Although looking like a deer in every respect, it was at least six feet high at the shoulder, and its head loomed far above Ryan's. Its rack was equally impressive, at least five feet across, and filled with dozens of sharp points.

The massive buck's eyes narrowed, and it pawed

the ground, its hoof, easily the size of Ryan's head, furrowing the dry earth underneath.

Ryan tried to keep its gaze locked on him as he moved his left hand slowly around his back to the butt of the Steyr rifle slung over his right shoulder. If he could just reach it, he could tip it down into his right hand, then bring it up and fire—if the buck didn't charge and impale him first.

The deer shook its huge head, the antlers shaking back and forth. Then, it reared up on its back legs for a moment before shooting forward, right at him.

Ryan's palm slapped the stock, and he pushed the rifle off his shoulder. The weapon fell into his right hand, and he twisted it around to bring it up.

The buck accelerated, gaining speed with every step, its pounding hooves seeming to shake the very ground as it hurtled toward him.

Ryan clapped his left hand on the stock as he raised and aimed the rifle, knowing there'd only be one shot before the animal was upon him. Dropping to one knee, he fixed the animal's chest in his sights, hoping to fire before it lowered its head to impale him on the sharp forest of bone rushing at his face and chest.

The deer was less than ten yards away when Ryan shot, just as it began to lower its head. The 7.62 mm bullet smashed into its nose, slicing through it into the mouth, where it split the tongue in two before continuing its tumbling flight, exiting the jaw and carrying a fist-sized chunk of its neck away, including severing the main artery that carried blood to the brain. Seconds away from dying, the gigantic deer stumbled and nearby fell, but its inertia carried it forward in one final lunge, as if it was trying to kill the lowly creature that had just destroyed it.

Ryan skipped back as the huge head slammed into the earth right where he had been standing, the body thudding into the ground right behind it. Sucking in a deep breath, he wiped sweat from his brow before cautiously approaching the massive animal. It tried to lash out at him one last time as he walked forward, but could only move its head weakly from side to side. Drawing his panga, and careful to avoid the lethal rack in case the buck was faking, Ryan knelt and slit its throat, his mouth watering at the idea of fresh meat. Within ten minutes he'd bled it out as best as he could, then hacked off a massive portion of a hindquarter, and hoisted it onto his back, heedless of the blood dripping on his new pants. He headed back to the redoubt entrance, his mouth watering in anticipated taste of roasted deer steak.

Chapter Fourteen

The next few days passed in relative comfort. J.B. and Jak responded well to Mildred's improvised antibiotic cocktail; both awoke the next day, and were strong enough to eat some of the venison soup with dried garlic and wild onion Ryan and Krysty had made in one of the giant stainless-steel pots in the kitchen.

After bringing his bounty back to the kitchen, Ryan had found a small handcart and several large black plastic bags. Pushing the load back out to his kill, he found a small band of savage, skinny coyotes already eyeing his prize. A few carefully placed shots had scared them away, and Ryan had taken his time carving off the best pieces before it spoiled in the hot sun, knowing there would be more than enough left for the scavenging pack to feast on after he was done. The refrigerator in the kitchen worked just fine, and he'd wheeled the whole cart inside and hung the cuts in the chill air. That night's meal, chunks of venison roasted over an open flame, was one of the best in his memory.

He'd spent the next couple of days exploring the rest of the redoubt, and some of the outlying buildings, always careful to keep the Steyr handy in case he ran into another big buck. Although he spotted some in the parched fields nearby, the stink of the decomposing deer's body had to have kept them away.

Most of the buildings were ruins, filled with rusty

remains of unidentifiable equipment that often crumbled to powder when he picked them up. However, one of the more promising ones was still intact, albeit with a rusty lock that broke in his hand when he picked it up. Ryan forced the resisting door open and stood next to the square of sunlight that pierced the interior gloom, just in case someone had beaten him to whatever was inside. When he was sure it was safe, he peeked inside and let out a low whistle.

The building was filled with vehicles, from the squat, tan Humvees Ryan had seen some wealthy barons use as heavily modified sec vehicles, to larger tracked personnel carriers and other wheeled vehicles, including two he thought might serve their needs if they were to drive out of here.

As soon as J.B. and Jak were well enough to walk, Ryan and the rest of the group went outside to the garage. The first thing the Armorer insisted on doing was finding out exactly where they were with the aid of his miniature sextant, calculating their longitude and comparing it on the laminated map he carried.

"According to this, we're on the west side of what used to be Wisconsin, right in the middle of the continent, about ten miles away from the Mississippi River."

Ryan got right to the point. "Where's the nearest mat-trans?"

J.B. licked his lips and pointed due west. "On the other side of the river are those jungles of Minnesota, and the nearest redoubt with a working mat-trans."

Even in the heat, Mildred hugged herself and shivered, although she tried to pass it off as the shadow from a cloud passing under the sun. Ryan knew all too well why that idea didn't hold much attraction for her. The last time they had visited the steaming rain forest to the west, where they had first found Mildred in her cryo-freeze chamber, they had also encountered a ville of brutal Vikings who had tried to sacrifice the black woman to their pagan gods. Ryan and the others had broken up the attempted murder before Mildred's blood had been spilled, and they'd left the area soon after.

"Course, that assumes we can ford the river. Even up here it's pretty wide, and if any bridges are nearby, they're probably heavily guarded. Take a lot of jack to cross, otherwise we have to search for another way."

As he leaned on his sword stick, Doc's eyes roamed the barren landscape before turning to the group. "Everything our stalwart companion has said indicates that going west, young man, does not sound like a suitable journey. Mayhap we can find a more suitable location to use as our means of egress."

J.B. brought his map close to his face, squinting in the bright light. "Remember Chicago? It's about four hundred miles away, if the roads hold up." He held the map out to Ryan. "We cross the state, should be there in four or five days, depending on what lies between us and it."

"What about mutie women there?" Jak piped up, his mane of hair restrained by a green army cap that shaded his sensitive eyes from the sun.

Ryan grinned at the mention of the underground tribe they'd encountered on their last trip through the nuked city. "I think we'll have something to dissuade them if they make a play for anyone again. Come on. I want to show you all something."

It took all of Ryan's, Krysty's and Mildred's efforts to heave the large garage door up enough for them to be able to drive a vehicle out underneath.

Although J.B. had been improving rapidly, the sight of the military vehicles ignited a fire that Ryan was all too familiar with. Adjusting his spectacles, the smaller man wandered up and down the rows created by the parked troop carriers and off-road vehicles, his lips moving soundlessly as he studied olive-drab profiles, weapons systems and mysterious acronyms.

After ten minutes, he emerged, blinking owlishly in the sunlight. "Well, all these were stored pretty well, for what it's worth. Like to get one of the bigger ones out, but I'm not sure it'll run. Otherwise, there's the four-wheel model there, a LAV 150 Commando, that would do the job, especially since it's amphibious, so we can ford any smaller streams we might come across. It's only supposed to hold a crew of three, plus two more, so it'll be a bit cramped, but we'll manage."

The rest of the day was spent jockeying the other vehicles out of the cavernous storage area to get at the larger vehicle—a LAV 300, J.B. called it—and see if they could get it running. Unfortunately, the electrical system was shot. No matter what J.B. tried—charging the battery, replacing fuses—the large machine's engine refused to turn over.

"Too bad. That would have been riding in style. Well, let's try the Commando tomorrow."

On that one they had better luck. J.B. spent the evening sipping broth and reading the thick manual, then Ryan and he took most of the morning to go over the engine, changing the oil, checking the spark plugs and making sure its fuel was good before trying to fire it up. The rumble of the gas engine split the hot silence outside, its exhaust belching white smoke that quickly dissipated in the still afternoon air.

"Let's take her for a spin." J.B. climbed into the

driver's seat while Ryan took the commander's position. As he passed the gunner's station, he noticed a joystick control and small monitor there. "Hey, haven't we seen this before?"

J.B. glanced back, and his lips split in a rare smile. "Yeah, I was gonna show you that in a bit. Now buckle up."

Ryan eased himself into the commander's seat, then J.B. depressed the clutch, shifted into gear, eased the Gas down and got the Commando rolling. The steering was stiff at first, but as the amphibious ground car warmed up, J.B. was able to turn the wheel with less effort. The engine sounded surprisingly good, but he drove it in a large circle, then back to the front of the garage, where he let it idle for a minute before turning it off.

"Well, that should get us most of the way there, at least. It's got a range of four hundred miles, and we'll bring extra gas, but who knows what the terrain is like between here and there. Figure we'll head out at first light tomorrow?"

"Yeah, use the rest of the day to load up and smoke the rest of that venison. Now, what's this device you're gonna show me?"

J.B. scrambled out of the driver's seat and into the gunners, moving as spry as a kid with his first blaster. Ryan settled back, ready for a torrent of words to spill forth on the only subject that got J.B. excited—munitions.

"This little number's called the XM101 Common Remotely Operated Weapons System, or CROWS for short. Basically, instead of a manually operated turret, where your shooter has to view their targets by eyeball, this system lets you acquire your target, rangefind and shoot from the comfort of your armored cockpit."

J.B. grasped the joystick and moved it to the left, then the right. Above them, Ryan heard a mechanical whirring as something moved on the roof. J.B. turned on the small LCD screen, which flared to life and showed the desolate landscape outside. "The camera is independently mounted from the blaster, so you can be tracking someone, but it can be pointed in a different direction. Less chance of scaring whoever you're looking at that way."

Ryan snorted. "Yeah, that option comes up so often out here."

"Well, at least you can watch your target before deciding to reduce them to a bloody smear. The gunner has full 360 viewing capability—eyes in the back of his head. It can also elevate to a sixty-degree angle, and decline to a twenty-degree angle, giving us a fantastic field of fire. But that isn't even the best part."

"Oh?"

J.B. flipped up a bright red switch cover, revealing a bright red switch underneath. He flipped it up, and a gunsight appeared on the screen, zeroing in on the leafless tree trunk. A number appeared in the upper right hand corner—43.71 yards—and the crosshairs flashed from red to green.

J.B. pressed the large trigger mounted on the front of the joystick, and a loud, rumbling burst erupted from the top of the vehicle. Ryan pressed his hands to his ears, but as soon as the cacophony had begun, it was over. Checking the screen, he found the tree had simply vanished. The waist-thick trunk had been blown into thousands of splinters, leaving only a jagged couple of feet of stump.

The Armorer's grin stretched from ear to ear. "The main weapon is the GAU-4 gas-operated Vulcan 20 mm rotary cannon. With a fire rate of 4000 rounds per minute and a range of at least three thousand yards, it's more than a match for any small to medium group we may encounter. It's devastating at close range, as you just saw. I just have to refill the hundred or so rounds I just used in that two-second burst."

Ryan still hadn't taken his eyes off the screen, and what was left of the tree. One second it had been there, the next it had disintegrated into toothpicks. "Just the thing to keep us covered on our drive through the countryside, you think?"

"Exactly."

Ryan made sure the rest of the group spent most of the day packing whatever they needed to head out at first light the next day. From Jak creating replacement throwing knives on a grinder in a small workshop to caching extra gas and water—and being careful not to mix the two up—to Mildred creating small packs of vitamin pills and practically ordering everyone to take them, everyone made sure they were ready to roll come morning.

After dinner, Ryan and Krysty took this last opportunity to get a little privacy by moving into one of the empty quarters. They had actually gotten the idea from J.B. and Mildred, who had slipped away earlier in the evening.

With full bellies and a pleasant, relaxed sense of security for once, their lovemaking had been slow and enjoyable. Krysty had taken the lead, straddling Ryan so that she rose above him like a glorious, nude Valkyrie, her dark red hair tumbling freely around her shoulders, just brushing the tops of her breasts. Ryan had filled his hands for several minutes, then moved on to other parts until they were both panting and satiated.

Afterward, he spooned with her on a pair of bunk beds they had pushed together for just this purpose.

"Haven't felt this good in a while, lover," she murmured sleepily.

"Mmm. Always best to enjoy the good times while you can. They're usually over all too quick." Ryan kissed her on the cheek, then allowed himself to drift off to sleep, for once unfettered by dark dreams or ominous thoughts of tomorrow.

Chapter Fifteen

The next morning dawned clear, bright and hot. The sky had turned a darker purple overnight, but the clouds had disappeared, leaving clear, violet emptiness stretching all the way to the horizon. No breeze stirred the grass, promising a hot afternoon inside the war wag.

While J.B. plotted their route, Ryan assigned positions. "Jak, take the front blaster. Krysty, you're on the back. A two hour shift, then I'll replace Jak, and, Mildred, you'll spell Krysty. Doc, I want you to be ready to take over either position if necessary. The blasters are simple enough, we're running with them loaded and ready, so just point and shoot. No air conditioning, but we got a wide enough field of vision and fire that we should be able to run with the hatches open, so it won't get too hot."

Jak turned his head and spit. "Bastard oven inside."

"Better than walking in this heat."

The albino nodded, his eyes straying to the black 20 mm cannon mounted in the squat turret.

"Not today, son, that's J.B.'s post. Mebbe you'll get a chance at it later."

Jak crossed his arms. "Who drive?"

"For the first stretch, me. Then we'll see."

For a moment, Jak looked as if he was going to push the issue, but then he shrugged, feigning disinterest, and turned back to the armored vehicle.

"All right, everyone got everything?"

"I daresay, Ryan, you have the interior packed so tight a body can scarcely wedge himself inside," Doc called from the entry hatch.

Ryan had crammed every kind of trade good he could think of, from clothing to ammunition to spices, into every storage space, nook, cranny he could find. "Yeah, it's tight, but I figure we'll be better off trading our way along than trying to intimidate our way through."

The one-eyed man had checked the redoubt door one last time. "Yeah, she's sealed tight. Time to ride." He walked past the remains of the giant deer he'd shot a few days earlier, now just large, white bones covered with gnaw marks and dried scraps of meat, bleaching in the sun.

After everyone else had got themselves situated more-or-less comfortably, Ryan swung up and into the already warm, cramped crew compartment, twisting himself around to fit into the driver's seat. As he did so, he dislodged a small container of pepper, which fell onto the floor and almost skittered under the seat before he stopped it with a boot.

"All this crap better be worth it," J.B. commented from the gunner's chair, surrounded by bundles of rolled-up fatigue pants and shirts.

Ryan didn't bother to reply, but hit the ignition button, the engine's roar splitting the early morning silence. "All right, where to?"

J.B. bent over a paper map of the region he'd found in one of the redoubt offices. He'd spent much of the previous night carefully laminating it with one of the several hundred rolls of vacuum-sealed clear plastic tape he'd uncovered in a storeroom. "The main gate is about a mile due south, just take something called W.

Thirteenth Avenue, and keep bearing right. It leads to State Highway 21, which, if still intact, will take us to road I-90, which will take us southeast toward what's left of what was the state capital—Madison—and then farther on to another large city, Mil-wauk-ee."

"Milwaukee?" Mildred piped up. "Home of the Brewers and Miller Beer. Back in the seventies and eighties people called it the armpit of America—or was that Cincinnati?"

"I doubt we'll be going there, since we'll be heading more southeast, but let's get off this base first before thinkin' about sightseeing." Putting the heavy vehicle in gear, Ryan let out the clutch and stepped on the Gas, slowly moving them out. The engine sounded as if it was in fairly good condition, but he proceeded forward slowly, keeping it at a steady thirty-five miles per hour.

As they approached where J.B. said the gate was, they saw more collapsed shells of buildings, picked over by time and scavengers until nothing but metal skeletons remained. Ryan drove down a wide thoroughfare, which could have held another two Commandos side-by-side, until they came to the remains of a large metal gate. Bare metal fence posts stretched into the distance on both sides. Except for the rumbling engine, nothing else nearby made a sound.

Ryan turned the wheel left and shifted, the large tires humming on the ancient pavement as they picked up speed. The wind stirred by their passage blew through the small ob ports, providing much-needed breeze. J.B. kept the turret moving, scanning the horizon ahead for any sign of trouble. Ryan didn't need to check with Jak or Krysty. He knew they'd sing out at the first sign of anything strange.

"Place called Tomah comin' up, where we join the highway," J.B. called out to Ryan. "Couple miles ahead."

Sure enough, less than ten minutes later the skyline of a small town appeared on the horizon. "Button up," Ryan called out, hearing the clanks of hatches being closed. "Everyone look sharp."

"Bridge crossing ahead—it's manned." J.B. said right afterward.

"We go in slow and easy, see what kind of reception we get." Ryan downshifted to first, slowing the vehicle to about twenty miles an hour until he was within a half mile of the bridge, then he slowed to ten miles an hour and drove forward until he was sure they had all of the guards' attention.

Bridges were a common toll point in the Deathlands, with villes often springing up on one side or the other of the natural barrier. An existing crossing was often the only one for dozens or even hundreds of miles in either direction, with hundreds of others having succumbed to the steady ravages of time or men. The communities near a bridge guarded and maintained it in exchange for a barter price, which Ryan and his companions were about to try to negotiate.

About one hundred yards away, Ryan brought the Commando to a stop and scanned their potential enemies. The guards in this case were patchwork militia, any able-bodied man and boy old enough to point a blaster pulling duty, about a dozen in all. They were armed with a bewildering variety of weapons, from battered hunting rifles, shotguns and homemade hand-blasters to melee weapons, including a pitchfork, with one even carrying a gleaming scythe. Everyone looked tense and ready for action—although Ryan knew they could have just mowed them down with the Commando without a shot, as nothing the guards carried could penetrate the war wag's armor. That was probably the only reason bullets weren't spanging off their ride just yet—they hadn't moved to attack just yet, so the guards were waiting for a more diplomatic approach.

At least, Ryan hoped that's what they were waiting for.

"J.B., where's that cannon pointing?"

"I got it aimed off the left and pointing down. Hopefully they'll think it's out of order."

"Good. Jak, you ready?"

"Good field fire. Take half down one burst."

"Keep your finger near, but not on that trigger unless I say so, you hear?"

"Yeah."

Ryan pushed up the top hatch and poked his head out, being careful to drop back down at a moment's notice. "Hello the bridge!"

One man stepped forward, a scoped longblaster held at port arms. "Hello, outlanders!"

"Like to cross. What's the toll?"

"Trade only, what kin y'offer?"

Ryan took a moment before answering, as if checking. "Got ammo, some tools, clothes, spices."

The man in front didn't react, but the line rippled in murmured wonder as the men whispered among themselves. The leader half turned and silenced them with a look. "We can barter. Ya mind comin' out to talk, mebbe bring a bit o' what yer carryin'?"

There was the crux of it. If these guards were cold-hearts looking to profit from any outlanders, then Ryan and anyone who came with him were targets to be taken hostage or killed for the wag, which was priceless. If they were decent men just looking to protect their ville, then there shouldn't be a problem, but still…

"Yeah, we can talk, but know this—I got more people in here, and we'll be covered by the wag's blasters, including this one."

At Ryan's words, the 20 mm cannon came to life, the six barrels elevating and swiveling over to point directly at the line. He saw several men ready their weapons, and one teenager even raised his rifle to his shoulder before the leader barked a sharp command. As one, the group set their weapons back to port arms, even those holding the close-combat ones.

"Fair enough, but y'all know this—if'n ya kill us, you'll never cross the bridge."

Ryan raised an eyebrow at that, but shrugged. "All right then, you and one other representative come out halfway, and me and one of mine'll meet you there." He dropped down through the hatch, locking it behind him. "Krysty, let's go. Mildred, take the rear blaster. Everyone else, watch for my signals."

The two women exchanged places without a word, and Ryan popped the side hatch and slid through it, then turned to see if Krysty needed a hand, which she didn't, slipping outside with her usual limber grace.

Ryan grabbed a selection of goods from the wag and distributed them between himself and Krysty, then they headed out. Being outside was a pleasant change from the already stifling interior of the wag. A breeze had kicked up that ruffled through Ryan's curly hair, cooling the sweat on the back of his neck as they approached the other pair.

As he came closer, Ryan saw the ville speaker appeared relatively clean-cut, with a neatly trimmed brown beard and hair, rather than the often-bushy growth many men favored. The man, who looked to be approaching the near side of middle age, carried the longblaster as if he knew how to use it, but although Ryan's hands were full, he was pretty sure he could drop the stuff he was carrying, draw and shoot the guy before he could fire.

They met in the road, halfway between the two sides. The man nodded in greeting, neither hand leaving his weapon. The other man held a rusty revolver, but it was also out and readied, carried in front of his chest.

As he'd figured, both men's eyes widened when they saw Krysty. With J.B. manning the cannon, and Jak's unusual appearance, Doc's shaky mental state, and Mildred's often sharp tongue rendering each of them unsuitable for the task at hand, Krysty was the best partner he could ask for at the moment, especially when bargaining with men.

Ryan gave the leader credit, he recovered fast, although he seemed to be staring at Ryan harder than was necessary under the circumstances. "Greetings, outlander. What ya got?"

Nodding to Krysty, they stepped forward and placed the various items on the road, then stepped back, keeping their hands in plain sight the entire time. The leader confirmed that his second was keeping an eye on the two outlanders, before walking forward to examine the goods. Although he tried to hide it, his gaze kept returning to the shells Ryan had set down, although he also showed interest in the small assortment of spices they'd packaged for the trip, including the more exotic ones like black pepper and vacuum-sealed containers of dried basil, oregano and sage, taken from the stores of the redoubt kitchen.

The man finished his review and stepped back. "How much .308 and shotgun ammo you carrying?"

Ryan rubbed his chin. "Mebbe fifty rounds of the ball ammo, and a hundred of the 12-gauge." He was lowballing—there was five times that amount for the two machine guns inside, but he saw no reason to mention it.

The man's tongue flicked out to lick dry lips. "We'll take forty .308 and fifty of the 12-gauge for passage for all of you and the vehicle. Disarm your weapons first, and you'd be welcome into the ville, where you could trade for any other items you may need."

"Sounds a bit steep—why don't we say twenty of the .308 and twenty-five of the shotgun? I'll even throw in a sample of the spices we're carrying for the womenfolk."

Ryan saw the second man—more a boy, really, barely out of his teens—wipe his mouth, and figured he had a deal. Only salt could be easily found in the Deathlands, crudely processed from the ocean. Spices like the ones he was carrying were worth their weight in gold—even more sometimes, since a person couldn't eat gold.

The man spoke up again. "Thirty bullets and forty shotgun shells—that's my final offer."

Ryan took his time replying, gazing first up the river, then down. "Could find another place to cross, then you'd have nothing."

The man smiled for the first time, revealing yellowed teeth. "Nearest bridge is more'n a hundred miles south, and they'd just as soon shoot ya as talk over there."

"Still, your price seems high. One bullet could get me a night's lodging and food in most villes."

"Times are tough," the second man said. "Caravans don't come by as often—"

The leader turned his head to stare at his backup. "Quiet, Jabe."

He turned back to Ryan. "Looks like ya got a destination in mind, and where yer going takes ya right through our ville. Could go around, but that takes a lot of gas. The toll is what it is—you kin pay and pass, or turn around and head back the way you came."

Ryan had been considering simply paying what had been asked—the bargaining had been tough but fair—but the man's dismissive tone had gotten his back up. He looked past the man's shoulder at the bridge in the distance. "Not sure what you're offering is going to do it. The wag's kind of heavy. It might bust your bridge right in half."

The man smirked. "She'll hold, I guarantee it myself."

"That's kind of you, but I'm not sure how I'd hold you to it if we end up at the bottom of the river with the fish nibbling our eyeballs. Nope, I think we'll find another way across."

His calm words took both men by surprise. "Like I said, if ya ain't crossing here, you're risking a lot more than a few bullets. Come on, be reasonable."

"We'll see you on the other side. Come on." Ryan scooped up the sample of goods, turned and walked back to the war wag, Krysty falling into step beside him.

"What's going on? The price for crossing wasn't that bad."

"Didn't like his tone, that's all. Besides, I think we can cross this river and not have to pay them anything."

"They see that, they might chill us all at being taken."

Ryan had reached the hatch of the wag by now, and opened it up. "It'd take a hell of a lot more than them to take us out. Let's go."

J.B.'s sweating face greeted them. "How'd it go?"

Ryan swung into the driver's seat. "We're crossing the river—just not over that bridge."

Chapter Sixteen

J.B. digested that for a moment. "They ask too much?"

Krysty glared sideways at Ryan for a moment. "Nothing we couldn't afford."

Settling into the driver's seat, Ryan silenced her with his own ice-blue gaze. "That bridge might not support the wag's weight—all eleven tons of it. If it breaks, we're out our ride, might even die trying to get out. J.B., you said this thing was amphibious, right?"

"Manual said so. You sure about this?"

"Yeah, let's move out." Firing up the engine, Ryan left the road, driving parallel to the river.

Mildred's voice called out from the back. "What's going on up there? Folks're climbing the bridge to watch us leave."

"Both blasters keep watch front and back. J.B., stay on the 20 mil."

"Hope you know what you're doing, lover."

"Don't worry about it, we'll be fine." The slightly nervous feeling in Ryan's gut belied his words, but he pressed on. "This should do."

The waterway had probably been a small stream decades ago, but decades of the water's relentless passage had widened it into a river, easily thirty feet across at this point, and probably ten to fifteen feet deep in the middle. The current was swift, the black waters bubbling and churning as it flowed toward the bridge. "Everyone make sure all hatches are secure, because we're about to go for a little swim."

Ryan had picked a section of bank that sloped into the water on both sides, rather than trying to ford the water off a small cliff. He gunned the engine while waiting for a reply.

"Front hatches secure," Jak called out.

"Rear hatches secure," Mildred replied from the back.

"Top hatch is secure," Doc said from the middle of the wag.

"Hold tight—here we go." Ryan dropped it into gear and pressed the accelerator, feeling the wag lurch forward. The river grew larger in his view, until it took up all of his vision, then, with a jolt and sudden tilt, they rushed down the bank and into the water with a large splash.

Ryan swayed in his chair with the sudden rocking motion as the Commando entered the river, but it kept powering its way forward, although more slowly now. The current lapped at his viewport, but otherwise the V-150 was unaffected by the water. Indeed, they were already almost to the other side, and with another bump, the wheels found the riverbed and Ryan floored it, sending the wag rocketing up the other side in a spray of water.

"Worked better than I thought," he said, turning back toward the town.

Krysty's face was drawn. "Just hope we haven't crossed into a whole mess of trouble with your little stunt."

"Only one way to find out." Ryan approached the bridge, slowing to a crawl as he came closer to the town. "J.B., best lower the cannon. We might scare them otherwise."

"Already doin' it." Ryan brought the wag to a stop a couple hundred yards from the bridge as the leader, who had already crossed the overpass, was trotting over, flanked by a half dozen men trailing him. Small children peeked out from around the corners of houses, and women hastily shooed them inside, slamming doors behind them.

"Let's see what they have to say this time." Moving to the top hatch, Ryan unlocked it, shoved it open and cautiously poked his head out again.

The bearded leader stood a dozen yards away, hands on his hips. "If you coulda crossed the river without us, why come out to barter?"

Ryan shrugged. "Wasn't sure I could in the first place. Besides, needed to know if you folks were honest or going to try a double cross."

"Ain't no reason fer that. We do all right out here fer ourselves, and trade for the rest of what we need." The man put one hand behind his back, and the rest of the men with him visibly relaxed. "Well, ya don't need to cross our bridge anymore, but I bet we got other stuff ya'd be willin' to trade fer. Why don't you shut yer wag down and come on in? At the least you all can break bread with us, share any news ya might have from the west."

Ryan considered the offer for a moment, then nodded. "Sure. Give me a minute, and we'll be right out." He disappeared into the cab. "Let's head in, blasters only, keep them in your holsters. They seem friendly enough, but we'll stick together. Watch their reaction to Jak. That'll tell right off what we need to know."

It took a few minutes of awkward scrambling, but at

last the group was able to exit the wag with a semblance of dignity. The guards greeted them with politeness, some hiding their surprise better than others at Jak's unusual appearance. At least no one made the sign of the evil eye or spit at seeing him, as had happened in other villes they'd come across. It said a lot about the people here, and Jak accepted it with stolid silence.

Ryan walked over to the leader and began making introductions, saving himself for last. When he did, however, the leader's eyebrows shot up.

"Ryan Cawdor? *The* Ryan Cawdor?"

Now it was Ryan's turn to be surprised. "You know me?"

"I knew it! I thought it was you! Lots of people here heard of you'n the Trader. Hell, I even met ya once, a long time ago. I was mebbe fifteen, and you were a few years older at the time. The Trader rolled into town and stayed here for a day or two. Good man—always treated us fair. Whatever happened to him?"

Ryan's mouth twisted at the question about his former mentor, but he quickly calmed his expression. "He and I parted ways a while ago. I've seen him here and there across the land, last time down south several months back. For all I know, he's still roaming around out there somewhere."

The last sentence was only partially true. When Ryan had last seen the Trader, he'd sacrificed himself to save Ryan and his group, making sure they had gotten on a raft while he stayed behind on shore to fend off the folks pursuing them. Abe, one of the last men to follow the Trader, had stayed behind with him, surrounded by murderous stickies and hostile locals. At the moment Ryan had no idea if the man was dead or alive. Still, the old man had an uncanny knack of wriggling out the tightest damn spots....

The leader's words jolted Ryan out of his reverie. "Too bad. If ya ever run into him again, be sure to send him up our way. We'd be happy to see him agin." The man held out his hand, which Ryan took and pumped once. "I'm Brend Towson." He introduced the rest of the men, with at least three others sharing his surname. "Welcome to Toma."

Half of the group peeled off to head back to the bridge, the others remained with the group as they headed into town. Before they left the wag, J.B. told Ryan he needed to check on the engine, and disappeared under the vehicle for several minutes. When he returned, he came up to Ryan and clapped him on the shoulder. "Runnin' a little hot, but it's fine now." The words were a subtle sign that he'd removed a spark plug, ensuring that the vehicle couldn't be stolen. They'd also removed the firing pins from all the blasters, rendering the wag an inert hunk of metal. But Ryan and his group would make sure to check on it during the night. Just because Brend and his closer relatives seemed friendly didn't mean everyone here would be.

"You the baron of the ville?"

Brend laughed. "No, not really. We have a town council that meets once a week to handle any issues, but everyone here pretty much keeps the peace among themselves."

"What about raiders?" J.B. asked.

"We're pretty much off the beaten track. You all are the only ones we've seen in the past month. With the bridge and the river, we don't see too much trouble, and all of the men are pretty good shots, so it'd take quite a force to actually do any damage here."

Ryan held his tongue, figuring it wouldn't do any good to mention that their lone wag could destroy the entire town if he'd chosen to do so. He simply nodded instead.

"So, where'd you folks come from? The I-90 road only leads to the ruins of Sparta and L'Crosse, then the big river."

Ryan exchanged a quick glance with J.B. before replying. "We were following one of our usual trade routes, coming down from Canada, around the Great Lakes, and over to this side of the Big Muddy. Heard rumors of a cache of predark stuff somewhere around here, thought we'd take a look-see. You know of anything nearby?"

Brend forced a laugh. "If we did—and wanted to risk our lives tryin' to get it—you think we'd be livin' like this?"

Ryan frowned at the reply. "We passed some kind of base sign on the road west of here. Anything in there?"

Brend's face darkened, and he turned to spit on the ground. "No one ever goes there. That's from before, ya know? Got enough problems livin' in the here and now. No need t'go stirrin' up any more trouble."

Now that Brend and the guards had cleared Ryan and his group, other members of the ville cautiously approached. Soon they found themselves surrounded by a small cluster of women and young children, all dressed in homespun garb in simple colors, mainly white, dark brown and dark blue. Jak attracted the most attention, his white hair and red eyes drawing whispers and stares. Doc also garnered his fair share of stares. With his antiquated clothes and manner of speech, he caused alternating consternation and fits of giggling from any of the women and girls he spoke to.

"Well, now we gotta start all over again with the barter," Brend grumbled, though his tone carried no malice. "Since ya don't need our bridge, is there anything ya *do* need?"

"Well..." Ryan drew the word out for a few seconds before smiling. "Actually, there are a few things we could use."

"Food—real food," Jak said, his arms folded, trying to watch everyone around them at once.

"And any information you might have about what lies to the east," J.B. said. "Particularly near the Great Lakes area."

"I think we kin do business—and at a price that works for ever'one. C'mon, we'll show ya around."

Chapter Seventeen

The rest of the day passed in strangely peaceful relaxation. Ryan was able to arm both women with plenty of reloaded .38-caliber bullets in exchange for a few original .308 slugs. Just to show there were no hard feelings about the bridge, he threw in a dozen shotgun shells, too. They traded more ammo and some of the spices for other food, dried fruits, canned vegetables in valuable glass jars, some fresh ones as well, and salted meat. Of particular interest were the crusty loaves of fresh-baked sourdough bread, baked from stone-ground wheat grown in the area and made from a starter that one of the wives boasted had originated more than fifty years ago.

The ville held a feast for the visitors that night, with everyone attending. There was plenty of venison, served several different ways, including several roasted haunches, a huge black pot of stew, and another pot slow-cooked and shredded for thick, sloppy sandwiches. They also served several other kinds of meat, including rabbit, squirrel, pig and chicken. There were plenty of vegetables: potatoes, tomatoes, zucchini, cucumbers and carrots. They even had fresh milk and butter, churned the day before. The real treat was thick, golden honey, collected from a large hive of mutie bees on the outskirts of town. The townspeople paid special reverence to the beekeeper family, who practically risked their lives every time they went out to collect it. They also distilled a strong, sweet mead from the honey, which left a pleasant, warm burn in the back of the throat after each swallow.

Ryan and his company ate their fill, with Jak almost getting sick after wolfing down three huge plates loaded with food. Afterward, there was dancing and music, with several people bringing out ancient instruments, including a violin, tin whistle and a tarnished snare drum, all forming a bizarre combo that came together with the ease of years of practice. They were mostly limited to hymns, but when the violin player sawed the opening bars of a fast-paced waltz, Doc rose and walked over to Krysty, bowing from the waist.

"Master Cawdor, would you mind if this old man asked Miss Wroth for a dance?"

Feeling full and expansive, Ryan was chewing on a sliver of oak after using it to clean his teeth. He glanced at Krysty, who had covered her smile with the back of her hand. "Permission isn't mine to give, Doc. The lady's right here, why don't you ask her yerself?"

The elderly man bowed again, all genteel courtesy, and held out his hand. Krysty rose to take it, and he led her out to the rough square formed by the rows of tables and benches. With a flourish, he drew her in close and swept the flame-haired woman around the floor in a whirl, his right hand around her waist, his left holding her right up and out at their side. Around and around they twirled, covering the floor in a series of circles, always moving counterclockwise on the floor.

"He waltzes well," Brend observed from beside Ryan.

"Better him than me." The one-eyed man thought about mentioning that Doc might have been around when this particular variation of the dance had been invented, but decided against it. Instead, he turned the conversation to more mundane matters. "You'd said you'd let us know what to expect east of here."

"That I did, but I'm not sure it's gonna be much use. None of us have headed out that way in the past few years. Villes round here look out for each other, and each helps all in time of need. Occasionally a caravan passes through from the east, and almost all of them have been carrying fresh and smoked fish—large ones—so either they're stocking up from the lakes, or someone over there is supplying them. But we've never taken that much interest—just trade with those that come through. It's a hard life here, but a good one, and we aim to keep it that way. One way to do that is to not go courtin' trouble."

Ryan nodded as he watched the festivities before him—Doc kicking up his heels as he waltzed a laughing Krysty around the hardpacked dirt, Mildred sitting next to J.B. down the table, their hands no doubt intertwined underneath. Jak off to one side, talking with some of the braver older children. For a moment he saw what all of the people here saw—a sense of community, a sense of place, of growing up where their fathers and their father's fathers had lived, of carving out a life from the land, of working with people you knew and trusted, and knowing that they would repay the favor when you needed it.

It could very well be a good life, but it wasn't the one for him. Not here. Not now. Maybe not ever. Ryan wasn't given much to introspection, but he knew himself well enough to realize that this sort of existence was, in reality, a trap. Although he could adapt to their simple existence well enough, it would chafe at him, the sameness of it, day in and day out, with nothing new over the horizon but the sun, rising and setting as it put another endlessly similar day to rest. No thanks. While he wasn't exactly sure what he was looking for, he knew this wasn't it.

The musicians finished the waltz with a flourish, and the dancers clapped in appreciation. Doc led Krysty back to the table, his eyes gleaming with what Ryan thought might be tears, but the old man quickly looked away.

"Thank you, Krysty. That was…that was wonderful. For a moment, I fair thought I was holding my dear Emily in my arms again as we did a turn around the floor."

"Oh, Doc—" she began, but he cut her off with a sniff.

"Never you mind, my dear, you should forgive the ramblings of a senile old fool." He straightened and cleared his throat with a phlegmy rumble. "I believe I shall take a brief constitutional down by the river."

Krysty nodded, and Ryan spoke up. "Don't go too far. Never know what animals might be out after dark."

"Your friend should be safe. We've taken care of any large predators in the area. If he stays near the river and town, he'll do all right," Brend said.

Flourishing his walking stick, Doc strode away. The musicians were about to strike up another tune when a loud voice cut through the night.

"Horse shit! I'm tellin' ya, no one can do that!"

Heads turned at the words, including Ryan's and Krysty's, to see Jabe, the young man who had come out with Brend at the bridge, pointing an accusing finger at Jak, whose pale ruby eyes glittered in the firelight. "I don't care what ya say, yer a shit-eatin' liar!"

Brend was on his feet in a flash. "Jabe! How dare you insult our guest!"

His son—for only a father would speak to kin that way—turned at the sudden silence, his feet shuffling on the dirt. He had one of the small mead cups in his hand, and Ryan figured it had been filled and emptied more than once that evening. He lifted his own cup at Jak in a silent question, and got a quick shake of the albino's head.

"Not liar. Said can do it, and can."

"Do what?" Ryan asked.

Jak nodded at the other teen. "Towhead said not hit thrown piece wood with knife. Said could."

Ryan draped an arm over the back of his wooden chair. "Sounds like a challenge to me."

Now both youths turned to him. "What'd ya have in mind?" Brend asked.

"I imagine your boy is a fair shot with a blaster."

The other man's chest puffed out. "None better. He can put out the eye of a chicken at one hundred yards."

"All right, then. Each gets one chance. Jak with his knives, Jabe with his blaster. Whoever hits the target wins. To keep it fair, one of you will throw for Jak, and one of us will throw for Jabe."

"Let's find a suitable target for these two," Brend ordered, his voice carrying across the square. Townspeople hastened to comply, some heading to the firewood pile, others scanning the ground for something that would fit the bill.

While they searched, Krysty leaned close to Ryan's ear. "You sure this is a good idea?"

Ryan shrugged. "Hell if I know. I'm sure Jak'll can win, no matter how good his kid is."

"Yeah, but Jabe seems to be spoiling for a fight, and he's been drinking, probably more than he should."

"Which gives our boy the clear advantage. Too bad these folks aren't the betting kind. I reckon we could clean up here."

"Ryan!" Krysty smacked his shoulder in mock disapproval.

Several people had returned carrying a variety of pieces of wood. Brend sorted through them, discarding any the unsuitable ones, and finally coming up with a piece about the size of his hand. "All right, we have a target. If no one objects, I'll throw for young Jak."

Ryan looked around, but no one raised a voice in protest. Hefting the chunk of oak in his hand, Brend stepped around to the front of the table. "Are ya ready, Jak?"

The white-haired teen stood so still he might have been carved from alabaster, his face completely neutral, the imitation of a statue broken only by the tiniest nod. Ryan knew exactly what that utter stillness portended, and leaned back in his chair. More than once he'd wondered where the frail-looking albino youth had learned his incredible fighting skills, but couldn't come up with any martial discipline or military program that would turn a teenager into such a devastating fighting machine. One thing he was sure of—he was damn glad Jak was on their side.

With a touch of the theatrical, Brend made sure all eyes were on him before continuing. "All right, I'll count to three, and throw. One...two...three...go!"

With a heave, the town leader pitched the piece of wood high into the air, sailing almost out of sight in the darkness. The throw was perfect, a steep arc rising over Jak's head. For a moment he just stood there, tracking it as it rose into the night sky. Every single person watching in the square seemed to hold their breath as well. Then his hands blurred, and a faint thunk could be heard as the chunk of wood fell back to the ground.

Brend walked over and gasped in surprise. Bending, he picked up the wooden lump and held it aloft for everyone to see.

Not one, not two, but three leaf-bladed throwing knives were stuck in the wood.

Gasps and whispers started at several places in the crowd and swelled, the men and women murmuring in stunned disbelief. Ryan, watching Jak's reaction, saw him frown, but the expression vanished as quickly as it had appeared.

Brend seemed shaken himself, but held up his empty hand for quiet. "Ever'one settle down now! That was— that was some kinda marksmanship, young Jak. A fine display." He removed the knives one at a time and handed them to the albino teen, who made them disappear with three twists of his wrist. "However, now we will be treated to a shooting ex'bition by one of the finest sharpshooters in Toma! Jabe, step forward."

The hometown boy polished off the last of his mead and walked out into the empty square to loud applause and cheers. Most the girls were cheering for the lad, but Ryan noticed one slim, dark-haired beauty had eyes only for Jak. He nudged Krysty, who nodded to indicate that she had seen it as well.

Brend let his son bask in the accolades for a few seconds, then raised both hands for silence again. "And who among our guests this evening will throw for him?"

"I will." Ryan was already standing, and he strode around the table to enter the square. Brend handed him the chunk of wood and retreated back to the table. Ryan hefted the oak in his hand, getting a good feel for it. He looked at Jabe, alone in the center of the square. "You ready?"

The young man nodded, already sliding his blaster, a well-maintained matte-black Ruger SP100, out of its holster. "Just make it a good throw, One-eye." His boots shuffled in the dirt, as if he was a bit unsteady on his feet.

Ryan's answering grin was tight, and he resisted the urge to chuck the wood at the kid's head or lobbing it so far into the night that no one would be able to see it. Instead, he leaned down and heaved the chunk into the air, straight up, the piece turning lazily end over end as it flew.

Jabe's blaster was up and tracking the wood as soon as it left Ryan's hand. His first shot split the night, and the wood lurched in the air, a puff of splinters bursting from it. A second shot followed as it reached the apex of its flight, but the wood only wobbled a little bit this time. A third shot came right after the second one, but now the piece was falling faster back to the earth. Ryan looked over at Jabe, who still had the piece in his sights.

At that second, Ryan realized the problem. In his zeal to beat the outlander, Jabe was either unaware or uncaring that his next shot would come perilously close to the people on the opposite side of the square. Certainly much too close for Ryan's comfort.

He launched himself at the other boy, but before he could lay a hand on the kid, a white-haired blur appeared under Jabe's outstretched arm and levered it up just as the youth triggered another shot, the bullet passing over the heads of a tight cluster of villagers on the other side of the square, making them all duck away, several of the women screaming in fear.

"Son of a— Goddamn mutie made me miss!" His words slurring, Jabe wrested his blaster arm out of Jak's hands and tried to bring the butt down on the albino's head.

It was his last mistake of the night.

Dodging the clumsy blow as if his attacker was swinging through honey, Jak stepped close and slammed his fist into Jabe's solar plexus. The other youth, although he stood seven inches taller and outweighed Jak by at least sixty pounds, dropped to the ground like he'd been pole-axed right between the eyes. His blaster dropped from his hand as he concentrated on trying to draw air back into his spasming lungs.

Jabe's eyes fell to his weapon, which had landed in the dirt a few feet away. He rolled over to it, but before he could pick it up, Brend stood over him, leaned down and swept it up in his calloused hand in one smooth motion.

"Dad! You saw! He tried to cheat—"

"What I see is a brave man who prevented my son from making a very big mistake." Brend turned to sweep the crowd with his piercing gaze. "And I'll have words with anyone who thinks otherwise." Opening the cylinder, he emptied the Ruger's load into his hand, then tucked the blaster into his belt. "I'll hold on to this until you get your wits about you. Right now, I'd suggest you git into the house and sleep it off. We'll talk about this in the morning."

Turning, Brend stalked back to the table without a backward glance at his son. "Let's have some music! Is this a cel'bration or what?"

The quartet scrambled to comply with Brend's order,

and a sprightly tune filled the air. The brunette girl was the first to walk out onto the floor, coming up behind Jak and tapping him on the shoulder. The albino youth whirled, stilling his hands before they unleashed a flurry of blows. She held out her other hand, and Jak took it gingerly, his other one curling around her waist. When the next measure began, they danced along with it, tentative at first, but Jak kept his eyes on the other dancers, and quickly picked up the intricate moves, with only the occasional misstep.

Rubbing his chest, Jabe had scrambled to his feet, all his attention on Jak, so much so that he started in surprise at the large hand that fell upon his shoulder.

Ryan leaned in and kept his voice low. "A word of advice, son—don't go looking for any more trouble tonight. You can go after that one all day long, and all you'll end up doing is eating dirt every time—assuming he doesn't grow tired of simply humiliating you."

The teen shrugged off Ryan's hand with a grunt. "Fuck you, outlander. Course you'd take the mutie's side. You travel with him, so you don't wanna see him get hurt."

He started to walk after Jak again, but Ryan stopped him again, a bit more forcefully this time. "Actually, boy, it's you I'm more concerned about at the moment." He put his lips next to the kid's ear. "Understand— I don't give a shit if you keep breathing or take the last train to the coast the second I let you go. But your father has shown us nothing but hospitality from the moment we arrived in your ville, and I respect that. I'd sure hate to have any more trouble over this little… misunderstanding."

With each word, Ryan's grip on his shoulder had tightened, until his large, calloused fingers had clamped down on the boy's collarbone so hard Jabe's clamped lips turned white with the pain. It was only with the greatest effort that he was able to remain standing. "Now the only thing I want to hear from you is a 'yes, sir, I won't cause any more trouble.'"

He pressed even harder on the kid's shoulder, eliciting a whimper of pain. "Yes, sir…I won't cause…no more trouble."

Ryan let him go, and Jabe dodged away in such a hurry he almost collided with the nearest dancing couple, avoiding them only by throwing himself toward the outside of the square. Shaking his head, Ryan walked back around the table and sat next to Brend, who was nursing a small cup of mead. Ryan refilled his and clinked his glass against the other man's.

"I 'pologize for m'boy, Ryan. He's at that age where he thinks the world should lie down at his feet, and though I try to convince him otherwise, it seems to be a lesson hard learned."

Ryan waved off his apology. "Boys can be trying at the best of times."

"You have children of your own?"

Ryan sipped the fiery-sweet mead while checking behind him to see if Krysty was listening. When he saw she was talking to Mildred, he turned back to Brend. "One boy, about twelve years old now. He's out west with his mother. I imagine pretty soon he'll be as much of a hellraiser as your boy seems to be."

Brend's smile was rueful. "That's exactly what I don't want for 'im. We need to educate the next gen'ration of men and women here, so theys can maintain and build what we started. I've worked too hard to see it all go to waste."

"Course not." Ryan shifted in his seat, unsure of

where this was going. "You seem to be doing all right. Just keep a firm hand, and don't let him get away with too much."

Brend digested this and nodded. "Good advice, Ryan. Thanks."

Chapter Eighteen

The rest of the evening passed uneventfully, except for a couple of glowering looks from Jabe at Jak, who was still hanging around the brunette. Ryan had realized the situation long ago, and when things started winding down, he gathered his people, thanked everyone for the good time, and retired back to the war wag. They were entreated to stay with families in the ville, but Ryan politely yet firmly turned down the offers, saying they were more than used to sleeping outside. The opposite was true—at least lately—but he had a feeling the evening wasn't quite over yet, and wanted to be where he could prevent anything untoward from happening.

The summer night was cool and peaceful, the oppressive heat of the day dissipated under the lavender-white moon. Ryan and Krysty walked back hand-in-hand, each savoring the quiet evening—and each other's company—in their own way.

"You see Jak come with us?"

Ryan glanced around. "Damn it, he was here when we left. He's probably sneaking off to see that girl he was dancing with."

"Could be trouble. Jabe could make things very uncomfortable if he gets more townspeople on his side."

"I wouldn't worry about that." Ryan tried to hide his smile from her. "Jabe and I had a little talk after he nearly blew one of the townie's head off."

"So that's what that was. I should have known."

"Just didn't want the kid getting himself killed over nothing, that's all. Life is short enough as it is. Besides, if Jak gets into trouble with the locals, you damn sure bet he'll be the one to come out of it in one piece."

"Speaking of the devil." Krysty nudged Ryan and nodded toward the war wag, where Jak leaned against one dusty wheel, hands in his jacket pockets, attempting to look nonchalant—and failing miserably.

"Where were you?" Ryan asked, his voice casual as he undid the main hatch.

"Walking with Delia." While he had to look twice, Ryan could have sworn the albino youth was blushing in the moonlight. "Not do nothin'."

"All right then, best get some sleep, we leave at dawn." Ryan got out bedrolls and set up a rough camp, rigging two tarps as ground cover and a tent, then tossing their blankets on top. They were behind the wag, with J.B. and Mildred ensconced in a similar tent rig a few yards away, and Doc, already snoring stentoriously in the tent he shared with Jak. The burbling river was just a few yards away, its soft gurgle providing a gentle undercurrent to the peaceful scene.

Ryan stretched out beside Krysty, taking the rare opportunity to sleep in just his shirt and pants. Still a bit too awake to close his eyes just yet, he bedded down next to Krysty and slipped a hand around her, his fingers exploring until they found her full breast.

"Mmm, that's nice, lover. Keep the slow hand for a while, will you?"

Ryan answered by leaning down over her and kissing her deeply, enjoying the unaccustomed luxury of not having to steal time for once, of being able to enjoy each other without having to look over their shoulders every minute, or worry about who or what might be coming after them. He slipped his hand under her jumpsuit, feeling Krysty's plump nipple stiffen into hardness between his fingers. Her breathing quickened as he delved further, drawing the zipper down until her chest was uncovered, her white skin gleaming in the moonlight.

Krysty, who hadn't been idle either, stripped his shirt off, and the two of them roved over each other for a good, long time. When she was ready, Ryan took the lead, moving up her tantalizing body an inch at a time, enjoying the trip as much as he had when they had first made love. He sank into her and it was as if they were two halves coming together to make a whole being, perfectly aligned, perfectly synchronized. Her hips moved in unison with his for long minutes, until neither could wait anymore, and their shared, shuddering climax was released in a chorus of low, urgent gasps, capped off by their tight embrace.

Afterward, Krysty lay with her head on Ryan's chest, listening to him breathe. "Perfect way to end a perfect day, lover."

"Near enough to suit me. Almost seems too peaceful out here, like there's a snake in the garden we haven't seen yet."

She lifted her head to stare at him with her emerald-green eyes. "For once I think we can take this at face value, and not have to worry about crazed villagers trying to kidnap one of us for sacrifice, or planning to force us to duel others—or each other—to the death for their twisted idea of entertainment. Just one time, I'd like to enjoy a day that doesn't begin or end with someone dying, all right?"

"Fair enough." Krysty moved off him and cuddled up under the blankets. Ryan curled a strong arm around her waist, holding his lover close until her breathing slowed to the gentle cadence of sleep.

Of course, as Ryan knew all too well, the night wouldn't be peaceful. There had been too much commotion already. He slipped into a light doze, able to gain enough rest from it while his subconscious remained alert for any disturbance.

THE FIRST SIGN was so quiet Ryan almost missed it. His eye opened at the soft brush of light footsteps over the dewy grass. Lifting his head, the SIG-Sauer already filling his right hand, Ryan pushed back the tent flap to see a familiar shadow outside.

His bright-white hair tucked under the army cap he'd found, Jak stealthily crept past. Intent on his progress, he didn't notice Ryan until the man cleared his throat. Jumping like he'd just been goosed by a stickie, Jak stood staring.

Jak had the grace to look somewhat abashed, although his guilty expression quickly turned to a frown as he leaned over. "S'posed be sleepin'," the albino teen hissed.

"So are you." The light dawned in Ryan's head. After all, he'd done the same exact thing more than once when he was even younger than Jak. "Just be back by dawn. And you're still taking your turn on the front blaster, too. I don't care how tired you are tomorrow."

Jak straightened, his dark expression turning to surprised relief at being let off with only a warning. "Thanks, Ryan." Turning, the boy ghosted away so fast Ryan was almost convinced he'd dreamed the conversation.

IT SEEMED LIKE only minutes, but might have been hours, when Ryan's eye opened again. This time the noise that had tripped his internal alarm was louder, the soft clink of glass on ceramic, followed by a stifled giggle.

Uncurling from Krysty's side, Ryan slipped out of the tent and pulled on his pants. A rustle of fabric made him turn to see J.B.'s head poking out of his tent, eyebrows lifted in a silent question.

Intruders, Ryan signed. Two to four, on other side of wag. You take front, I take back.

With a nod, J.B. slipped out, mini-Uzi in his hands as he stalked silently toward the war wag's nose. Just as quietly, Ryan padded around the back, homing in on the hushed voices conferring on the far side of the vehicle. As he drew closer, he saw several shadows near the back tire of the wag, and heard the clink of metal, tools, most likely.

A cold fire ignited in Ryan's gut. It was one thing to try to impress your folks by walking tall in front of visitors, but sabotaging a vehicle—potentially leaving their group to die in the middle of nowhere—was something else entirely.

He eased around the cold, metal corner to see a cluster of four boys fiddling with the wheel hub, which came up to their chests. One of them giggled, only to be hushed by the ringleader.

"Hush, ya stupe! Don't wake 'em! Hurry up with those bolts. Let's see how the old fucker likes it when he tries to leave and the goddamn wheel falls off." The kid raised a jar of mead to his lips, not even bothering with a glass.

In one fluid motion, Ryan rose and stepped over to Jabe, pressing the cold circle of his blaster's muzzle into the back of the boy's neck. "I can tell you the 'old fucker' wouldn't like that one bit."

Caught in midswallow, Jabe choked in surprise, spraying the mouthful of booze over his companions, all of whom looked up in shock. The one working on the wheel staggered backward, staring at the black-haired demon that had materialized out of thin air next to his buddy. His face contorting with fear, he turned to run toward the front of the war wag, but had only taken a single step when he collapsed to the ground, out cold.

Ryan glanced over to see J.B. step out from the wag's shadow, his mini-Uzi leveled to cover the other three boys. Jabe's two cohorts had fallen to their knees, mouths opening and closing soundlessly, too terrified to talk. Ryan heard a strange, hissing sound and realized one of the boys had pissed his pants.

"Fireblast! You just don't know when to quit, do you, boy? Come here." Using the pressure of his blaster as a prod, Ryan separated him from the other two. "Turn around."

Jabe complied, his eyes widening as the barrel of the SIG-Sauer, only inches from his face, filled his vision.

"Raise your hands."

He did so, one of them still holding the empty mead bottle. His eyes flicked to it in surprise, and Ryan read his mind as easily as if the kid had tried what he was thinking. "Twitch that bottle at me, and I'll take every broken shard and shove them so far up your ass you'll shit glass for a month."

The boy's fingers slowly opened, and the bottle rolled out of his hand to land in the grass at his feet. Ryan wasn't through, however.

"Open your mouth."

Jabe blinked in confusion, his eyebrows knotting in puzzlement.

"Open—your—mouth." He pressed the end of the

blaster into the kid's teeth, forcing his jaw open, and inserting the barrel until it brushed the back of his throat. "Now, don't move."

The boy was as still as death itself. Reaching up with a thumb, Ryan cocked the hammer, the click ominously loud in the silence, broken only by the nervous breaths of Jabe and his two comrades.

"Answer me with your head only, and be careful, because my finger's on the trigger. Answer too hard, your buddies'll wear your brains. Ever been this close to death before?"

Jabe shook his head slightly, tears welling in his eyes.

"Ever been shot?"

Another shake.

"You taste the gun barrel in your mouth?"

A nod, the tears spilling down his cheeks winking silver in the moonlight.

"Taste good?"

Another head shake.

"What's on your tongue right now is the second before a bullet carves through the back of your throat, right there—" Ryan pressed the barrel in until he hit the boy's soft palate, making Jabe gag in terror "—and drills a tunnel through your brain before exploding out the back of your skull. Still with me?"

Another nod, accompanied by a now-familiar odor. Ryan glanced down to see Jabe's pants darkening, as well.

"Good. Normally I don't let folks in this situation walk free, which means the next thing for you would usually be a shallow grave. Hell, I'd probably just dump your body in the river and leave, letting your father wonder what might have happened to you for the rest of his life, and his imagination would play worse tricks than I ever could. However, and this is the only reason I haven't pulled the trigger, I happen to like and respect the man. So from this moment on, every time you feel the urge to disobey him, or back talk, or bully strangers that stop by to trade with your ville, you remember that it was only by your father's good graces that you're still alive to see the sun rise every day. You got that?"

A final nod. Jabe sobbed silently, his tears mingling with the snot dripping from his nose. Ryan withdrew his blaster from the boy's mouth and cleaned the glistening barrel on his homespun sleeve. "There's steel in you, boy, I can see it. Mebbe you should dig down and find it yourself, become the leader your father wants you to be, instead of throwing your weight around like a spoiled baron's brat. Think about it. Now get the fuck out of here, and take your bully boys with you."

Wiping his nose on his sleeve, Jabe motioned to his friends, who scrambled to their feet, one almost falling over in his haste to put some distance between themselves and the two stone-cold chillers. Ryan let them get a few yards away before calling out again. "Jabe."

The teen twitched like he had been shot, then, shoulders hunched, slowly turned. His two friends, their already frayed nerves breaking, took off into the darkness. "Yes, sir?"

Ryan held up two fingers. "That's twice now. There won't be a third time. You understand?"

"Yes, sir." Jabe stood there silently, waiting for something.

Ryan stared at him for a few seconds before realizing what the youth needed. He waved him off. "Get the hell out of here."

Jabe whirled and shot off into the darkness like a

terrified rabbit. Ryan turned and walked over to J.B., who stood over the unconscious fourth member of the group. "Sure you didn't kill him?"

The Armorer leaned down and swiped at the kid's mouth with his finger. "Drool's still warm, so he'll be okay. Have a bastard headache when he comes to. Some friends he's got, runnin' off and leavin' him here. What do you want to do?"

"Better drop him off somewhere away from us, otherwise we might get blamed for this when all we did was try to instill a little backbone in Brend's boy."

They picked up the limp body and hauled him away from the war wag. Finding an alley between two houses on the outskirts of town, they set him down against one of the walls. A wooden barrel of water sat nearby, and Ryan sniffed it to make sure it wasn't stagnant, then scooped up a handful and dashed it in the kid's face. After the second splash, he started coming around, and that was the signal for Ryan and J.B. to depart.

Ryan caught J.B. regarding him out of the corner of his eye as they headed back. "What?"

J.B. shook his head. "Nothing."

"Think I was too hard on him?"

"Too hard? A few years ago you probably would have kneecapped the kid just for looking at you wrong. And to find him touching the war wag… Yeah, that Ryan most likely would have put him in the ground just to make sure he didn't come after you later."

"Fireblast, J.B., that kid isn't a threat."

"No shit? If you let me finish, I already knew that. Now what the hell was my point? Oh yeah, what I was saying is that you did the right thing, that's all. Black dust, if he don't take *that* lesson to heart, boy's too stupe to live much longer."

Ryan nodded. "Good, for a second I was worried you thought I was getting soft."

J.B. snorted quietly. "Not likely, I've seen Krysty's satisfied expression when you two join us for breakfast lately."

His head swiveling to stare at his friend, Ryan's mouth gaped in shock. A joke from J.B. was as rare as an honest baron, and it literally made the tall man stop in his tracks. Not missing a beat, the Armorer slapped him on the shoulder. "I'm gettin' to bed. Long day tomorrow." Ambling back to his tent, he ducked under the flap, and vanished inside.

Ryan glanced around, hoping, praying for a witness to the miracle he had just witnessed. Of course, the area around the wag and tents was completely deserted. "Figures. No way anyone'll believe me." Shaking his head, Ryan slipped back into his tent and curled up next to Krysty. She stirred next to him, throwing her leg over his.

"That sly little son of a bitch." Krysty's low voice made Ryan smile in the darkness.

"You heard that?"

"Heard him? I was covering both of you from underneath the wag—just in case they decided to really get stupe. Why do you think my feet are cold?"

"No shit?" Ryan hadn't even been aware of her presence during the confrontation. "Pretty sly yourself. J.B.'s comment bother you?"

"No, besides, I've seen Mildred's lazy smile more than once in the recent mornings, as well. He just better be careful with what he says, or I might bring that up one of these days."

"Then we'd see another rare sight—J.B. blushing."

Ryan's snicker was contagious, and soon Krysty shook against him as she joined in his laughter.

When they stopped, she ran her fingers down his chest. "Well, I'm too awake to go back to sleep now."

Ryan grinned as her hand drifted lower. "Why, Miss Krysty Wroth, whatever did you have in mind?"

In one fluid move, she rolled on top of him, nipping his lips with her teeth. "Me on top of you for a while, that's what."

Running his hands up her smooth sides, Ryan lay back as she kissed his chest, enjoying the feeling of her strong legs intertwining his. "One hell of a way to start the morning, that's for sure."

Chapter Nineteen

Despite the evening's various activities, Ryan and Krysty managed to catch a few more winks before dawn. However, they were up soon after the first glimmers of light broke over the horizon, mostly due to the tantalizing aroma wafting into their tent.

"Damn, that smells delicious," Ryan said as he pulled his boots on. "Wonder who's cooking?"

A small wood fire burned inside a ring of stones a few yards away from the wag, the white smoke curling up into the dark purple sky. The clouds had turned during the night, and a front was rolling in, with fluffy, lime green cumulus clouds puffing several thousand feet into the air, darkening to the color of the Lantic Ocean at their center. Ryan sniffed the air, his nose wrinkling. "Smells like rain coming."

"Breakfast is ready. Come on, get it while it's hot." Mildred waved at them from where she stood next to the fire.

Her smile was wide that morning, and Ryan nudged Krysty as they walked, earning an eye-roll in return. When they got closer, however, his attention was drawn to the food: slabs of batter-dipped bread browning in a large, cast-iron skillet, surrounded by thick strips of crackling bacon. A blue-enameled pot rattled and steamed as whatever was inside boiled. "Looks good. Uh, what is it?"

"Something I haven't tasted in about a century, give or take—homemade French toast, with, get this, real butter and true maple syrup." Mildred held up an ancient glass jar that was three-quarters full of dark brown semiliquid. "I was talking to some of the women and learned they had all the fixings, so I did a little trading last night to borrow all this. I, uh, also used a bit of the coffee. Hope you don't mind, Ryan."

He shrugged, getting a good look at the meal as his stomach growled. Although they usually traded coffee for more vital necessities, he wasn't averse to enjoying a cup every now and then if available. "That's all right. What it's there for."

"Anyway, J.B. was kind enough to build the fire this morning, and here we are. Grab a plate and dig in. You haven't had anything until you've tried this."

Mildred had gone whole hog. There was a stack of beaten-up tin plates next to a pile of ancient silverware and a half dozen enameled mugs. Ryan armed himself and used a fork to spear a steaming piece of bread out of the pan, along with some crisp bacon.

Turning the latest batch of sizzling toast, Mildred pointed to a small ceramic pot. "Some folks like butter with their syrup, but me, I just take it straight up." Sitting on the ground, she doused her serving with a liberal helping of the brown stuff, then cut off a piece and ate, chewing slowly, her eyes closed.

Following suit, Ryan added the syrup, sawed off a chunk with his knife, and put it in his mouth. Crisp on the outside, tender on the inside, the bread's pleasant sourdough tang was muted by the egg coating and the sweet syrup. Ryan didn't waste any time, but devoured everything on his plate, washing it down with sips of strong coffee, and looked for more when he was done.

Mildred had also finished hers and was cooking up more, with another half a loaf sliced and ready to go. "Keep coming, there's plenty more where that came from. Where's Jak?"

Ryan swallowed and glanced around. "He's not with Doc?"

J.B. had also joined them, his grease-smudged hands testifying to his work getting the wag ready to roll. "I woke Doc when I went over to check on him. He was all by his lonesome."

Mildred and Krysty exchanged knowing glances.

"What was that?" Ryan asked, although he already knew.

"It was hard to miss that dark-haired girl—Jabe's sweetheart, I learned—hanging all over him last night."

"Oh, that one." Ryan suddenly busied himself with his breakfast. "Hadn't noticed."

Mildred frowned. "I hope he didn't do anyth— Oh, hello, Jak."

The teen joined them, his still-dripping wet hair sleeked back from a morning swim. Plopping down cross-legged on the ground, he snagged the syrup jar and looked at it for a second before tilting it up and pouring some down his throat.

"That's not—" Mildred got out before being nudged into silence by J.B. just as the stream of sticky sweetness gushed into the young man's mouth. Jak's eyes bugged as the syrup overwhelmed his tongue. Swallowing as fast as he could, he tossed the bottle aside and looked for something else to drink. Seeing Ryan's mug on the ground next to him, he grabbed it and raised it to his lips.

Even Ryan couldn't let that go. "Wait, Jak, it's—"

Too late. The albino teen took a huge gulp of the black liquid, then bellowed in pain, the coffee spraying out of his mouth and down his shirtfront as he leaped up and bolted for the river, where frantic splashing could be heard.

For a moment, silence reigned around the fire. Mildred was the first to break, her throaty chuckle rising to become high, loud laughter. Ryan was next—as much as he tried to hold it in, he couldn't stop the helpless amusement, which spread to Krysty next. Even J.B. wore a wide smile as he sipped his coffee. The four of them were speechless for a minute as they tried to catch their breath before catching each other's eye and collapsing in laughter again.

"Oh—oh shit, he's coming back. Everyone shut up." Mildred waved at them with one hand while hiding her smile behind the other.

Jak stalked back over, his face wet and lips red. Without a word, he grabbed a plate and scooped three pieces of toast and several strips of bacon onto his plate. Making a sandwich out of the whole mess, he began eating, blowing on his meal to cool it while trying to shove large bites into his sore mouth. The other four exchanged covert glances, but managed to hold their tongues.

Then Doc joined them. He'd also apparently bathed in the river, for his hair was still damp and stringy around his shoulders. His knees cracked like dry sticks as he settled by the fire. "Good morning, all. I trust everyone rested comfortably last night?"

Ryan, Krysty, Mildred and J.B. all nodded or mumbled affirmatives. Jak was the picture of stony, injured silence. Doc poured himself a cup of coffee, then leaned over the skillet. "And who do I have to thank for this delectable-looking repast?"

Ryan cleared his throat. "That'd be Mildred."

Doc sketched another of his elegant bows. "If it tastes half as good as it looks, 'twill be ambrosia upon my hungry lips."

He picked up a plate and silverware and helped himself, then noticed Jak off to the side. "Jak, my good man, I didn't see you when I awoke this morning."

"Was out." The boy barely glanced up from his plate, white hair falling across his eyes.

"Courting a fair, ebony-haired maiden, were you?"

"What you say?" Jak's head snapped up at this, his crimson stare boring into Ryan, who shook his head and held up his hands, fighting to keep a smile off his face.

Doc shrugged. "Oh, no matter at all, I merely commented because I noticed the young woman left traces of her lipstick upon your mouth. You should be more careful if you want to keep your dalliances discreet among these ruffians."

Now Jak frowned in puzzlement, one hand going up to his lips, which were still bright red from the scalding coffee. Mildred lost it first, laughing so hard she fell over, whooping for air. Ryan and Krysty were next, leaving J.B. shaking his head and chuckling quietly.

"Not fuckin' funny!" Snatching the remains of his sandwich, Jak threw down his plate and stomped off, leaving the other four gasping for air, and a befuddled Doc looking around at all of them, his brow furrowed.

"Was it something I said?"

That just set the others off all over again.

JAK RETREATED to the sanctuary of the war wag, settling himself in the front blaster's position, and refusing to come out until they were on the road.

J.B. shrugged. "Probably just as well. If he did get any action and Jabe finds out, likely there'd be another duel, and Brend's son'll end up on his back, staring into the sun."

His blunt assessment of the situation sobered everyone, and Ryan cleared his throat first. "Yeah, time for us to hit the road anyway. Let's pack this up, get it back to whomever it goes to, and get moving."

"Might be too late." J.B. nodded past Ryan, who turned to see Brend and several of the other bridge guards walking toward them. Everyone was armed, but no weapons were out.

"Everyone stay cool, and be ready to move on my signal." Ryan turned to face the group, aware of the odds stacked against them if anything did go down. Although he was armed, and he was sure Krysty and J.B. were as well, the same couldn't be said of Mildred and Doc, even though they were supposed to carry everywhere they went, even in a "safe" ville.

Brend came up to him and nodded. "Morning, Ryan." He nodded to everyone else. "Mind if you and I talk for a minute?"

Ryan's gaze flicked down and back up the other man, trying to fathom his intent. He didn't get the sense that Brend was about to try a bushwhack, so he nodded. "Let's walk."

Deliberately turning his back on the other man, Ryan led the way downriver, knowing that if the ville leader was going to try something, that would be the time— and he'd be killed by J.B. before he could get a shot off, leaving Ryan to try and distract the rest of the guards.

Although his demeanor was relaxed, Ryan couldn't help feeling his shoulder blades tense in expectation of a bullet ripping through them.

But that didn't happen. The sun shone on Ryan's face, a light wind ruffled his hair, and the two men kept walking until they were out of earshot of the rest. The last thing Ryan heard was Mildred playing peacemaker in the simplest way she knew: "Any of you boys hungry?"

When he figured they were far enough away, Ryan turned to Brend, planted his feet and waited.

The ville leader wasted no time. "After the…unpleasantness that happened last night, I saw ya exchanging words with my son. Like to know what ya told him."

"I warned him against trying to go after Jak in his condition. Seemed he'd had a bit too much to drink. He wouldn't have had a chance, you'd be burying your boy today, and there'd be a lot of bad blood between mine and yours, which I didn't feel like having. Especially after the hospitality you've shown us."

Brend nodded. "That's all—you didn't say anything else last night?"

Ryan debated for a second just how much to tell him about the second encounter. "I came across Jabe and some of his friends later in the evening. They were looking to blow off steam after what'd happened in the square."

"Not aimed at you or your group, was it?"

"Not at any one of us, no." Although it was stretching the truth, Ryan kept going before Brend could think about his answer. "I had a bit of a talk with Jabe, told him I thought he had the makings of a good leader, and mebbe he should try that route instead of running around causing trouble."

Brend stared at him for a long time, and Ryan didn't flinch or drop his gaze. At last, the other man nodded. "When I saw him this morning, he was…different. Whatever you told him, it musta sunk in deep. Hell, he was washin' his own pants in the tub when I woke up. Hasn't done since forever."

Ryan rubbed his mouth to erase the smile that had sprung to his lips. If Brend noticed, he gave no sign. "Just wanted to thank you for whatever you said to him. Already he seems like another person than who he was last night, almost as if he came to some life-changin' decision."

Ryan shrugged. "Doubt I had anything to do with it, but if something I said or did helped, hopefully that's all for the good."

"A'right, then." Brend clapped him on the shoulder. "That's that. Ya all headin' out today?"

"Yeah. We're going to keep heading east, mebbe find those traders along the Lakes, the ones you mentioned last night."

Brend snapped his fingers. "That's what I was gonna tell ya! Something was niggling my brain last night, but I couldn't grab it till the morning. If ya stay on the main road out of town, you're gonna follow it down toward what used to be the capital of this area, a large city called Madison, mebbe sixty, seventy miles away. Caravans coming through've said to steer clear of the city itself—heard cannies're campin' out there."

Ryan grimaced at the thought. He'd just as soon shoot a cannibal the moment he saw one. He held out his hand, which Brend clasped and pumped. "Thanks, we'll keep a sharp eye out for them. And if we're ever back in the area, we'll be sure to drop by."

"You and yours are welcome here anytime."

With a nod, they headed back to find the rest of Brend's men clustered around the fire, polishing off the last of Mildred's breakfast. When they had finished, the plates and utensils were washed, and the men said they'd make sure the cooking gear got back to the right people. Everyone said their goodbyes, then Ryan and his crew finished cleaning up their campsite, packing up any remaining items and basically making sure nothing remained of their passage but tire tracks and, Ryan hoped, a bit of good sense.

Leaving the ville was a drawn-out affair, with small knots of villagers dropping by to say goodbye. Ryan even caught Jabe standing at the back of a small crowd that had come to see the war wag start up, since they rarely saw self-powered vehicles around anymore. The young man regarded him with a steady, emotionless stare. Meeting his gaze squarely, Ryan inclined his head. Jabe nodded back, once, and Ryan turned to continue directing the packing.

At last everything was secured, and the group was ready to leave. Ryan shook Brend's hand one last time, then hoisted himself through the hatch into the driver's seat, made sure everything was ready and fired up the engine.

Putting the vehicle in gear, Ryan eased out along the riverbank until he came to the cracked, highway, Number 90, according to J.B.'s maps. It would take them southeast to Madison, then east to the former city called Milwaukee and from there south to the blackened plain of Chicago and the hidden mat-trans.

J.B. kept the ville of Toma in his camera view as they slowly accelerated away, until the buildings and their waving inhabitants were mere specks on the horizon.

Chapter Twenty

They stayed ahead of the storm blowing out of the west for the first hour, pushing up to about forty miles an hour on sections of highway that weren't too badly damaged. But the clouds grew larger and darker behind them, with lightning bolts arcing from the thunderheads to the ground, and claps of thunder heralding the impending storm, until Krysty and Doc both suggested finding a safe spot, preferably under cover, until the tempest passed over.

Ryan was for pushing on, until J.B. brought up the fact they were in a big rolling piece of metal, and, although grounded by the tires, a direct or nearby lightning strike could easily knock out the engine or electrical system, stranding them in the middle of nowhere. "We're running just fine now, and I don't want to blow it because you have a hard-on to get another ten miles down the road," were the Armorer's exact words, making Mildred and Doc smile, and Ryan flip his old friend the finger without taking his hand off the wheel.

In the end, however, he went along with the group consensus and found a highway overpass that seemed stable enough, since it held the Commando's weight when they drove across it. Easing carefully down the crumbling off-ramp, he pulled around underneath just as the first patter of rain hit the war wag. They rolled to a stop into the center of the concrete structure just as a freakish blast of wind howled through the man-made tunnel, and then the skies opened up. Even through the wag's metal skin, they heard the rain pounding down all around them, with a gust of howling wind blowing sheets of water over the Commando. J.B. showed them on the blaster cam just how bad it was outside—driving sheets of solid water that cut visibility to a few yards at best.

"Least it's not acid," Ryan commented, drawing a grunt of agreement from J.B. Out west, particularly along the border of what used to be Mexico and the U.S. the infrequent rains picked up alkali and other chemicals that brewed into toxic, deadly precipitation that could strip a person to the bone in under five minutes. Once, when he was barely out of his teens and working in one of the pestholes along the Tex-Mex border, Ryan had had the unfortunate chance to see one of these storms in action as it deluged a poor drunk who had been caught away from shelter. The caustic liquid had flayed the man's skin and flesh from his bones as he had run for cover, turning him into a seared, blind, deaf, mute wretch by the time he had reached the reinforced doors. One of the other bouncers had taken pity on the poor lump of meat and put him out of his misery with a bullet. Ryan had never forgotten the sight of the guy beating on the door with his melted hands, his screams of pain muted to incomprehensible moans. And there were other times....

"Ow! Son of a bitch!" The commotion came from the front blaster port, with Jak cursing, followed by the clank of the blaster port slamming shut. They all heard the hiss of a knife being drawn, then nothing.

"Jak? You okay up there?" Ryan called from the driver's seat. He was about to get up and maneuver his way over when the albino teen's head appeared, glowing reddish-white in the dim light from the instrument panel.

"Bastard bugs, or whatever's out there!" The youth was favoring his left hand, and when J.B. produced a small penlight and shone it on his injury, they saw a dime-sized injury on his palm, bleeding profusely.

"Fireblast! Mildred, get up here, Jak got bit again."

She came up to see, her eyes widening in surprise at the wound. "My God, Jak, trouble is drawn to you."

"Just tryin' to get drink rain water. Hot up there, no vents open."

Ryan and J.B. exchanged a knowing glance. "So you decided to cool off, right?"

The youth glared at them while Mildred tended to his hand. "Was just gonna stick hand out. Next I know, something landed on it, hurt like hell. Pulled in, stabbed fucker with knife, flicked it out the port, slammed shut." His expression grew pensive. "Saw more out there. Lots, black, small." He made an o with his thumb and forefinger. "'Bout that big."

"Insect swarm, lookin' for shelter from the storm?" Ryan guessed.

"Whatever they are, they don't strike like any insect I've ever seen," Mildred said while bandaging Jak's wound. "This wasn't made by a proboscis, more like some kind of leech, with some kind of rasping tongue to scrape off layers of skin until the bleeding starts."

"One way to find out." J.B. turned to the blaster cam and fired it up, moving the turret to scan back and forth. "What the hell are these things?"

The area around the war wag was filled with small, black, floating creatures, looking like a dark globule of gum or dirt, drifting lazily in the air. Occasionally one would pass by the camera, seeming to writhe in the air, as if it was steering in some instinctive fashion.

"My word, isn't that interesting." Doc had managed to squeeze his lanky frame into the cramped main compartment, and stare at the monitor. "Reminds me of the famous Kansas City, Missouri, incident in 1873, whereupon the entire city was pelted with live frogs during a freak rainstorm. Of course, at the time I don't expect anyone suffered the indignity of a bite like young Jak."

"Think we're in any danger?" Krysty asked.

J.B. snorted. "Not unless they can rasp their way through plate armor."

Just then, however, the engine hitched before resuming its normal rhythm, making J.B. frown. "Unless they're attracted to a heat source…"

The engine hitched once more, then died with a snort, shaking loudly enough that the entire wag vibrated, as well. "And clog up the main exhaust pipe."

Ryan had already leaned over into the driver's seat and turned off the engine. "Better get out there and clear it. Looks like the rain is subsiding, so we can get back on the road, too."

"Yeah, these little bastards are floating to the ground—definitely not lighter than air. Let's give them a couple more minutes to settle, and we'll head out."

Mildred put the back of her hand to Jak's forehead, who shook it off with a grimace. "You feeling all right so far? We don't need another incident like we had with those damn pig-rats."

"Fine, not worry 'bout me." Jak looked around at the cramped quarters and shuddered. "Go outside and clear the pipe. Want stretch legs."

"In a minute or two, we'll all get out, three at a time."

Ryan gave it another few minutes before moving to the hatch. "Jak, J.B., you're with me." Opening the metal cover, he swung it out slowly, careful to avoid the few little black creatures that had been resting on the top edge of the hatch itself. He peeked out to see the ground alive with a moving carpet of squirming creatures.

"Here we go." Ryan stepped out, his feet crushing dozens of the slugs, boots sliding unsteadily on the goo. When his feet hit the ground, the nearby creatures began crawling toward him, undulating their bodies as fast as they could.

"Hand me a blanket from inside, would you?" J.B. obliged, and Ryan swept it over the roof, dislodging a wave of the slimy creatures that rolled down over the front of the wag to the ground. Using the bottom of the entry hatch as a step, Ryan hauled himself up to the top, brushing away the slugs before they could start coming for him. Once he had cleared a space to stand on, he scrambled onto the roof and flicked the blanket out, sending the invaders tumbling off the top of the vehicle until the area was clear.

"All right, come out, but stay on the roof. Jak, once you're on top, get clearing that stack so we can get out of here."

The albino teen crawled out onto the roof with ease and trotted to the smokestack, which was still crawling with the loathsome creatures. Many had been cooked by the heat of the pipe, but there was still a head-size lump of them wriggling all over it.

"Use one of your knives," suggested J.B., who had just come up as well after closing the hatch.

"No shit." Jak drew a pair of his throwing blades and began scraping the mass off the pipe. Ryan and J.B. kept a careful watch around them, looking at the large, black mass of leeches below them.

"Hate to fall into that," the Armorer muttered.

Ryan nodded, then turned back to Jak. "How's it coming?"

"Almost done. Fuckers don't give up easy."

"Hey, Ryan, look at this." He turned to see J.B. examining one of the animals, which was slowly floating toward him in midair. "I'll be damned. They're like little leech balloons."

The storm had passed enough to let some wan sunlight into the underpass, enough to illuminate the strange creature. It was about three inches long, and looked for all the world like a banded leech, black and segmented, with a questing mouth on one end, large enough for Ryan to see three tiny plates in its mouth that also moved every time its maw opened, coming together to form a rough surface that could easily strip off skin. The really strange thing was the small sac on its back, filled with what he assumed was air, that allowed it to float on the breeze.

J.B. moved out of its way, but it turned as well, as if coming after him. Pursing his lips, J.B. blew at it, sending the floating creature drifting away.

Seeing it so close prickled a vague alarm in the back of Ryan's mind. "I thought all of them had settled to the ground. Is this a straggler?"

J.B.'s gaze flicked from the little parasite to Ryan. "Mebbe. Unless—"

Both men had the same thought at the same time. Lifting his head just enough to look upward, Ryan beheld a nightmare above them.

The top of the bridge was made of poured concrete sections that supported the road above. They were spaced like giant rows, with a space between each pair of braces. Each space was filled with hundreds, maybe thousands of squirming, writhing leeches, held up by one another's mass as they wriggled around.

"Attracted by—" J.B. began.

"Heat. Jak, run now!" Ryan didn't wait to see if the albino teen listened, but was already heading toward the front of the war wag, planning to jump off and head for the hopefully leech-free ground outside the underpass.

He had just taken his first large step when the deluge came down.

In a heartbeat, the air was filled with hundreds of the leech-creatures. Although many of them had filled their air bladders to float down at their leisure, just as many had taken the quicker route, falling from the ceiling in hopes of landing on a meal. Moving between them was like trying to dodge big, black, hungry raindrops.

As he moved, Ryan kept his head down, mainly concerned about his eye. Just one of the things blowing into it could seriously injure, or even blind him. He would have closed it, but he still had to get off the wag, and jumping blind would invite a sprained or broken ankle or worse. And the one thing he knew he didn't want was to fall into the layer of bloodsuckers on the ground. He waved his arms around his head, feeling his hands bat several of the things away, and at least three latched on to his fingers, instantly sending burning pain through his hands as they went to work on him.

Reaching the edge of the wag, Ryan slid down the front, aware he was both crushing and picking up more as he went. His boots thudded on the ground, turning dozens more to paste under their treads. He tried to run, but nearly fell over, and only saved himself from toppling with a supreme effort. Everywhere he looked, he saw little black bits in the air, dozens of bloodsucking paratroopers zeroing in on their objective—him. More settled on his head, moving around in his hair, seeking the warm, blood-filled scalp. He felt them land on his shirt, on his shoulders, on his pants, everywhere they could get to him. He tried shaking them off, but they clung like they were coated with glue.

Ryan Cawdor didn't scare easily, but this onslaught would have made even the strongest man break as the dozens of slick, black leeches came at him, each one seeking his warm blood. He burst from the dark tunnel into the sunlight, tearing off his shirt and flinging it away as he did so. The greedy parasites on his hands were the first to go, torn off with scrabbling fingers. Next he ran his hands through his hair, sloughing off at least a half dozen of the creatures and whipping them onto the ground. He saw J.B. out of the corner of his eye, cursing and capering as he swatted away his own army of attackers. Ryan couldn't waste time spotting Jak, but was sure he was in the same boat.

"Hold still, Ryan—on your back!" As he heard the words, Ryan felt a sting as a pair of them latched on, their greedy mouths scraping through the skin. They'd landed right in the small of his back, and Ryan was about to draw his panga and scrape them off, cuts be damned, until J.B. ran over and tore them loose, flinging them to the ground and stepping on them.

Having cleared his head and hands, Ryan moved to his arms, dislodging each leech he found and stomping on it. He checked J.B. as well, finding one that was about to head south down the back of his pants. Grabbing it between two fingers, he threw it away. The sight made him immediately check his own fatigues, which were thankfully leech-free.

"I imagine you'd know right away if one of those fuckers went after your privates," J.B. said, giving Ryan a last, careful once-over. "Thanks."

Jak had joined them, as well. His arms and neck weeping blood from several wounds. His hands blurred as he found the leeches and ripped them off his body "Fuck, fuck, fuck!"

"Got that right." Even though he was pretty sure he was safe, Ryan kept checking his arms and legs every few seconds, thinking he could still feel one or two crawling on his skin. "Never wanted a hot bath more in my life."

"Yeah, with a heavy dose of salt—that'd take care of the little bastards." J.B. had finished scraping the last ones off his trusty fedora, which had once again saved him from suffering the worst of the attack. One last check of everyone found a straggler lodged in Jak's armpit, swelling to triple its normal size as it gorged. Whipping out his knife, the teen impaled the parasite on the tip, sending a spurt of dark crimson onto the ground. He flicked it away, letting the blood run down his side.

"Didn't you feel it?" J.B. asked.

Jak shrugged. "Too busy dealing with dozen others."

"Did you clear the exhaust pipe?" Ryan asked.

"Think so. Course, all comin' down coulda plugged again."

"Yeah, mebbe." Ryan walked back to just outside the shadow cast by the tunnel. He noticed that none of the leeches on the ground had ventured onto the sunlit ground. "Krysty?"

"Yeah?" Her voice was muffled by the wag's thick armor. "Where are you?"

"Outside the tunnel. Got some leeches on us, but we're okay now. Start the wag and drive it out." Ryan wasn't about to head back underneath that overpass if he could help it.

"All right." The engine turned over, then fired up with a roar, echoing loudly in the confined space. Ryan, J.B. and Jak stepped to one side as the vehicle slowly emerged from the darkness, clumps of leeches clinging to it. Grabbing his dirty shirt, Ryan cleared the hatch and brushed more of the creatures off. The hatch opened, and Krysty poked her head out. "Why are you— Gaia, what happened?"

Ryan pointed at the overpass. "Big colony of the bastards must have blown in with the storm. They fell on us while we were cleaning the exhaust—"

"While *I* cleared exhaust," Jak broke in.

Ryan continued. "So we ran out here, got cleaned off fast as we could. All of us got a few bites taken out." Ryan looked at his hands, which still oozed blood. "Don't seem to be stopping as fast as I'd like."

Krysty got out, making room for Mildred, who had grabbed the first-aid kit, stocked with additional items she had pulled from the redoubt. "Not surprising, considering the little bloodsuckers probably have an anti-coagulant in their saliva, to keep dinner flowing faster." She handed tape, cotton, alcohol and gauze to Krysty. "Clean up, Ryan, and I'll handle the other two."

"Probably should start with the pair on my back." Ryan turned, aware of a warm trickle down his spine.

"Ryan!" Krysty admonished while wiping up his blood.

"Hey, as I recall, none of us asked to get covered in leeches and have our blood sucked out."

"I know, I know, it's just—never mind. You just seem to find more trouble than Job himself. Find a stick or something. This'll sting a bit."

Ryan almost turned to see if she was kidding or not. He couldn't imagine cleaning the bites would be more than a minor nuisance. When she swabbed the bites with the alcohol, he learned her prediction was correct, although he manfully tried to control his wince. She bandaged the wounds on his back, then moved to his hands.

"You're going to be some sight after all this." Krysty swabbed and bandaged and taped until Ryan was dotted with patches over all his wounds. J.B. and Jak were similarly bedecked, the three of them looking exactly like what they were—survivors of a very odd skirmish.

Krysty, Doc and Mildred stared at the trio until Ryan couldn't stand it any longer. "What the hell we standing around here for? Let's get moving."

Chapter Twenty-One

With the storm quickly outpacing them to the east, Ryan was able to drive without incident on the highway for another hour. Occasionally they had to detour around broken sections of the road, but for the most part, they kept heading due southeast.

The sun blazed high overhead when they stopped for lunch and to give the engine a rest, pulling into the overgrown gravel driveway of one of the long-abandoned farmhouses that dotted the countryside. After sweeping and clearing the area, Mildred and Krysty laid out a spread of cold meats, cheese and a loaf of bread, and everyone enjoyed thick sandwiches, along with a jar of clean-looking water that Ryan purified anyway, just to be sure.

After lunch and cleanup, Doc and Jak lay underneath towering oak trees for a nap—Jak due to tiredness from the previous night, and Doc simply because he was Doc, muttering something about the "pastoral locale and Little Boy Blue." Krysty and Mildred wanted to poke around in the tumbledown house and barn, and J.B. settled down with his maps to plot the next leg of the journey, conferring with Ryan on the best route.

"How solid you think Brend's information was on Madison?" the one-eyed man asked as he sucked on a hollow tooth.

"Depends. It's not like they get out much, so info's

always second- and thirdhand. Don't see much use in convoys misleading the ville, so it's probably got some truth to it."

Ryan scrutinized the map, tracing the red line of the highway they were on as it led into the vicinity of three lakes where the onetime state capital had sprung up. "If we turned off here—" he tapped an intersection of Interstate 90 and State Road 60 "—we could avoid the city altogether and keep heading east. Maybe check out this place—" He pointed at a patch of green labeled Poynette St. Farm Home. "Might be a good place to hole up for the night."

"Seems like we got plenty of those places around right now. Just pick a farm, and you're good to go. Can't count on everybody bein' as friendly as the last ville."

"Never do. We'll give the sleepyheads another half hour, then get back on the road. Let's check out that farm place anyway. It's far enough away from Madison that we shouldn't have to worry about any cannies."

Carefully folding the map, J.B. regarded him. "How're your bandages?"

"Itch like hell, but I'm not gonna give the women the satisfaction of seeing me scratch them. You?"

"Same. Feel like my luck hasn't been all that great the past few days."

Ryan shrugged. "Bound to turn soon enough."

J.B. frowned. "Damn well better. If it gets any worse, it's liable to kill me."

The two men went to find their respective women, who were returning from their recon of the ruined house. Mildred and J.B. went to relax a bit before they hit the road again, leaving Ryan and Krysty to walk around the barn and through one of the overgrown fields, as much to steal a moment together as to get the lay of the land.

Finding a small hillock, they climbed it and stared out at the gently rolling hills around them, which were slowly baking brown in the summer's heat and dotted with the crumbling ruins of farms that had once sustained a long-ago nation. Ryan didn't give the landscape more than a passing glance, but when he turned to Krysty, he noticed her staring out at the hills absently, her eyes unfocused, as if lost in thought.

Carefully he approached her. "What's going on?"

She shook her head, crimson hair fluttering in the light breeze. "Oh, nothing—for a moment I thought of Harmony ville in summer. It looked much the same as this—the hills parching under the summer sun, fields tended to begin the harvest soon. Just—took me by surprise to be reminded of it like this. It seems like a lifetime ago since I was last there."

"Yeah." Ryan didn't bring up how they'd had to rescue Krysty's home ville from a small gang of killers who had blown into town last time they were there, or how her childhood lover had been killed during the trouble, as well.

"You think we'll ever settle down somewhere someday, Ryan?"

"Mebbe, if we ever find the right place. Don't think this is it, though."

Krysty nodded, staring at the ground. "I was watching you at dinner last night. You were like a wolf among pet dogs. Difference clear as night and day."

He shrugged, walking close to her and putting his arm around her shoulders. "Some folk are born to grow and create. Some aren't. You know which side I fall on."

"I do. Good thing you tend to leave most places we pass through on the better side."

"When possible." He turned her gently back toward the wag and their campsite, unwilling to admit he'd also entertained the thought of holding still recently. "When the time and place are right, we'll know."

She looked up at him, her expression neutral. "Will we?"

Ryan didn't have an answer for her that time.

AFTER A QUICK CHECK of the engine, they fired it up again and set out, heading south until they found the crossroads to take them due east.

The surrounding landscape was more of the same, the bright sun painting the hills vermilion and purple through the violet sky. Along with the farms, they passed several deserted small villes along the highway, and one larger one that had a strange collection of tall, curved pipes that rose dozens of feet into the air, some broken and bent, some still upright. Since there weren't any signs of life, they didn't stop to investigate.

Ryan found the country roads to be in overall better condition than the highway; although rough and rutted, they weren't falling apart like the asphalt and concrete road. Route 60 was straight and level, enough so that he edged up to around fifty miles an hour on one stretch, just to see what the Commando could do. He didn't keep it there long, however, not wanting to stress the engine. He was pleased with the vehicle's speed, however, since it ensured they could outrun just about anyone they might encounter.

About an hour before dusk they stopped again, J.B. wanting to check the wag's coolant levels. They all grabbed a bite and discussed pressing forward or finding a place before night fell. J.B. estimated they were about ten miles from the ville of Poynette on the map, and could probably reach it before dark fell, although if there were folks there, they might not like seeing folks approach after dark. Ryan thought they could press on a bit farther—if they didn't make it, no doubt they could find a suitable camping spot without too much trouble. "Besides, we haven't seen a soul for the entire day, so its not like we're on a well-traveled path out here."

In the end, the decision was made to keep moving, and a few miles later, when Ryan saw smoke rising into the sky to the north, he called back to the rest of the group. "Looks like a settlement to the north. Might as well check it out."

A few hundred yards farther, he came to the intersection of what J.B. said was Route 51, which would take them right into Poynette. At least, that was what the hand-carved sign said by the side of the road. Ryan turned left, and headed up the well-maintained road.

Five minutes later, they came to a checkpoint, lit by blazing torches and manned by several guards—six on the ground and another six on horseback—all armed with longblasters. Ryan downshifted and pulled to a stop about fifty yards away again. Scooting out of the driver's chair, he called out, much like he had done at Toma.

"Hello the guards!"

"Hello yourself. Where you coming from?"

"West, over the Big Muddy, near Toma. We're headin' farther eastward."

"What's your business?"

"Trade, mebbe a place to stay the night if you have a place."

"Sure, but you'll have to leave the wag outside of town. Elders' orders."

Ryan's eyebrow went up, but he went along with it for now. "All right."

"Some of the boys here will escort you to a place you can leave it, then they'll take you to a house you can stay in. In the morning, we can do some trading."

"Sounds good."

"That was a bit odd." Ryan turned to see J.B. wearing the same skeptical expression he'd had. "No toll for coming inside the ville?"

"Maybe these people are overflowing with the milk of human kindness, and do not see the need to tax visitors for the privilege of walking their streets," Doc suggested from the back.

"Mebbe, but everyone keep your eyes open regardless," Ryan said, waiting for the gate to open. A quartet of horsemen had formed up on the other side, a pair on either side of the road, standing at quiet attention. Another one galloped off toward the ville in the distance.

Krysty nodded in appreciation of the horses. "Well-trained. They're not even spooked by the engine noise."

"Not care well trained. Machine gun burst to chest would do 'em." Jak said.

"Let's not get trigger-happy unless they give us a reason," Ryan said. Once the way was clear, he proceeded forward, finding the lights on the wag and flipping the switch to illuminate the road. Next to it was another hand-carved wooden sign: Poynette—Pop. 174.

"Certainly take pride in their ville," J.B. noted.

The riders escorted them to a side road a few hundred yards north of the guard post, pointing them into a grassy field where Ryan parked the wag. "J.B."

"On it soon as we're outside. Weapons?"

"The usual. They'll probably have a place for us to hold them at the boardinghouse." Ryan grabbed the bag of goods to show, then got out, grabbing his Steyr and slinging it. The rest of the group followed suit, with J.B. disappearing underneath the wag again.

"We've sent for a wag to take you into town. What's your friend doin'?" the lead rider asked.

"Wag runs a little hot. He's just checkin' the water level."

"Haven't seen one of those kind in a long time. Usually only steam wags comin' through."

"Had this one awhile, been lucky enough to find gas here and there. Don't suppose you folks have any?"

The rider smiled without showing his teeth and patted the neck of his horse. "You're lookin' at the main vehicles here, friend. They eat just 'bout any crops we grow, and don't require nearly as much upkeep."

"Probably right." Ryan stepped forward, holding out his hand. "Name's Ryan."

"Caleb." The rider introduced the rest of his group, and Ryan did the same, first names only. When they were finished, a wooden wag, drawn by a team of four horses, pulled up, driven by a boy barely into his teens, his eyes widening when he saw his passengers.

"'Zekiel? Take our guests over to Grandma Flannigan's house. Let her know they are guests of Poynette this evening." He nodded at the group. "Enjoy your stay."

"Thank you." Leading the way to the wag, Ryan ushered everyone else in first, making sure no one, Doc especially, hurt themselves getting into the high-sided vehicle. When everyone was situated, the boy clucked his tongue, twitched the reins and turned the team around to head into the ville.

Chapter Twenty-Two

The place itself was as neat as the road, with well-maintained wooden houses lining the streets, the intersections lit by torches. Even at this relatively early hour, there weren't a lot of people out and about, the neat sidewalks and roads devoid of activity. Ezekiel turned down a side street a few blocks in, neatly labeled with a wooden sign that proclaimed it Hudson Street, then clip-clopped three more blocks to the crossroads of Hudson and Lincoln, where a whitewashed house sat with kerosene lanterns burning in its windows. Another carved wooden sign out front read Grandma Flannigan's Boardinghouse.

"Here we are, folks. Grandma runs a nice, clean house, and she'll take care of you right." Jumping down from the buckboard, Ezekiel ran to the back to let down the tailgate. Everyone got out, and followed the boy up the concrete steps to the front door. He had just raised his hand to knock when the door swung open.

"Guests at this hour? Welcome and come in, you all must be tired." Grandma Flannigan, if this was her, didn't fit the image Ryan had in his mind. She was a tall, whipcord thin woman with iron-gray hair and a stern demeanor who was dressed in a homespun cotton dress over which was an apron with several unidentifiable stains on it. "Goodness, I've barely had time to clean up after our last visitors, but I'm sure we can find room for you all."

"Caleb said to tell you they're guests of the ville," the boy piped up.

The old woman's lips curved up in a smile. "That's all I needed to hear. Please take your coats off and hang them in the hall there." Upon seeing the various blasters, she nodded. "I'm afraid I'll have to ask to you hand over your blasters while you're under my roof. They'll be kept safe, you have my word."

There was a pause, and J.B. and Krysty's eyes flicked toward Ryan, who nodded, unslinging his rifle. Unloading it, he slipped the magazine into his pocket, then did the same with his SIG-Sauer before offering both firearms to her. It was a matter of trust. Either side could have done the other in long before this.

"You can set them on the table there." The rest of the group did the same. Ryan noted the proprietor didn't request that they surrender their knives, even though J.B.'s flensing knife was visible on his belt.

"You all must be hungry. I was just about to sit down to dinner."

Ryan and the others had eaten less than an hour ago, but one of the cardinal unspoken rules in the Deathlands was to eat whenever food was available or offered. After all, a person never knew when he might get the chance again. "We'd be happy to sit at your table." He took a moment to introduce everyone, with Doc sweeping his arm out in a courtly bow that nearly knocked Jak off balance next to him.

"Ezekiel? Go set six more places at the table, now!" The boy took off into what looked to be a dining room off the entry hall. The smell of something cooking drifted into the hall.

"You manage this place by yourself?" Mildred asked, looking around at the spotless wooden floor and ancient yet clean rug in the middle. The candelabra overhead held several candles, the melted wax catching in metal holders at the base of each one.

"The boy helps out, and for larger groups some of the women come in and assist with the cooking, but there's plenty for you folks tonight. Come on."

She led them into the dining room, where Ezekiel was just finishing placing bowls around the table. Grandma motioned for them to sit at the table, then disappeared through a swing door into what had to be the kitchen. She emerged a minute later with a large tureen, steam wafting off its top.

"Go on, sit down." She set the tureen down in the middle, disappeared into the kitchen, and returned again carrying a tray of flatbread and bowl of honey. Setting it down next to the pot, she ladled out servings of a thick, light-green soup into the bowls. "Afraid this is all I have ready at the moment."

"It's smells heavenly," Doc offered gallantly.

Once the elderly woman was done, she sat down and waited for everyone to watch her before bowing her head. Ryan did the same and suddenly much of the ville's appearance—the clean streets, the drab clothes—fell into place. Small groups of the religiously inclined often found a ville that they could remake in whatever fashion they desired. Ryan counted his blessings that both this place and the last one weren't one of the more zealous groups. There didn't seem to be much chance of Jak being accused of consorting with demons here or worse, of being one himself.

The evening prayer complete, he bent over the earthenware bowl in front of him. Picking up the clean spoon on the wooden table next to it, he scooped up a bite, all the while sniffing the liquid for any sign of drugs or other additives. Again, the broth didn't have any real odor, malign or otherwise. He sipped cautiously; it was all right, with bits of what might have been finely chopped yet unidentifiable vegetables swimming in it.

Jak hadn't wasted any time, blowing on the soup to cool it before shoving the spoon in his mouth. Grandma noticed and raised an eyebrow. "Boy's got a powerful appetite. I daresay he looks a mite skinny for his age."

Ryan hid his smile as he exchanged a covert glance with Krysty. Despite his odd appearance, Jak often brought out the motherly instinct in older women for some reason. J.B. had once opined it was because the kid looked like a half-starved, half-drowned cat. Jak hadn't spoken to him for a week afterward. "He eats as much as the rest of us. Who knows where it all goes?" Ryan stirred his meal, waiting for any sign of incapacitation. He caught J.B.'s eye as he ate, and the bespectacled man gave the slightest shrug. Everything seemed to be on the level here.

The sound of conversation broke Ryan's thoughts, and he realized Krysty was replying to the old woman's question. "We came from the west, over the river, and straight through. Heard talk of cannies near Madison, so we thought we'd avoid the city altogether."

Grandma Flannigan stiffened in her chair as if she had been slapped, then crossed herself. "Filthy creatures. Eaters of the dead. They haven't been seen around here in a long time. I hope to never set eyes on one for the rest of my life." She set her spoon down on the table, as if the conversation had made her lose her appetite. "So, Krysty said you were traders. What might you have for barter?"

Ryan took this one. "Ammo for your men's rifles, fishhooks and line, a bit of spices, clothes, tools, some other odds and ends. Ought to be just about something for everyone."

She nodded, her iron-gray head bobbing. "I would be interested in seeing what spices you could part with. Your first night here is courtesy of the town, but anything afterward will be paid for, of course."

"Of course. I'm sure we can come to a suitable agreement." Ryan sipped at his cooling soup, reaching for a piece of bread to mop up the remains. Jak had already pushed his bowl forward in hopes of receiving another serving, and Grandma obliged.

"You'd mentioned another group of visitors, madam. We didn't see any people heading west when we were approaching your fair town."

"They had come from the east, true, but decided to try their luck north instead of continuing on to the river. It was a small caravan, only staying a few days before moving on."

"What does your ville have to trade?" Ryan asked

"We are a simple community, living primarily off the bounty of the earth, and trading for whatever we need with those who stop by in their travels. We offer fresh vegetables, candles and honey from the local bees and—" her mouth pursed in disapproval "—fruit of the grain, or distilled corn liquor."

Ryan stilled his eyebrows before they could rise much higher in disbelief. Next to jack and drugs, moonshine was another highly prized commodity, but he wouldn't have expected this place to traffic in it.

Finishing his soup, he mopped up the bottom of the bowl with the soft flatbread, then leaned back in his chair and stifled a belch. "I think we can certainly do business."

"Good to hear." Grandma suddenly pushed back her chair. "The days are long here, and our work begins well before sunup. If you'll follow me, I'll show you to your rooms. Ezekiel will clear the table."

Ryan rose, and everyone else followed suit. Carrying a candle in a metal holder, Grandma Flannigan led them single file into what was a parlor or living room, furnished with hand-carved furniture surrounding a stone fireplace, currently cold and dark. On the other side, a staircase led to the second floor.

"Who does the carving around here?" Ryan asked as he ran his hand up the polished wooden banister. "Got a real talent for it."

"The Ephraim family's been supplying furniture for the town for six generations, since before the harrowing."

Ryan caught Krysty's raised eyebrow, and waved her off. These insular communities often had their own terms for skydark, as the rest of Deathlands called the nuclear catastrophe that had maimed the world.

Doc, however, didn't catch the subtle gesture. "Beg your pardon, madam, but I do not believe I'm familiar with that particular word."

"The harrowing was God's plan to cleanse the land, and everything that man had created on it, and all those who dwelled in it in the flames of his holy fire. Those who are not worthy in His eyes will be destroyed, and those who are worthy, those who worship Him, will receive their just reward in heaven." Her voice hadn't changed in timbre or tone, but Ryan felt that strange shiver curl around his spine whenever he was in the presence of religious zealots. Since Doc was behind him as

Ryan ascended the stairs, he wanted to turn and motion him to shut up, but Grandma had already reached the top and had turned to face them as they came up.

Fortunately, Doc had the sense to not pursue the matter further. "Ah—I see. Thank you for the elucidation, it is much appreciated."

They were at the second-story landing now, and Grandma pointed at three doors, one behind her, and the two right next to her in the hallway. "Rooms are all the same. One mattress only, so I hope the men don't mind slumbering together."

"Not at all, it's common enough in our group."

"Good." Grandma stepped to the first room and opened the door. "I think the ladies will be quite comfortable in here."

Ryan opened his mouth, but was forestalled by the iron-haired proprietor. "Mr. Cawdor, I do not care what sort of arrangement you may have outside of this establishment, however, under my roof, you will obey my rules. As I do not see any sign of matrimony, neither a ring nor a collar, the men and the women will sleep separately. If you do not agree, you are more than welcome to find lodging elsewhere."

Caught, Ryan couldn't do anything but glare at Jak as he sniggered behind his hand. They could leave the house, but that would sour relations with the entire ville, and not gain them anything. Besides, it was only for one night. "We have no wish to cause insult." He waved Grandma into the room. "After you." With her back to him, Ryan caught Krysty's eye and signaled her to have one person stay on watch through the night, then caught Jak's eye and passed the same message to him.

The Armorer had walked into the room, followed by Ryan. Grandma Flannigan had lit the candle by the bedside table, illuminating the wooden floor, a lone hardback chair and lumpy mattress, most likely stuffed with straw, and covered with a homespun quilt. "If any of you have to do your business, the chamberpot is underneath the bed. The closet is there." She waved at a small door on the far wall. "Sleep well, and I'll see you in the morning." With that, she walked out, closing the door behind her.

Ryan stared across the bed at J.B. "Certainly isn't how I figured things'd work out."

"You're telling me." The pale man had crossed silently to the door, pressing his ear against it for a few seconds. "She's gone, back down the stairs." He tried the door, which opened under his hand. "Least she didn't lock us in."

"Yeah, which also means anyone can come in."

J.B. nodded. "You want first watch?"

"No, you take it. Wake me in four." Ryan stretched out on the bed, sinking into the mattress, which didn't rustle underneath as he'd expected. "Goose down mattress, whattya know?" Within seconds he was fast asleep.

RYAN COULDN'T REMEMBER the last time he truly slept. He rested certainly, but years of protecting his life and others' had turned it into combat sleep, from which he could come awake at a second's notice, ready to destroy any attacker.

It was this rest he came out of when J.B. touched him lightly on the shoulder, stepping back when Ryan rose, the handle of his panga in his hand. Memory of where he was flooded back to him, and he nodded at his old friend. "I'm up, I'm up. Anything?"

The Armorer yawned widely. "Other than watching you sleep, it's been as quiet as a grave."

"Nice choice of words."

"Suits this place." J.B. sat on the bed, testing it, then lay down, putting his battered fedora over his face. Just like Ryan, he was asleep in seconds.

Ryan walked over to the chair, picked it up and set it against the wall that had the closet door in it, and sat, crossing his arms as he watched the room. He sensed it was the darkest part of night, and J.B. had been right—everything was dead silent. The night outside was calm and still, without a hint of a breeze. Even the house didn't creak, which surprised Ryan, as it had to be at least a hundred fifty years old, maybe more. Maybe the Ephraims also did house repair.

The minutes crawled by, and Ryan amused himself by watching the moonlight drift across the bed, bathing J.B.'s legs in silver. He tried to see shapes in the light, finding a crude war wag, then a running horse, then, strangely enough, a patch that looked an awful lot like Krysty's face.

Despite this diversion, he wasn't caught off guard in the slightest when he heard the creak of a floorboard, soft, as if someone had stepped on its edge. No, the surprising thing was where it had come from.

Inside the closet.

Ryan's hand stole to his panga as he rose and stood next to the chair, sliding the eighteen inches of honed steel out with barely a whisper. On the bed, J.B. hadn't changed position or breathing, but Ryan would have bet his life the Armorer was completely aware of everything going on nearby.

Seizing the moment, he stole across the room and lay on the bed, concealing his blade at his side. Keeping his eyes slitted, he watched the closet door crack open. Minutes passed before it moved again, testifying to the patience of their assailants. Ryan didn't move, but felt J.B. shift in the bed as if turning in his sleep, dislodging his hat. He also spotted the telltale glint of the flensing blade, now drawn and waiting.

For long moments, nothing stirred. Then the closet door opened wider, and a pale hand curled around it to stop it before it went too far. One figure, then two crept into the room, both swathed in black, including masks over their faces, making them blend with the insubstantial shadows.

Ryan had to give them credit, they stalked their targets carefully, stepping only when they were sure the bed's occupants were asleep. And he was willing to give them all the time in the world to reach him.

Step by step, they edged closer, slim knives clenched in their hands. Ryan figured they planned to stab J.B. and him in the heart, causing instant death without soaking the mattress in blood. After all, they had to keep the room clean for their next victims.

By now Ryan's attacker was almost right next to him, with only a few feet separating them. Keeping his breathing slow and even, he adjusted his grip on the panga handle ever so slightly. Just a bit farther now, and—

The killer paused, as if scenting the air, then took that last step to the bed, his knife sweeping down.

Ryan's left hand flashed up and grabbed his wrist, pulling the weapon down to his side. Caught off balance, the man was forced down near Ryan's body. He opened his mouth to cry out in surprise, but never got the chance to even draw a breath.

The moment Ryan's free hand grabbed his attacker's

and pulled, his right hand rose into the air and brought the panga down on the man's neck, the razor-sharp blade sinking deep into his flesh and severing his spinal cord.

The man was dead before he even knew what had happened. Ryan kept his hold on the man's wrist and maneuvered him onto the bed before he thumped to the floor. He didn't have to look over to know that J.B. had dispatched his own enemy without a sound as well.

Lowering the corpse to the floor, Ryan rose and padded quietly to the closet. It was empty, but he noticed a panel of wood in the back wall that didn't seem to be quite lined up with the rest of them. He picked at it with his finger, and felt it give under his touch.

He sensed J.B. near him. "Candle?"

"Not yet."

"They'd probably light it to signal the deed was done."

"Yeah, but the folks outside don't know how long it'll take. Besides, we have to check the others first." He stalked to the door and pressed his ear to the wood, trying to hear anyone outside. "You check Jak and Doc, I'll take the women."

Turning the knob slowly, Ryan eased the door open, his panga ready to cleave at the slightest sign of anyone in the hallway. It was deserted, with only blackness greeting him. Ryan slipped outside just in time to hear what sounded like a pained grunt come from the women's room. Sticking close to the wall, he sneaked over to the door, grabbed the knob, opened it and burst in.

Ryan had scarely taken a step when he almost tripped over a lifeless form sprawled on the floor in front of him. Sensing someone nearby, Ryan looked up to catch a glimpse of dark hair, red-black in the moonlight, and knew it was Krysty coming at him.

"Shh! It's Ryan!" Along with his hissed warning, Ryan threw his arm up, in case she was wielding steel, too.

"Ryan! I almost stabbed you!"

"You two all right?" Ryan's night vision revealed another two bodies, one hanging half on the bed.

"Of course." Krysty's voice dripped with disdain. "Lecherous bastard thought he'd cop a feel before killing me, so I broke his jaw before breaking his skull. Mildred took hers out with a scalpel to the throat. Decided to arm herself after the pig-rats."

"Good. J.B.'s checking on Jak and Doc. It's time to go."

"Ryan? You should see this," Mildred whispered.

Frowning at the delay, he strode to her. The woman had pulled her dead body's face so it was in the moonlight and had pulled back its lips.

Yellow teeth shone in the moonlight.

Yellow, pointed teeth.

"We didn't avoid the cannies in Madison," she hissed. "We let ourselves be driven right into their fucking town!"

Chapter Twenty-Three

"Even more reason to get the hell out," Ryan whispered, snatching up the pair of slender knives. "Come on, we've got to get the blasters."

He led the two women to the door, checking the hallway, and especially the stairway to make sure a rear guard wasn't cutting off their escape. Everything was deserted and silent. The whisper of a door opening caught his attention, and Ryan saw J.B. exit the far door, leading Jak and Doc to the middle room. Ryan waved Krysty and Mildred to go and slipped out behind them, closing the bedroom door behind him.

Once he was inside, he closed their door as well and wedged the chair underneath the knob.

"Why are we in here? We're trapped now!" Mildred whispered.

Ryan put his finger to his lips, then picked up the body next to the bed and began stripping it. He waved Jak over and pushed the dark shirt into his hands.

"Feel like taking them on straight up?" He nodded toward the closet and showed the albino teen the pair of knives he'd taken off the bodies.

Jak's feral smile gleamed white in the moonlight. "Fuck yeah. Tired all pussying around." Grabbing the shirt, he wriggled into it.

Ryan rolled across the bed and started stripping the second corpse. As he did, he waved J.B. over. "When the shit goes down, you, Doc and the others'll get to the main floor and meet us at the kitchen. It's most likely where she's stored the blasters. Chill anyone in your way."

"Want to tell me something I don't know?" the Armorer grunted. "We'll give you a sixty count, then we'll go. Don't be late."

Ryan yanked the black cloth mask over his head, grimacing at the sticky blood on it. "See you down there."

Jak had already gone to the closet and was about to head down. Ryan stopped him with a hand on his shoulder. "Fake like you've been wounded. Take them by surprise."

"No shit—not stupe!" the albino teen hissed through his mask. Grabbing the wooden ladder inside the narrow passage, he clomped downward, holding his side convincingly as he went. Ryan gave him about ten feet, then swung onto the ladder as well, knife clamped between his teeth. He caught the flicker of candlelight below, and heard the soft thud of someone trying and failing to move quietly.

Beneath him, Jak groaned in simulated pain, causing a head to poke into the shaft and hiss. "What's taking so long?"

"Uh, they awake. Surprised me." Jak was laying it on thick, but the ruse had the desired effect.

"Damn it, get back down here, and we'll take them—urk!"

Jak had reached the bottom before the man could finish his sentence, and then the teenager finished him. The boy stepped out into the room, and Ryan finished clambering down, snatching the knife from his teeth while drawing his panga as he burst out, armed for bears, cannies and anything in between.

The kitchen was dead silent, except for the last hissing breath of a man slumped over the wooden island in the middle of the room, the wooden handle of one of the flensing knives jutting from his nose. Ryan spotted another body beside the opening to the hidden tunnel, the second knife buried in his throat. He gurgled once, a gush of blood bursting from his lips before he expired.

Edging around the island, Ryan saw a third man down near the doorway to the dining room. Jak crouched over him, pulling a throwing knife from his neck. He looked up and smiled. "What took you, old man?"

Aware of how he looked, Ryan stabbed the flensing knife into the butcher block of the island, pulled off his mask and shirt and tossed them aside. "Find the bastard blasters."

The pair quickly tossed the kitchen in under a minute, but all they found were utensils and cooking supplies. "Shit, where the hell are they?" Ryan whispered.

"Ryan." Jak pointed to the back of the room, where a narrow wooden door was set into the wall.

Ryan moved to one side of the door, panga ready, waved Jak to the other side. When they were both set, he yanked it open. Behind it was darkness. Ryan grabbed the candle from the counter and held it up. Narrow concrete stairs led down. The air drifting up from the basement was chilly and redolent of a strange, meaty smell.

"Stay here. I'll be back." Holding the candle high, Ryan edged down the stairs, straining to see anyone in front of him. The odor got stronger the farther he went, until it was almost overpowering. When his feet hit the bottom stair, it was all he could do to not throw his arm over his mouth to breathe through his coat. That, or simply throw up.

The basement was an abattoir. Human carcasses in various stages of dismemberment hung from hooks attached to the ceiling. A bloody table took up the center of the floor, stained and crusted from who knew how many butcherings, a set of well-used knives scattered on its surface. In the corner was a steel barrel that Ryan wouldn't have been surprised to find was full of human blood.

Glancing around, he spied their weapons, piled haphazardly in a corner. Sheathing his panga, he ran over and slung the Steyr longblaster, then grabbed his SIG-Sauer and slammed in the magazine. The click-clack of the action as he pulled it back to chamber a round was one of the more satisfying sounds he'd heard lately. Shoving blasters in his belt and pockets, he grabbed J.B.'s mini-Uzi and ran back upstairs.

Jak stood at the dining-room entrance, turning to him as he emerged. "Anything going on?"

"Not yet. Think we got all?"

"Looks that way, though I haven't seen the old woman. Come on." Handing Jak his .357, Ryan led him through the dining room and into the main room, where J.B., Doc, Krysty and Mildred were coming down the stairs. The weapons were quickly distributed and loaded, and Ryan turned to head out the main door. "Let's go, quick and quiet."

He was at the foyer entrance when he heard Doc at the back. "Madam, you are not safe here. Come with us, quickly."

"Who's he— Shit!" Pushing past the others, Ryan got to the living room entryway to see Doc just inside the room, holding out a hand to Grandma Flannigan, who stood framed in the doorway leading to another room opposite the fireplace. Although Krysty tried to move him along, Doc refused to budge, beckoning to the old lady with his fingers.

"It's all right, madam. We shall escort you from this den of killers."

"Doc, she's one of th—" Ryan began, but was cut off by the old woman.

"When the enemy shall come in like a flood, the Spirit of the Lord shall lift up a standard against him. No weapon that is formed against you shall prosper, and every tongue that shall rise against you in judgment you will condemn. This is the heritage of the servants of the Lord, and their righteousness is of Me, says the Lord. You have come among us to sow destruction and hellfire, and for the wicked there is only one punishment!"

Her voice rose as she spoke, until it was an eldritch screech of insane rage. During her rant, Ryan had been trying to edge around Doc to get a clear shot without setting her off, but hadn't been able to line up the kill yet. Now he feared he might be too late, as Grandma Flannigan launched herself at the old man, the bloody carving knife hidden under her apron raised high to bury into his chest.

Ryan leaped to one side, tracking her with the SIG-Sauer but before he could squeeze the trigger, he saw Doc raise his ponderous Le Mat, the hammer already cocked.

"No, Doc!"

But it was too late. With an ear-blasting roar, the ancient blaster's scattergun barrel went off in a plume of smoke and fire, the grapeshot tearing a fist-sized hole in the old woman's abdomen. Staggered by the blast, she stumbled sideways, almost reaching Doc before crumpling to the floor, the knife skittering from her hand. Her mouth opened and closed soundlessly, revealing her pointed teeth as the mad, glittering light faded from her rheumy eyes.

"And the wages of sin are death indeed." Doc crossed himself with his smoking Le Mat. He turned to Ryan as if seeing him for the first time. "Ah, Ryan, there you are. Shall we depart?"

Grabbing the other man by the arm, Ryan hauled him toward the front door. "Fireblast, yes, we need to 'depart.' That shot'll probably bring the whole bastard town here. Move!"

They hit the front door and found their companions clustered tightly in the shadow of the stairs. "Lights going on." J.B. pointed at the surrounding houses with the muzzle of his Uzi.

"Around the corner, let's go, now. J.B., take the rear." Ryan led the way into the shadows, cutting behind the boarding house of death and the home behind it to come out on another street. "Got mebbe five minutes before they raise the alarm, but we can be halfway back to the wag by then. Take the back way to the main road, then head out to our ride. Stay low, and only shoot if we're about to be discovered."

Ryan took point, cutting through backyards and sticking close to the dark shadows cast by the houses they passed. Once he was about to signal the all clear, when the front door on the house they were hiding next to slammed open and heavy boots tromped down the front steps, fading as their occupants headed back to the boardinghouse. Ryan gave it a ten-count, then kept the group moving again, prowling through the night.

A small group of mounted men met at the intersection

of Hudson Street and the main north-south road, talking loudly enough so Ryan could hear them.

"What happened?"

"The outlanders killed Grandma and everyone at the boardinghouse, and now they're loose in town! You two, guard this road. You, go warn the gate guards to watch for them! And send a group to guard that wag of theirs. They'll be trying to get back to it for sure."

The group split up, with the main contingent heading toward the boardinghouse, a pair of them staying put, and a lone rider heading toward the checkpoint.

"Whoever's running the show doesn't lack brains," J.B. said.

"So what now?" Mildred asked. "If we stay here, we're dead for sure."

"We need those horses. We can use them to fake out the guards at the wag, take them by surprise." Ryan rubbed his jaw. "Just need the right distraction."

"I'll do it," Krysty said.

"Hell, no!" was Ryan's immediate reply.

"Why not? There's no cover to sneak up on them, and any man they see'll be shot on sight. Besides, they'll want to capture me to learn where the rest of you are. I can take one out by myself, it's the other one that'll be the hard part, especially without any shooting."

"No way, you can't risk yourself."

Krysty's response was to unzip her jumpsuit and tear open the T-shirt underneath, revealing a generous expanse of cleavage. "Don't think I'm going unarmed, lover." She kissed him quickly, then ran out before Ryan could grab her.

"Shit!" Ryan was about to go after her, but was restrained by J.B.

"Where the hell you going?" the smaller man demanded.

"Stoppin' her."

"Krysty knows what she's doing. The best thing you can do is help when she needs it, not fuck everything up by running out there now."

Knowing J.B. was right but not wanting to admit it, Ryan let himself be pulled back into the shadows, watching while she approached the pair of riders, her arms held high above her head.

"Don't shoot, I give up!"

Her words caught the men by surprise, but they quickly wheeled their horses around to cover her with their longblasters. "Stay right where you are!"

Krysty did, but slowly turned. "I don't have any weapons. I need yer help! Please, he's crazy!"

"That might work." Mildred nodded in grudging admiration. "Amazing how you boys always seem to fall for a damsel in distress, particularly one with her, ah, assets."

Ryan estimated the distance between him and the nearer horseman to be about thirty paces, a hard shot under perfect conditions, and nearly impossible at night. Breath hissing through his teeth, all he could do was watch in frustration.

The conversation had quieted so much as to be inaudible now, with Krysty gesturing frantically while she talked. The riders seemed to be discussing what to do with her, and Ryan couldn't help noticing how each one was more than a bit distracted by the very attractive woman in front of them. Finally they reached a decision, with one of them holstering his rifle, then reaching down and pulled her up onto his horse in front of him. The second rider turned and began cantering down the side road back to the boardinghouse.

"Get out of the way!" Ryan took off back around the house, rounding the corner and skidding to a stop at the corner that hid him from anyone coming down the street. Holding his blaster up in front of his face, he concentrated on the thud of the horse's hooves as it approached, visualizing the rider, estimating how tall he was, how he sat in the saddle. One more second and—

Ryan stepped out and aimed at the lead man, not more than fifteen feet away. The rider glanced over, his mouth opening in surprise as the one-eyed man triggered two shots. The first hit the rider high in the shoulder, snapping his collarbone as it tore through flesh. The second entered his mouth, breaking off his front teeth as it ripped through his soft palate and into his brain, killing him instantly. Dropping his rifle, the man fell from his saddle, one foot tangling in his stirrup. Without pausing, his horse kept going, dragging him down the road.

Ryan was already tracking the other one in his sights, but Krysty had the situation under control. Although little appeared to have changed in the few seconds they'd been riding, her captor's face was pale, his mouth gaping in shock as a dark red stain bloomed on his side. Pulling the flensing knife out, she stabbed him again, hard enough to push him off the horse. The man flopped to the ground, vainly trying to suck in enough air to scream a warning.

"Grab the other horse!" Ryan hissed as he ran to the second man and planted a boot on his neck, shaking his head. Drawing his foot back, he kicked the man twice in the temple, breaking the thin bone there. Grabbing a foot, he dragged the body back into the shadows. Krysty followed a few moments later, leading the other horse by the reins, the lifeless body of his rider still dragging along beside it.

"Not bad," J.B. said.

Ryan didn't say a word, but the look he gave Krysty said they'd discuss this later. "Get their shirts off. We can fake the rest." They stripped the two bodies and J.B. pulled one of the shirts on. Ryan tossed his to Krysty "Put it on. You're taking Mildred with you."

"What are you—"

Ryan held up a finger. "No arguments! J.B., you take Doc. Jak and I'll follow quick as we can. Get to the wag and take them out fast, then get it up and running. Soon as we get there, we'll get the hell out. Now go!"

Her face dark, Krysty held out an arm for Mildred to grab and pull her up onto the horse. J.B. had a harder time, having to dismount and get Doc on his mount before he could scramble up behind the old man. Clapping heels to hide, the foursome trotted off into the night.

Ryan scanned up and down the street, which was still quiet, although he heard shouts and galloping horses on the other side of the ville. He was just about to rise when the night's stillness was shattered by the loud clanging of a church bell.

"Well, that tears it." Ryan glanced back at Jak. "Ready to move?"

The albino youth's teeth flashed as white as his hair in the moonlight. "Quicker'n you ever be."

"Let's go."

The other side of the main road held no homes, just a bare expanse of fields. Ryan led Jak into it, running out about forty paces, then turning south to parallel the road.

As they dashed through the dark, he heard blasterfire ahead, the staccato burst of J.B.'s mini-Uzi interspersed with the flatter blaster shots from the women, along with a couple of longblaster shots from the defenders. Glancing over his shoulder, Ryan saw a cluster of bobbing torches thunder down the road and turn onto the main highway.

"Keep going, Jak! Get to the wag!" Skidding to a stop, Ryan unslung the Steyr and chambered a round as he dropped to one knee. Trying to steady his rapid breathing, he sighted underneath the lead light, led it by just a fraction and squeezed off a shot. The lead horse screamed and the torch went flying as the rider pitched headlong, the one behind him also going down. The rest of the party kept going, swerving to miss the tangle of horseflesh and humans.

Ryan worked the bolt, sending brass flying, and sighted the next rider. Another shot boomed, and he went down, too. The others scattered, not even returning fire as they wheeled their mounts toward the ville and galloped for cover as fast as they could go. Ejecting another shell, Ryan stood to sight another rider and squeezed the trigger, watching through the smoke of his longblaster as he threw up his arms and slid off the saddle. He took slow, careful steps to the side, weapon at the ready, scanning for any movement from the town. A part of his mind registered that the firing from around the wag had died down, too.

After seeing no movement or blasterfire from the streets for several seconds, he ran into the darkness.

Chapter Twenty-Four

Ryan loped across the fields, the Steyr held loosely in his hands, ready to shoot again if necessary. He still heard noise back in the ville, but the church bell had stopped ringing—a small mercy.

Jak had left him far behind, and as Ryan approached the war wag, he was pleased to see it ready to go, the engine idling and parked in the field. Dark forms littered the ground around it—two men and one horse, all dead.

Ryan stepped into the clearing, his longblaster still out in front of him. The turret on top immediately swiveled toward him, and he stood perfectly still, waiting for J.B. to recognize him. After a few seconds, the rotary-barrel 20 mm cannon turned away, and the main hatch opened.

Ryan jogged over, handing his Steyr up and climbing inside. Everyone was there, and a cursory check showed no one was injured. Without a word, he settled into the driver's seat, gripped the wheel and began hauling it over to the left to take them through the checkpoint and out of town.

He stopped, his hands frozen where they had started their task. They had parked the wag in the middle of the lot, and Ryan saw the pinpoints of torchlight in the distant ville as the people reorganized. For a moment, his memory brought up that nightmarish vision of the boardinghouse basement and the horrors it contained, and his gorge rose at the sudden thought that they might have partaken of some of that, as well. He restrained it with an effort, telling himself that it was only vegetable soup they'd eaten. Even he wasn't sure he believed that, but he clung to the thought like a drowning man, for to lose it was to risk a descent into madness.

But if they turned and left, what would stop this hell-town from continuing their atrocities on the next convoy that came through the area? What might happen if they killed everyone around? Would they begin foraging farther for human flesh to eat?

Would they fall upon Toma like the slavering wolves they were, gorging themselves at that waiting feast?

If they had taken another route, it was likely they would have passed this quaint little ville by, and never been the wiser, but they hadn't, and now here they were, with two paths to choose from—one leading to freedom and safety, and letting a monstrous evil survive to prey on the unknowing, and the other down a dangerous path that could see them injured or even killed. The first was obviously the wiser choice, but Ryan didn't think he could live with himself if he drove away and let this ville continue to exist.

Sensing movement beside him, Ryan felt Krysty slide up next to him. "Ryan?" He didn't acknowledge her presence, but just stared straight ahead for long moments, until he said the only thing he could say.

"We're going back in."

She didn't protest, but just kissed him on the cheek. "I'll spread the word and man the rear gun." She started to turn, but was stopped by Ryan's hand on her arm.

"No, I'll do it. Get to the rear."

She did, and Ryan turned to face the others. "We're

going back. I want to wipe these hellspawned cannie bastards from the face of the earth. Kill anyone you see lifting a weapon against us. Make sure no one gets close. Wipe them all out."

No one said a word at first, then J.B. asked. "Burn them?"

"Not unless we can do it from the wag. No one's going outside."

"Give me a minute. I have to swap the belt in the main gun for tracer rounds."

"You got ninety seconds."

Except for the sounds of J.B. switching the ammo, no one else said a word. Ryan didn't care how they were preparing for what they were about to do, as long as they were getting in the right mind-set. A few moments later, J.B. dropped into his chair. "Turret's ready."

"Front blaster ready," Jak sang out.

"Rear blaster ready," Krysty called from her position.

Ryan heard muttering from Doc that was probably a prayer, but at the moment, he didn't care. He pulled out onto the road, driving slowly back toward the ville. Ryan's mouth was dry, and he swallowed to ease his throat. He'd chilled many before in his life, including some extremely evil bastards, but could think of few who deserved it more than these people, who extended a hand in seeming peace and friendship, only to cut your throat with the blade hidden in the other.

"Going a mite slow," J.B. observed.

Ryan stared out into the darkness. "I want them to know what's coming. Soon as you have targets in range, light them up."

The rotary cannon roared immediately after, with J.B. putting short bursts into the buildings lining the left side of the road. The tracers flashed out like giant orange fireflies that punched through doors and walls to roost in each home. Moments after each one hit, flames flared in each home, causing small forms to spill from the doors, and in several cases, jump from second-story windows. The Armorer was methodical, spraying each building with short, controlled bursts until it ignited.

Ryan turned left down Hudson Street and proceeded until they were at Grandma Flannigan's boardinghouse again, with J.B. torching every building they passed along the way.

"Destroy it," Ryan said.

J.B. sent a long burst into the house, ensuring that it caught. By now the entire southeastern quadrant of the town was burning, with the wind from the east spreading the hungry flames to more buildings. Ryan relentlessly kept on his path of destruction, finding the ville's main street and turning onto it. J.B. was about to continue his controlled burn when he noticed what was ahead of them.

A double line of horsemen, about twenty in each row, had assembled in the street about fifty yards down, every rider carrying with a firearm and a torch. Catching furtive movement in the shadows of storefronts and on rooftops, Ryan glanced around to see more armed townspeople taking up positions for their last stand.

"Ryan—" Jak called from up front.

"The second you see one fire, unload on them. J.B., take the roof positions out. Krysty, make sure no one gets behind us."

For several long moments, no one on the street moved. The only sound heard above the idling engine was the crackle of flames as the cannies' town burned around them. Then one of them held his longblaster above his head and screamed, a long, loud savage war cry that rose and fell in the night air. The rest of the mounted men followed suit, the street reverberating with their shouts and yells.

The leader kicked his horse forward into a full charge, bringing his weapon to his shoulder and firing at the armored war wag. The rest of the line hurried to catch up, weapons leveled, bullets pinging off the thick armor plate.

A second later, all hell broke loose.

The wag shuddered as Jak opened up with his 7.62 mm machine gun, spitting full-metal-jacketed death at the line, chewing into the ragtag cavalry galloping toward them. Ryan hadn't been idle either—as soon as the first man had burst forward, he'd tromped on the Gas, the wag accelerating toward the suicidal men and horses. The front blaster kept chattering, sending men and animals crashing down in tangled piles of horses and riders. But there was still enough left to form a weak barrier when the wag swept into them.

The already panicked horses screamed as they were mowed down by the ten-ton behemoth. Their riders flew through the air, either killed from the wag's impact or when they hit the ground. If by some miracle they were still alive, they were crushed under the inexorably advancing vehicle, belching fire from its front, top, and back like some strange, three-headed monster.

At the end of the street, Ryan cranked the wheel and turned the LAV. The main thoroughfare of Poynette was now a ravaged killing field. Bodies of men and horses littered the street, either pulverized by bullets, crushed by the war wag, or both. Storefronts were riddled from dozens of light-machine-gun rounds, many with smoking bodies sprawled on the sidewalk outside, or dangling half out of windows. Several buildings were already on fire, and J.B.'s efficient manning of the 20 mm cannon was lighting up the rest.

The air inside the wag was hot and smoky, and Ryan's throat was parched. Still, he cruised down the street one more time, trying to draw out any last pockets of resistance so they could be destroyed. The front and rear blasters chattered only sporadically now, with Jak and Krysty mopping up any stragglers.

J.B. tapped him on the shoulder. "Nothing more to do here. Fire'll burn the rest."

"Yeah." Ryan turned down a side street and drove back to the main road out of the ville, heading toward the guard post. Along the way, they saw the carved wooden sign: Poynette—Pop. 174.

"J.B.?" Ryan asked.

A short burst from the turret obliterated the sign and post, leaving only a shattered stump behind. Ryan revved the engine again and drove past.

The guard post was deserted, the men most likely lying dead on Main Street. Ryan drove straight through the wooden barrier, which shattered under the impact, and headed down the road, the red and orange flames of the burning ville lighting the night sky behind him.

Chapter Twenty-Five

They drove for another hour, with J.B. keeping an eye out behind them for any signs of pursuit. The sun was just starting to glimmer over the horizon when they stopped for a cold meal and to reload the blasters. The wag's engine was idling rougher now, but other than topping off the coolant with water, there didn't seem to be anything that could be done about it.

J.B. estimated they were about sixty miles from what used to be the city of Milwaukee, and after their last encounter, Ryan didn't find much resistance when he suggested they skirt the town completely, cutting to the south and east to make a beeline for Chicago. Doc had been muttering darkly about nests of snakes in the garden of Eden, and Ryan figured it didn't pay to stick around here any longer than necessary. No one else mentioned what they'd done, and the atmosphere inside the wag was somber and silent as a result.

The bright sun didn't last long, being overtaken by a thick bank of green-tinged clouds by midmorning. The air grew hotter as the day passed, turning thick and still. J.B. had also noticed his rad counter showing traces of radioactivity in the area, not enough to be concerned about, but edging toward the top of the green safe zone.

They followed the decrepit highway east, looking for a turnoff, or even a clear path across the country. Ryan was just about to turn off and start carving his own path through the fallow farmlands when he heard a fusillade of blaster shots in the distance to the north. Turning, he saw a thin plume of dark smoke on the horizon.

"What now?" he muttered. "We've already done our good deed for the day."

"Too far away too get a look with the camera. If that fire catches, could be days before it burns itself out in this weather," J.B. said. "Don't want to wake up one morning breathin' cinders and ash."

Ryan sighed, resigned to J.B.'s implacable logic. "All right, we'll get close enough so you can see what's going on." He turned the wag toward the noise, figuring they wouldn't lose too much time by the detour. A few minutes travel brought them to the crest of a hill that would give anyone on top a decent view of the surrounding countryside, including the battle zone. Parking just below the crest, he and J.B. crept up to see what was going on.

Ryan watched the aftermath as J.B. surveyed the scene with a pair of Zeiss binoculars he'd scavenged from the redoubt. Two groups of people were clustered around the still-burning remains of a charred building. "Looks like a group of raiders trapped some other folk in a farmhouse and smoked them out. Filthy looking bastards. Mebbe three or four survivors. What the…it can't be…"

"What?"

J.B. passed Ryan the glasses in response. "I, uh, didn't get a good look, but check out the tall one in the middle. The really tall one."

Ryan raised the glasses to his eye, focusing on the abnormally thin, tall man being prodded along by one of the raiders. He had long, gray-white hair, and wore a familiar pair of aviator sunglasses.

"Fireblast! That can't be…Donfil?"

Donfil More was an Indian shaman the group had encountered on one of their adventures in the Southwest, where they had gone up against a blackhearted bastard named Cort Strasser, whom Ryan had encountered more than once in the past. In the stark desert, Strasser had styled himself after a long-dead military leader, and had been leading a war of extermination against the local Apache populace. Once his group had been destroyed, More had accompanied Ryan and his companions until settling down in a whaling community on the East Coast. Seeing him again after all this time was more than a surprise—it made Ryan's jaw drop.

"You know any other seven-foot-tall Mescalero Apaches in the area? What the hell's he doing here?"

"Only one way to find out," Ryan said, pushing back from the hilltop and trotting to the wag. "We go in fast and take them by surprise. They'll never expect it."

J.B. followed Ryan back to the wag, and they told the others who they'd just seen in the clearing. They were predictably surprised. Gunning the engine, Ryan hit the Gas, sending them roaring down the hill. As he'd suspected, the sight of the wag coming straight for them demoralized the formerly jubilant predators, most of whom took off into the surrounding trees, helped along with a few short bursts from the front machine gun. The former prisoners also took off in the other direction, but Ryan slipped to the hatch and poked his head out.

"Donfil? Donfil More! Wait, it's Ryan Cawdor!"

The tall man had been shooting for the tree line as fast as his skinny legs could carry him, but at the shout of his name, he instinctively glanced back at the wag, his mouth opening in shock as he spotted the man calling out to him.

"One-Eye Chills?" He slowed to a stop and came back "Is it really you? By the Great Spirit, it is good to see you again!"

"None other. What the hell are you doing out here? Last we saw you, you were setting up with those whalers on the Lantic."

"My journey since parting company with you has been a long and strange one, my friend. Please, let me get my other friends back here first, and we will go back to Waukee and catch up."

"Sounds good to me." Ryan kept a tight watch around them, in case the bandits were dumb enough to counterattack, while Donfil called to his fellows in the woods, eventually rounding up three of them. When they got closer, Ryan noticed that each one had minor mutations—one had what looked like a set of vestigial gills on his neck, the second's head was bald, except for what appeared to be a small dorsal fin that started at his forehead and swept back to his neck, and the third who had webbed fingers and a distinct scaled pattern on his skin. Donfil made introductions, and they all nodded tentatively to him.

Donfil wasn't all that concerned. "The others know how to find their way back to the ville, or we might come across them on the way. Let us go and talk. There is much to discuss."

"You got that right. You and your group can hitch a ride if you don't mind sitting on top."

"Most generous of you, One-Eye Chills." After a brief conference with his comrades, Donfil led them to the wag and climbed on top, settling himself as comfortably as he could beside the cannon. The rest of his men followed. "Head due east, and you will come to the Great Lake. Once there, turn south and you will take us back to our ville much faster than we had left."

Ryan waited until everyone was secure before pulling his head back inside and engaging the wag's gears. He kept it to around fifteen miles an hour, not wanting to spook anyone above into falling off.

They drove for about ninety minutes, and located the missing fourth member of Donfil's party on the way. Afterward, Ryan bulled through the thin forest to find himself near a cliff that overlooked a great, muddy-green expanse of water that stretched out over the horizon. There were several watercraft on the lake, their patched sails up as they skimmed along the surface. The wind blowing off the lake was redolent of algae and rot, with an underlying hint of metal. He heard a thump from up top, then Donfil's muffled voice.

"Welcome to the Great Lake Michgan. Follow the shore south, and we'll be at our homestead soon."

Ryan obliged him, and they began traveling along the shoreline, careful to avoid the crumbling cliff edge. After several miles, they found a rutted dirt road, and Donfil yelled to take it. Ryan did so, and came across the ville of Waukee a few bone-jarring minutes later.

From what he understood of predark maps, the shoreline of the Great Lakes had taken a terrible battering from the Russian nukes. The area around Chicago had been reduced to a radioactive wasteland, black and empty. The city of Milwaukee had been badly damaged by the reshaping of the coastline, with much of its original waterfront destroyed long ago. The rebuilt port had grown up around a large concave bowl of land that might have been formed from a long ago landslide into the dark-green water. Crude wooden docks poked

into the lake like fragile fingers, holding strange looking, low-slung boats between them like toys in a giant's
hands.

The majority of the buildings around the harbor were
houses, sturdy-looking, weathered cubes of wood with
angled roofs and heavy shutters that could be pulled over
the mostly open windows. Two larger buildings, each
one several times larger than the biggest home, dwarfed
the rest of the surrounding structures. The smell of lake
water and fish hung over everything.

Donfil directed him to the smaller of the two large
buildings, where they parked the laboring wag, and
waited for the group to get out of the vehicle before he
headed inside.

The interior was a communal room, filled with long
tables and rows of benches. Several women, all dressed
in heavy, plain skirts, blouses and white bonnets, bustled
around. When they saw Donfil and the group in the
doorway, a few of them stopped in surprise, then they
all clustered around him, chattering excitedly. Some
also noticed Ryan, Krysty and the others, and eyed them
cautiously, particularly Jak's and Krysty's hair.

While Donfil held up his hands to calm them, Ryan
was also looking around. He noticed that all of the
people in the room had a small mutation of some kind,
from variants of the three he had seen earlier, to silver-
eyed children and fish-mouthed girls.

Donfil had finally gotten the milling women around
them to quiet, holding his spindly arms above his head
to placate them. "Just a minute—settle down, everyone.
These are friends of mine that I met many moons ago,
and have been rejoined with by the wisdom of the Great
Spirit. I cannot say if they have been sent to help us—
indeed, I have not even asked them if they would—but

I must confer with the town elders first. While I see the elders, I would ask that you make them as welcome in our home as you have made me."

Ryan caught J.B.'s eye and picked up his surreptitious nod, indicating that what Donfil had said about their "helping" the ville hadn't gone unnoticed. Brow furrowing, he decided to ask the tall shaman just exactly what he meant by that at the first opportunity.

A stern-looking matronly woman with a silver-scaled pattern on her face and hands shooed the others back to work, nodding respectfully to Donfil. "Will our guests be staying for dinner?" Her voice had an odd, sibilant quality to it.

Donfil nodded, and the woman smiled, revealing needle-sharp teeth irregularly spaced in her mouth. "Then we shall prepare the best of the day's catch for them." With that she bustled off to oversee her charges.

The scarecrowlike Donfil then turned to his friends, his head bowed to regard them. "My apologies, my friends. Our town has had some troubles recently. That was why I was inland this morning. I was looking for help with our problem and was hoping that perhaps another community might be able to offer a solution."

Ryan repressed a shudder as he thought of these relative innocents wandering into the hellhole of Poynette. Would have been hung up and gutted before night had fallen, he thought. "Right, but first things first, Donfil. Like, how'd you end up here? Like I said, last time we saw you, you were pretty well set in that whaling town on the Lantic."

Donfil nodded, his iron-gray hair bobbing around his face. "Yes, I thought I had found my place in this world, and for a time, it was a good life. Unfortunately, the Great Spirit turned his face from us, and the whales grew harder and harder to find. The ships were staying out longer and longer, and returning with nothing to show for it. I had been saving up to buy a stake in a vessel myself, but when the good ship *Phoenix* was attacked by a large school of killer whales and nearly sunk, I knew my time there was at an end. A group of traders was planning a trip down the Lawrence, and I hired on with them to sail to the Great Lakes. We moved among the shore communities for several moons, until I found my place here, among these fishermen, and have remained ever since."

"Okay, so what's the problem you all have?" J.B. cleaved right to the point, as usual.

Donfil lowered his voice, leaning close to Ryan, J.B. and the rest of the group. "Since Waukee was rebuilt many, many moons ago, its people have lived in peace with the lakes, taking what they need and knowing that the waters will replenish themselves. Lately, however, it seems that the Great Spirit is angry with us again, for boats go out on calm days, and a sudden storm will arise from nowhere, destroying our ships and men. The pike, trout, salmon and sturgeon that once filled these waters now seem to elude us, letting our boats come home empty time and again. When they are running, we set our lines, yet they come up empty, or even worse—cut clean off. On night sails, when the spawning fish run under the moonlight, men have disappeared without a trace, on deck one moment and gone the next. A few days ago, a large boat went out and was found floating on the water with not a single hand on board."

He shook his head. "I am even starting to wonder if I am the cause for this—first the whales leave the coast, and now this village suffers when I arrive. If we do not uncover what is behind this soon, I feel that I will have to leave this place, perhaps head to the Great River to find a home." He stared at Ryan with that strange, penetrating gaze of his. "Perhaps the Great Spirit has brought us together again for a reason, eh?"

Ryan didn't give much credence to the vagaries of fate, but he also saw no reason to disillusion his old friend. "Mebbe. Are we supposed to meet with these 'elders' of yours?"

"Yes, actually, they wish to see everyone who visits our town, so that they may take their measure, so to speak. If you wish, we could take care of that right now."

"Yeah, probably the best idea. Let's go say hello."

Chapter Twenty-Six

"What do you think?" J.B. asked as they walked a few steps behind Donfil and Doc, both of whom were enjoying a spirited philosophical discussion pitting Native American philosophy against more traditional Western schools of thought.

Ryan shrugged. "Seeing Donfil sure distracted Doc from his depression, that's for sure. 'Bout the rest of it, who knows? Mebbe the fish have wised up and just don't live around here anymore."

Mildred, close enough to overhear their conversation, frowned. "Maybe, but what about the disappearing people? I never heard any stories of fish developing a taste for human flesh. Unless these folks are suddenly getting real clumsy, something else is going on."

"Yeah, but that don't necessarily make it our business either."

Mildred snorted. "Says the guy who didn't hesitate to kill half the population of the last ville we came across."

Ryan turned his head to stare at her. "Difference between there and here is no one's tried to chill us yet. If that happens, my response will most likely be the same."

"Why don't we meet the elders and see what they have to say before making any decisions?" Krysty asked. "We're probably only about a hundred miles or so away from the mat-trans and aren't that hell-bent to get there, so maybe staying here a day or so wouldn't hurt."

"We'll see." Ryan lengthened his stride to catch up with the other two men as they headed toward the second large building. "Donfil?"

The gaunt shaman stopped with his hand on the door. "Yes, One-Eye Chills?"

"Anything we need to know about these elders before we go in?"

Donfil shook his head. "Just answer any questions they have honestly. There is nothing to fear."

"Never said there was. Let's go."

Donfil opened the door, and the first thing to hit Ryan and the group was the rank, almost overpowering smell, a sharp stench of guts and blood. This room was set up like the other one, but its long tables were given over to processing of giant tubs of freshly caught fish. With machinelike efficiency, rows of men and women gutted, filleted, skinned and deboned carcasses with precision, completing their assigned task before sending what was left on to the next station. They worked quietly, and the large fish bodies were reduced from their natural state to rows of pale white fillets. Not even the presence of the visitors caused them to lift their heads from their work. Ryan picked out more marine abnormalities, including more than one person who had only one working limb, with the other being what he could have sworn was a fin, but that might have been just a trick of the dim light cast from the high windows on a withered hand and arm.

The smell was most pungent where they were standing, and Donfil smiled as he led them to the back of the cavernous room, the swish and chop of the knives on the human disassembly line loud in their ears. "You get used to it after a while. Of course, coming in where the fish guts are piled doesn't help any either."

"Excuse me, Donfil, but I fail to see the problem here," J.B. said. "Looks like everyone's busy enough, plenty of fish to go around, so where's the trouble?"

"To you it may seem busy, John Barrymore, but this is the only shift that is still operating—we used to have two. We have been trading with other communities both around the Lakes and inland, using our extra fish, and if we only have enough to feed ourselves, then our trade suffers as a result."

"Makes sense."

Ryan thought about throwing a sleeve over his nose in an attempt to block the stench, but decided against it. No sense having to talk to these elders with his arm over his face. He followed Donfil up a staircase on the wall at the back of the room. At the top was a rusty metal door with a rectangular wire glass window in the middle. Raising his walking stick, Donfil pounded on the door, loud enough to be heard over the din on the processing floor.

The door opened, and what might have been a man or woman's face peered out—it was that hard to tell. The doorperson was one of the more severe mutations they'd seen so far, completely hairless, with wide, bulging eyes mounted on either side of a flat, narrow head that somehow tapered down into a normal human neck. The rest of his or her body was normally proportioned.

"Donfil More to see the elders, please." The shaman had bowed his head as he spoke, making Ryan's eyebrows rise.

The person spoke with a watery gurgle. "Enter and be welcomed here."

Donfil walked through the doorway, with Ryan and

his group entering behind him. This room was much smaller, and smelled of freshwater shallows. It was dimly lit, and Ryan heard a gurgle as he walked in, as if someone were slowly pouring out a jug of water.

At the far end, five people sat in small circles of light provided by a row of round, high windows mounted along the left wall. The right wall was dark, but Ryan got the impression of a large pane of glass of some kind mounted there with something large behind it, perhaps several hundred gallons of water. But he gave it only passing attention, his gaze drawn to the people before him.

The five people that made up the elder group basically resembled old, wrinkled fish mutants. They were certainly human, but their aquatic features were more pronounced than the rest of the villes' inhabitants. As Donfil walked up, one of them reached down to a bucket next to him and picked up a dipperful of water, pouring it over the set of opening and closing gills in his neck.

Donfil approached the row of watchers and nodded to them. "Elders, I have returned from my mission, and, brought with me a possible answer to our problem." Introducing Ryan and the others, he quickly recounted his group's encounter with the bandits and their subsequent rescue.

The second one inclined his head to Ryan and the others. "We owe you a debt of gratitude for saving our people. We would ask that you stay with us tonight, and be fed and housed, and any other needs you may have will be taken care of, if they are within our power."

Ryan nodded, as well. "Thank you. Not that we don't appreciate it, but Donfil mentioned a problem you all are having recently. I don't want to give anyone the wrong impression here, but I'm not sure if there's anything we'd be able to do about it."

The third elder leaned forward. Although his mouth was small, he spoke very well. "We cannot ask you to do anything more than you have done already. We know well the cost of hired men and women such as yourselves, and it is an option we have considered."

The member on the other end of the table stiffened and looked away from the rest. Ryan didn't need a sign to tell he wasn't happy about that last part.

The third elder continued as if he hadn't noticed the movement. "However, we could tell you of our problem, and perhaps you could share your knowledge with us. As of yet, we haven't even been able to discover the cause of the disappearances, either of the fish or our townspeople."

A spark of light flared in the darkness to everyone's right, and Ryan started back in shock as a humanoid form was revealed in the phosphorescent glow.

Like the doorperson, the sixth elder combined the strangest traits of human and fish into a completely new appearance. Perhaps four feet long, he had no legs to speak of, but a fish tail that waved back and forth in the water as he moved. His arms were a combination of human limb and fin, with a segmented elbow joint that allowed him more flexibility as he swam around the tank. His body, limbs, and tail were all outlined in an eerie, blue-green luminescence, making him appear partly translucent. His face combined what might have been the best or worst of both races, Ryan couldn't be sure, with a gaping mouth that opened and closed to suck in water, and huge eyes that seemed more designed for a lightless environment than the surface.

"My God," Doc said, entranced. He slowly approached the tank, his gaze never leaving the fish-being inside. It in turn swam up to the glass, regarding him with one pale, unblinking eye. Doc reached out a tentative hand to gently touch the barrier, which was answered in kind by the creature rolling over to extend a flipper to him in greeting. "Sentient, or I'll eat my hat. The wonders of this world never cease to astound me."

That wasn't the only wonder either, for the elder on the far end, nearest the tank slowly stood. "Our brother may be about to speak—he usually lights up beforehand. He will do it by contacting your mind, so just relax and open yourself to him. He does not mean any harm."

"Wait a minute—" Ryan began, but it was too late.

The fishman rose in the tank until he could see everyone in the room, his internal light glowing even brighter as he did so. When everyone was bathed in its radiance, Ryan didn't hear a voice, but saw a series of images in his head: The village on a bright summer day, the sun shining over the houses, the buildings and the water, making it glitter like someone had scattered a handful of diamonds on the lake... Boats sailed out, the occupants fishing like their ancestors had, and their ancestors before them... A shadow suddenly fell over the harbor, the village, everything in sight...it came from the east, and grew from a speck on the horizon to reality in seconds—a gargantuan, massive tidal wave, seventy feet high, a churning, roiling cascade of bile-yellow, foaming water...people saw it...only had time to point and scream before it was on them...devouring the town under its pounding force, shattering the docks, washing away houses, caving in one side of the processing building...washing away both it and all inside, sweeping them all back out to the implacable waters…leaving shattered debris, broken planks, and lifeless, floating bodies behind—

WITH A START Ryan jolted out of the vision, coming back to the room around him. The pictures in his head had been so real for a moment, he found himself tensed to try to do the impossible—outrun the mammoth wave that had come crashing through his mind.

He glanced around to see his friends similarly shaken. Krysty's hair had coiled tightly up around her neck, J.B. had taken his fedora off and was running a hand through his hair. Mildred's eyes were wide as she stared at the rest of the group, while Doc barely repressed a shudder at seeing the watery death engulf the town. Jak simply wrapped his arms around himself, his head down, having seen a foe that even he could have no effect against.

Ryan cleared his throat, which had gone strangely dry, even in the damp room. "He a doomie?"

The second Elder considered the question. "To a degree. Some of what he foresees does come to pass, enough that we must take every vision he chooses to impart to us seriously."

"Yeah." Ryan rubbed his chin, also choosing his words carefully. "Look, if what's on your horizon is something like what we just saw, there's nothing we can do about it. Seems like the best idea would be to think about pulling up stakes and moving elsewhere."

His suggestion brought urgent muttering from the elders, all of whom leaned toward one another to confer among themselves. Ryan looked at the rest of his group and shrugged, earning puzzled looks from the others in return.

After a minute or two of impassioned discussion, the five elders turned back toward the group. "That choice has been discussed as well, and then, as now, we have decided to stay here, to try to find a way to stop this from coming to pass."

Ryan halted the snort of derision rising in his head, turning it into a cough instead. He was still trying to find a diplomatic way to point out the folly of their decision when an urgent banging on the door startled everyone.

The doorperson walked over and opened it to see a new person, slick with sweat and panting hard, as if he had run a good distance to get here. He clutched a cloth-wrapped bundle to his chest, the lower end leaking some kind of noxious, black fluid.

"Elders, please, forgive my intrusion. There's been another attack—Melob's boat—and they have brought something back. You must see!"

He was waved into the room and entered hesitantly. When he reached the center, he knelt and unwrapped the stained cloth from what it had been holding.

On the floor lay the forearm and hand of some kind of lizard creature. The fingers were webbed, but each one also ended in a sharp, black claw. The arm was covered with thick, dark green scales, each as wide as a fingernail, and overlapping all the way down. Black ichor still oozed from the injury that had severed the limb, staining the floor.

The elders reacted with expressions ranging from anger to surprise to shock. There was a clamor of noise as each one tried to speak at the same time. Only when the sixth elder glowed brightly again, lighting up the room, did the rest quiet down.

"Tell us what happened, Qualen," the elder on the left end said.

"Don't know whole story. They were north of the harbor and set upon by one of these things as they were hauling in their lines. It was creeping up on one of the crew when it was spotted. Made a grab for him anyway, and that's when its arm got cut off by someone with a 'chete. Dived off fast enough that no one got a good look at it. They hauled in their lines and sailed back fast as they could."

Ryan had been keeping an ear on the conversation while he leaned over the limb, drawing his long knife to poke at it. The hand contracted sluggishly, fingers curling in response to the stimulus. Straightening again, he drew the toe of his boot through the black blood and waited for the elders to finish talking among themselves again.

"Yes, Ryan Cawdor."

"Well, I don't know what we can do about that wave that may or may not be coming at you, but this is a damn sight different."

"Oh?"

Ryan's answering grin was cold. "These things bleed, so they can be hurt. And if they can be hurt, they can also be killed."

Chapter Twenty-Seven

The conversation was tabled until after the communal meal was served. Ryan and the others headed back to the other hall, where they were served a thick seafood chowder, filled with chunks of fish, what looked like large crayfish, and an array of vegetables. Baked oat scones accompanied the dish, which many used to sop up the soup. Despite the wide array of mutations, the villagers were polite and civil to each other, with several stopping by the table where the attacked boatmen ate, to clap them on the shoulder or offer their commiserations.

Although the men and women ate separately, the ville didn't request the same of Ryan's group, and once they had helped themselves from the large tureen nearby, they sat together and discussed the situation.

"Well, what you think?" J.B. asked between bites.

Ryan blew on a spoonful of soup before eating it. "Donfil hasn't changed a bit since we parted ways on the coast."

"That's not what I meant and you know it."

"Yeah, yeah. Been thinking about it all."

"It's just after that pretty speech you gave upstairs, I figured you'd be hell-bent to go out there and save them from whatever's causing the trouble."

Ryan stared at the bespectacled man over his soup bowl. "Mebbe we'll just use you for bait, see what comes out to nibble on your toes."

The corner of J.B.'s mouth twitched in acknowledgment of the joke, and he returned to his own meal.

"Donfil's a friend, and that carries some weight. But if these people are about to be destroyed by some kind of natural disaster, what's the point of helping them now? Hell, what we ought to be doing is packing up and hitting the road, before whatever's coming for them catches us, too."

Mildred stifled an unladylike burp behind her hand. "Yeah, but the elder said only some things the fish-man saw came true. What if our presence here is the thing that stops it?"

Ryan fixed her with his cold blue stare. "Yeah, and what if our presence here is the change that causes it?"

The woman didn't back down, holding his gaze with her warm brown eyes. "Stalemate, Ryan. You can't prove your idea is true, and I can't prove mine is either. I've seen a lot of weird stuff since y'all thawed me out, and the only thing I can say with certainty is that there isn't any certainty in this world. No one bats one hundred percent, not back in my time, and sure as hell not now. Maybe that doomie is right about the killer wave, but it might not happen for years, maybe long after this generation is dead and gone. And if you think you're going to wipe out a town just by entering it, then you got a pretty high opinion of yourself, mister."

Ryan's face didn't even change expression as he replied. "Tell that to the good people of Poynette."

Mildred opened her mouth, then closed it again with a snap. Her lip curled like she wanted to cuss Ryan out, but instead she returned her attention to her bowl, scooping up succulent chunks of seafood and shoveling them into her mouth.

"Friend Ryan," Doc said suddenly, "If these people are in need of our assistance, would it not be remiss to neglect them in their direst hour?"

Ryan tossed his spoon on the table, his appetite gone. "Fireblast! You know, lately between the three of you, it's like I'm surrounded by walking consciences every minute of every single fuckin' day."

His eye fell on Jak, who was busy scraping the bottom of his second bowl. "What about you—you must have something to say about all this."

The albino youth flipped a lock of lank, white hair out of his face and grinned. "Boats look like fun."

"That's about what I figured. What about you, Krysty, since this has suddenly turned into some kind of communal democracy?"

Doc opened his mouth, no doubt about to point out the impossibility of Ryan's statement, when he winced and grabbed at his shin, his face grimacing in pain as Mildred, sitting next to him, smoothed her features into the picture of innocence.

"You don't need my take on it. You're going to do what you like anyway—just like Poynette." Krysty turned her level green gaze on Ryan, and he felt that same strange flutter inside, just as he had the very first time he'd first seen those emerald eyes. "However, my mother always told me the sign of a true man—or woman—is when they see the path they want to take clearly before them, but they turn onto the right path whether or not it was what they'd wanted."

"Hell, that's just as bad." Ryan ran his hand through his hair. "And I suppose someone here has a plan to take care of the problem, too?"

J.B. cleared his throat. "Not till you mentioned the idea of hangin' me out for bait—"

"Even more tempting now," Ryan growled.

"We'll make a bait boat instead. Send out a couple, all within sight of each other, and put two or three of us on each one. Haven't seen a decent blaster here yet, so ours should make the difference. Lizard men come up, we put a round into their scaly foreheads, and send the bodies back down to wherever they came from. Problem solved."

"Works for me," Mildred said.

Ryan held back the first remark he thought of—naturally she'd agree with J.B. The only problem was that he was inclined to agree with it, too. As usual, the pragmatic Armorer had come up with a very practical solution to the problem. If they couldn't bring the lizard-things to them, then they'd have to go to where the lizard-things were.

He nodded. "We can stay here a day or two, help Donfil and his ville out. I suppose you all want to head right out there after lunch, see if we can't mop this up before dinner?"

J.B.'s eyebrow lifted in surprise. "If you're so all-fired up to get back on the road again, I figure that'd fit your plans just fine."

"I think we're forgetting one thing," Krysty said. "What makes any of you think that just stopping these creatures on one or two boats will prevent them from coming back once we're gone? If they are a threat to this ville, someone would have to track them back to their home and deal with them there."

J.B. pushed his empty bowl away and picked up his fedora. "Not necessarily. If these things have at least rudimentary intelligence, the presence of a better-armed and capable force that stops them from attacking the boats could drive them to seek easier pickings elsewhere."

"We wont know either way until we find out what's going on." Spotting Donfil walking toward them, Ryan pushed his chair back and stood. "Sooner we get to it, the better."

The skinny shaman greeted all of them with nods. "I hope your meal was enjoyable?"

"Really good, thanks. Haven't had anything like that in a long time."

Donfil hesitated, rocking back and forth on his heels, as if unsure how to continue. "Ryan, I just wanted you to know that it was not my plan to get you involved in what is happening here. It's just that, well…"

Ryan reached out and clapped the other man's shoulder. "Don't worry about it." He let his gaze fall upon the rest of the group. "We've decided to see what we can do to help."

The tall Apache stared at Ryan like he didn't believe what he had just heard, then quickly nodded. "Thank you. Our thanks to all of you."

Ryan cut him off with a wave of his hand. "Save it for when we've actually done something, okay?" He took a few seconds to outline their plan. "Why don't you take us down to the boats so we can get a look at what we're going to be riding on?"

Donfil's face split into a genuine grin. "Your thoughts and ours are as one. I was hoping that might be your next request. I want you to meet the captain of the two boats that have already volunteered to serve as your decoys this afternoon."

Turning, he waved to someone behind Ryan. A few seconds later, a relatively normal-looking man walked up to them, his face browned from exposure to the sun and weather. Ryan was debating whether to say anything about his average appearance when he stepped into the sunlight. Under the bright afternoon beams, his skin gleamed as if he was covered in silver. After shading his eyes from the glare, Ryan blinking a couple of times and refocused on the man, who was covered in what appeared to be thousands of tiny fish scales that flashed iridescent in the light.

"Ryan Cawdor, meet Saire, the best fisherman in town. If he can't find them, the fish are simply not to be found."

Ryan extended his hand, finding the other man's grip to be exactly as he expected—callused and hard from years of working on the lake. "Donfil told you it's not fish we're going after this time."

Saire nodded. "Lost my first mate to those scaly bastards a few days ago. Been achin' to get some payback."

Ryan turned back to Donfil. "Well, then, let's go fishing."

Chapter Twenty-Eight

After lunch, Saire led the group through the ville to the docks. Donfil had begged off accompanying them, saying he had things to attend to. Ryan wasn't sure if that was the truth, or if Donfil was really afraid his presence would affect the trip—or what they hoped to find. Either way, he didn't blame the man. If the boats they'd be sailing on were anything like the usual vessels, Donfil's height would be more of a minus than a plus.

Other than the ever present, slightly brackish smell of the nearby lake, the ville was neat and orderly, reminding Ryan uncomfortably of Poynette. But he dismissed his twinge by the simple fact that Donfil would never have fallen in with cannies, and it was obvious that they all subsisted on and made their living from the wideopen expanse of water stretching beyond the horizon.

The sturdy wooden dock shook under their feet as they walked out to take a look at the craft they'd be using. The ship was about forty-five-feet long, and appeared to be flat bottomed, with a main mast containing two reefed sails, a large one on a jib in front, and a smaller one behind the mast. What at first glance looked to be a crazy tangle of lines snaking every which way turned out to be, upon closer examination, neat groups of ropes that controlled the sails and held the mast in place. There was a very small belowdecks area, but no cabin that Ryan could see. It looked large enough for about a half-dozen people to work comfortably. Four men bustled about on the deck, clearing lines and readying the vessel to make way.

"A Dutch barge!" Doc exclaimed. "I haven't seen one of these for—well, a long time, anyway."

Saire nodded approvingly at the old man. "You know your boats, white-hair. The *Lament* was hand-built by my father from the plans we've kept safe for the past seven generations. She's the sturdiest, fastest vessel on the lake, and should be the perfect bait for those things."

J.B. slowly walked from the foredeck to the aft section, most likely measuring lines of fire. He glanced up after his inspection. "Got any idea where we'll most likely run into them?"

Saire nodded at a boat with faded red sails on the other side of the long dock. "Those boys who returned before lunch, part of the *Gravelax*'s crew, said the one they took the arm from was found north of here, 'bout ten miles up. Figured we'd start there and work our way down the coast, see what we reel in either way—fish, amphibian or both."

"Donfil said you had two boats. Any objection to sending them both out, that way if one's in trouble, we have backup from the other?"

Saire nodded at the ship next to his, which might have been the *Lament*'s twin. "No one goes out alone anymore, not since these attacks began. The *Banshee*'s ready to sail, too, so all we need is to figure out who's going on which boat."

Ryan stroked his chin as he pondered that exact same question. If he had his druthers, he would have left Doc on shore, maybe Mildred as well. However, she would be good in the event anyone got injured, and Doc... Well, even Ryan had to admit that, as much as he liked him, sometimes the old man seemed sort of like a millstone around his neck. But, just when he thought the old man's train had finally gone off the rails for good, he pulled something out of his hat—like that crazy torch in the rat's lair, without which Ryan was sure none of them would be standing here right now. With a shrug, he assigned their places.

"Krysty, you and Jak'll sail with me on the *Lament*. J.B., you, Mildred and Doc will go on the *Banshee*. Everyone got what they need?" After everyone nodded, Ryan turned to Saire. "Ready when you are."

The other man leaped aboard, his exposed skin flashing in the sunlight. "Welcome aboard the *Lament*. As soon as you're secure, we'll cast off."

Ryan stepped onto the barge, expecting to feel the boat shift under his feet, but was pleasantly surprised to find the deck solid and sound underfoot. The boat rocked a bit on the water, but overall felt as sturdy as the dock itself. He extended a hand to Krysty, who stepped aboard a bit gingerly, her face lighting up as her boots touched the deck. Jak vaulted the low rail with a flourish and leaped up to the roof of the cabin, already scanning the horizon for their planned route.

"Prepare to cast off!" Saire walked to the captain's wheel at the rear of the boat and snapped out more commands. "Cast off bow line! Cast off aft line! Hoist sail!" After each one, the crew moved in perfect synchronicity to prepare the small ship for sailing. With the last command, the furled sail was released from its gaskets and raised to catch the wind. Saire guided them away from the dock with minute movements of the wheel. In a few minutes, the barge was heading smartly out to deep water, leaving the coast farther behind. Behind them, the *Banshee* trailed about a quarter mile off the port side.

For the first part of the trip, Ryan concentrated on getting his sea legs. The lake was calm, and the boat's keel cut through the water smoothly, but he knew fighting at sea was tricky at best and lethal at worst. While he'd never consider himself entirely at home on the water, so far this was the most pleasant experience he'd had, particularly compared to previous encounters. Being attacked by the loathsome Pyra Quadde on her whaling ship in Claggartville where they'd left Donfil, or getting caught in a power struggle among various pirate empires in a chain of tropical islands was not his idea of a good time. This, however, with the warm afternoon sun on his face and the barge slicing through the placid water, was pretty close to perfect at the moment.

Lost in his memories, he almost missed Krysty's light touch on his arm. "You might want to watch this before Jak does something really stupe."

Shading his eyes from the late afternoon sun, Ryan looked over to see the albino teen balancing on the narrow rail of the boat as easily as if he was out for a stroll after lunch. As if he knew eyes were upon him, he arched back into a graceful handstand, walking back and forth on his palms. One of the crewmen was watching in open admiration, but Saire wasn't nearly as amused.

"Cawdor! Get your man off my rail! We tack over and he's not ready, he'll end up in the drink, and you can go in after him!"

Ryan was loath to stop the teen's fun—he figured Jak could probably handle the change in direction better than some of the crew—but called over anyway. "Jak!"

Without looking at him, the youth pushed off the railing high into the air, turning a complete somersault before landing on the deck with hardly a sound, just as Saire called to the crew.

"Ready bait lines!"

The others picked up wooden poles as thick around as Ryan's wrist and set them in heavy-duty metal brackets bolted to the deck. Each had a thin line attached to one end, and the other end of the line held a large, steel, three-pronged hook, about as big as Ryan's closed fist. As he watched, the men baited the hooks with large chunks of fish, then readied them to go overboard.

One of the mates, a lanky fellow named Rubon, noticed Ryan's attention. "Now you'll see how we bring them up on the lakes, lubber!"

"Cast bait lines!" Saire shouted. As one, the four men tossed the hooks overboard, the meat-laden snares vanishing into the green-blue depths.

"We troll for the large ones out here. The bait hooks moving through the water attracts the fish's attention, it moves in for what it thinks is a tasty snack, and wham—" Rubon smacked his hands together "—we got him. Then the real fun begins."

Ryan thought of the large hook, and of the size of a fish that would take that bait. He started to reach for his holstered blaster for backup, but stopped at the other man's snort of laughter.

"Don't even bother using that pea-shooter. It'd barely bother the fish we catch." He picked up a nasty-looking harpoon, a two-handed weapon easily six feet long, with a triple-barbed iron head at the end. "We have to play them until they get tired and surface, then finish them off with this."

"Sounds like fun—" Ryan's words were cut off by the other man.

"Got one!" Just as he announced it, the boat heeled

over sharply, resisting Saire's efforts to hold the wheel steady. Rubon felt the taut line and grinned. "A big one!"

"Stop yawpin' and get on the winch!" Saire snapped. "I'm not letting the best fish we've caught in three weeks get away!"

Rubon looped the free end of the line with the fish on it to a large cylinder with a handle on the end. Once lashed tight, he began cranking on the handle, drawing in the line with each turn.

The winch clicked with each revolution, and Ryan saw that it had teeth to lock the cylinder in place, so the line couldn't play back out unless the operator released a small catch. The tight line quivered as Rubon played it back and forth. Then it suddenly slackened, dropping to the deck.

Ryan frowned. "What happened? You lose him?"

The whipcord-thin man scooped up the harpoon and went to the side. "Nope. He's comin' up. There!"

Ryan looked out in time to see a slim, torpedo-shaped fish burst from the water about twenty yards away and arch, wriggling, into the air. It was a dull brown monster, easily twenty feet long, and he marveled at its size as it reached the apex of its leap and fell back into the lake.

"Huge muskie! Get on the winch!" Rubon hefted the harpoon in his other hand and waved Ryan at the crank. "Take in the slack!"

Grabbing the handle, Ryan turned it as fast as he could, watching the line tighten again as he cranked. Shouts from the other side of the boat told him they had something else hooked as well. The boat shook as the pair of huge fish pulled it one way, then the other.

"He's coming up again! If he's close enough, I'll try to spear him!" Rubon leaned over the side of the barge, harpoon at the ready. The line slackened again, and Ryan cranked hard on it, trying to draw the huge fish as close to the boat as possible.

"Here he comes!" Rubon tensed, trying to judge where the fish would leap so he could strike with the greatest accuracy. The water erupted a few yards off the starboard side as the huge fish launched itself into the air again. His arm cocked, the fisherman hurled the harpoon into the animal, the triple barbs sinking deep into its body just behind the head.

"Got him!" Rubon ran back to the winch mechanism and grasped it, his hands over Ryan's. "Crank hard and fast!"

The two men put their backs into it, turning the winch as fast and hard as they dared. The rope grew taut again, then even tighter, making them use all their strength to move it. The thick rod was bent in a large curve, but it showed no signs of breaking.

"We must have him right next to the boat!" Rubon said. "Come on, let's have a look!"

Grabbing a gaff hook, he ran to the side and leaned over. "Yup, got him. C'mere, Ryan, you'll wanna see this."

Ryan made sure the winch was secure before going to the side of the barge. Rubon was leaning over, reaching down with his hook to apparently snag the giant fish. Ryan was only a step away when the water exploded over the side, drenching him. He had just enough time to duck away as another fish, easily as large as the one they had just caught, reared out of the water. Its mouth agape, it heaved its upper body over the railing and caught Rubon squarely in the needle-sharp teeth of its open jaws.

Chapter Twenty-Nine

The poor man didn't even have time to scream as the mutant muskie's stilettolike teeth sank into his chest. The momentum of the fish's body sent it back into the water, and Rubon was dragged off his feet and into the lake. One moment he was there, the next he was gone, even before the water drops thrown off by the giant fish had finished falling to the deck.

"Fireblast!" The moment he'd sensed the danger, Ryan had hit the deck, blaster in hand. "Man overboard!"

The rest of the boat was still distracted by the battle for the second hooked fish, but Saire, still at the helm glanced over at Ryan. "What?"

"Said man fucking overboard!" Ryan rolled to the rail and peeked over, scanning for the killer fish. The body of the caught muskie was floating parallel to the *Lament*, and he saw no sign of the one that had gotten away—and taken Rubon with it. No blood, no body parts, no froth; it was like the man had simply vanished. "Another big bastard fish came up while we were securing the first and grabbed him! *That* ever happen before?"

"Blind NORAD, no!" Saire crossed himself rapidly, then grabbed the wheel as the entire boat shook from a large impact on its hull. "What the hell—they're ramming us!"

"Who is?"

"The goddamn fish, that's who!" Saire lashed the wheel in place and grabbed a gaff hook, walking toward Ryan as he did so. "I'll be damned if I let them sink my ship! Look out!"

Feeling a shadow fall over him, Ryan ducked and rolled forward, away from the rail, just as he heard a *thunk* behind him. Twisting as he came to his feet, the one-eyed man rose and came face-to-face with the enemy.

The lizard-creature was short—perhaps five feet tall—but broad and very muscular. Covered in scales so dark a green they seemed almost black, it had the standard two legs, two arms and a head, with a short, thick tail lashing the air behind it. Its face was a distinct blend of human and lizard, with a segmented fin atop its hairless head, no ears to speak of, just a small hole on either side of its skull, wide, black eyes, a vestigial nose that was little more than two tiny holes, and a lipless mouth opened wide in a hiss that revealed double rows of small, serrated teeth. A biowep?

A short, rusty harpoon was clutched in its clawed, webbed hands, which it thrust at Ryan with amazing speed as he tried to line up his blaster on its chest. Backpedaling to avoid the barbed tip, Ryan stumbled on a coil of rope and lost his balance, throwing out his free hand to avoid falling on his back. The mutie pressed its advantage, jabbing the spear at him, then drawing back just as fast, the edge slicing into his blaster hand. Ryan tried to keep his grip on the weapon, but his fingers popped open, and it slid from his grasp. Grabbing the slick shaft of the spear, the one-eyed man wrenched it to one side as his other hand went for his panga, knowing it was probably too late, and expecting his enemy to lean in and impale him at any moment. But he wasn't going to make it easy for the lizardman.

A roar from behind him startled both Ryan and the mutant, who looked up in time to see a gaff hook swing at its head. The thick pole cracked into the creature's skull, making it stagger to one side. Saire followed up his attack by reversing his weapon and coming at the humanoid again, leading with the butt end. At the same time, Ryan used the distraction to shove the spearhead into the deck and scramble to his feet, drawing his panga in one smooth action as he did. Unfortunately, as he rose he realized that Saire and he were facing off against not one of the aquatic attackers, but three.

"Shit!" Ryan quickly glanced behind to make sure no more of the scaled bastards were trying to sneak up on them. On the other side of the boat he heard grunts, a brief shout, and an agonized scream that didn't sound human before being cut off by the thunderclap of a large-caliber blaster. Over the side, he heard splashes as either more of the giant fish or the next wave of lizardmen approached the boat. But at the moment, he only had eyes for the three monsters in front of him, and every fiber of his being was attuned to making sure he survived the next few minutes.

He stood at a slight angle to the boat captain, Ryan facing left, Saire facing right, forming a two-person wedge. The captain kept the two on his side at bay with tight jabs at their faces. Besides the spear, one had a rusty hatchet lashed to a pole, making a crude halberd, the other carried a pair of foot-long knives, one up and one down, and moved like he had some idea how to use them. Ryan marked him as the most dangerous at the moment, since he could defend and attack at the same time.

The three paused for a moment, as if taking stock of the situation, then rushed the two men. The halberd-wielding one blocked Saire's gaff hook, trapping it with the bottom of the hatchet blade and forcing it to the deck. His partner with the twin knives came in over the tangled weapons, one blade flashing in the sunlight as it came down at Saire's head.

The captain dropped his weapon, leaving the first lizardman to try to untangle the two shafts. Engaging the immediate threat, his hand snaked behind his back to draw a slender blade and stab at the lizardman's throat while blocking the blade coming at his face. Both moves succeeded, but he unfortunately left himself open to the second blade, which slashed deeply into his chest, making him grunt in pain. Impaled on the blade, the mutie thrashed and bucked, its sudden, limp weight driving Saire to the deck.

Ryan had his own problems, as his attacker was using the spear's longer reach to try to get around his guard while avoiding the panga's heavy, slashing blade. The lizardman bobbed and weaved, trying to catch Ryan's arm or face. Hearing Saire's grunt, Ryan moved to end his duel fast. The next time his opponent jabbed at his head, he grabbed the shaft, making sure his fingers were well behind the head. As he'd suspected, it was metal, affixed to a wooden handle.

Caught by surprise, the lizardman tried to jerk the spear out of his hand, but Ryan moved forward with the weapon, shoving it up into the air. As soon as it was high enough, he reached underneath and swung his panga out in a broad arc—not at the lizardman, but at the weapon's handle. The thick blade chopped into the wood, splintering it and separating the spearhead from the wooden haft. Still pulling, the lizardman stumbled backward, clutching the broken piece in his hand.

Pivoting, Ryan reversed the spearhead so the point faced down and drove it between the shoulder blades of the halberd-holding mutie, who had just gotten his weapon untangled from the gaff hook. With an agonized croak, he shuddered once and slipped to the deck, black blood spurting onto the wood.

Ryan checked on Saire, who was shoving the lifeless body of the third lizardman off him. Bright blood stained his shirt, but he waved Ryan off. "Get that other bastard."

Needing no more encouragement, Ryan stalked forward toward the third mutant, who had gripped the haft like a club in front of him, and was making a low, clicking noise in its throat. Ryan stopped just out of reach of the club, balanced on the balls of his feet, waiting for the creature to come to him. Glaring at him, the lizardman sprang, but not directly at him. Instead, it leaped to the edge of the cabin, gripping the roof with its clawed toes and pushing off in an all-or-nothing attack, the club raised high to brain his target.

It was almost too easy. Sidestepping the falling mutie, Ryan lashed out, his panga sinking deep into the lizardman's knee. The blade hacked through muscle and sinew, destroying the joint and sending the creature smashing hard onto the deck, squealing in agony. The club skittered from its fingers. Ryan brought the panga down on its head, cleaving through the skull and into the brain. A rush of vile-smelling fluid spurted over his hand as the mutant spasmed and died.

"Ryan!" The shout whipped his head around to see Saire trying to fend off another pair by bracing his gaff hook over his prone body. One lizardman was about to break through his defense, while another was already charging at Ryan.

Ryan brought his blade down on the mutie's back, but it was already on top of him, and slammed into his midsection even as the panga bit into its flesh. The impact drove Ryan back against the side of the cabin, making the breath whoosh from his lungs. He raised the short machete again even as his opponent reared up, trying to slam the top of his head into Ryan's jaw. Twisting his head, Ryan got an eyeful of the mutie's hissing face up close, one of the most disgusting sights he could remember. Rotting scraps of fish were stuck in its mouth, and its fetid breath almost made him vomit. It lunged forward, its needlelike teeth snapping at his nose, and Ryan jerked his head back just in time.

The lizardman got his hands around Ryan's throat, claws digging in to tear out skin and flesh. Realizing he had only one chance, Ryan snaked the panga's blade under the lizardman's chin and drew it across his throat in one quick slash. The keen metal opened a second mouth in the mutie's scaled skin, and another gush of cool, foul-smelling blood poured over him. Its mouth opening and closing in a vain attempt to suck in air, the mutie released him, its hand clutching at its throat in a vain attempt to stem the black tide flowing out between its fingers. Ryan lifted his foot and shoved the dying creature back toward the side of the ship, grinning as the backs of its legs hit the wooden rail, and it fell overboard.

Even as it disappeared from sight, he was already moving toward the second mutie, who had just torn Saire's broken gaff hook out of his hands, and was about to brain him with the jagged hook end. In one giant step, Ryan moved right behind him and swung the panga with all his strength. The heavy blade hacked into the creature's shoulder joint, pulverizing the entire ball-and-socket in a crunch of shattered bone and spraying blood. The lizardman wailed in agony, the hook slipping from its hand as it turned to swipe at Ryan with its good arm. Evading the clumsy claw, Ryan wrenched the panga blade out of the rubbery hide and swung at its free arm, severing the hand at the wrist. The creature screamed again, a strange, burbling sound that grated on Ryan's ears. Shoving the end of the panga blade at the mutie's open mouth, he herded it back toward the railing, and with one final push, sent it over the side into the churning sea.

After confirming there were no more lizardmen attacking, a second quick glance told him that both Krysty and Jak were all right on the other side of the boat. Only then did Ryan go to Saire's side. "How you doing?"

"It'll take more than that to put me in the dark deep for good." The captain had torn his shirt into strips and created a makeshift bandage to stem the blood flow. "Who's at the wheel?"

Ryan poked his head up to see the lashed ship's wheel with no one behind it. "No one."

"Well, get me up and over there. I'm not letting these overgrown minnows tear my ship apart!"

Slinging Saire's good arm over his shoulder, Ryan hoisted him to his feet and helped him over to the wheel. Spying Jak at the railing, looking over at the teeming mass of fish below, Ryan was about to warn him to step away when a gust of wind made the barge heel over to the port, tipping the deck precariously.

At the exact same time, a thunderous crash reverberated through the entire hull, shaking the deck and mast. Jak had just kept his balance when the boat had leaned over, but the impact knocked him off his feet and over the side. Twisting in midair, he clamped a hand on the railing, hanging on as his lower legs hit the water.

"Jak!" Krysty was already reaching for him, and Ryan pitched Saire toward the wheel and leaped onto the roof of the cabin. He needed only a few seconds to get to the teen and pull him back up.

Ryan hit the deck with a crash and lunged forward, but just as he reached the railing, a slim shape burst from the water. Mouth gaping wide, the muskie hit Jak around the midsection, its teeth sinking into the albino as the force of its jump knocked his grip loose, taking him with it into the roiling lake.

Chapter Thirty

There was no time to think, only react. Even as his feet touched the rail, Ryan dropped the panga, drew his knife with his free hand and shoved off over the side, burying his blade up to the hilt in the side of the huge fish. He held on with all his strength, knowing if the mutie threw him off, his chances of survival were as slim as a minnow's at feeding time.

The giant muskie kept going, and the sideways jerk as it landed in the water nearly yanked Ryan's arm out of its socket. His hand a clutching claw on the knife's hilt, Ryan used it to thrust himself forward, aiming his free hand toward the muskie's huge gills.

He had just enough time to close his mouth before the water enveloped him, chilling him to the bone. His clothes were instantly soaked, and his boots, while not filling with water, turned into weights on his feet. Ryan tried opening his eye, but immediately squeezed it shut again when he realized all he could see was the rush of bubbles and roiling water caused by the fish's movement.

Wedging his hand into the fish's gills, Ryan made sure his grip was secure on the knife handle before pulling it out and bringing it in front of him. It was dark now, and he figured the fish was most likely diving, so the sooner he freed Jak and got him back to the surface, the better. Forcing the blade into the fish's gills, Ryan hacked with all his strength, not sure what he was hitting, but simply trying to damage the gigantic animal as much as possible. His lungs started to ache with the effort of holding his breath, and Ryan flailed even harder with the knife, feeling resistance as the blade met the fish's innards, then nothing as it cut through them. The muskie bucked and thrashed, its wild movements slowing as the internal damage caught up with it. With a final spasm, it arched one last time, then stilled as death took it.

Ryan pulled his knife out and was able to look around for the first time since hitting the water. With the fish's giant body still, he let a brief burst of bubbles out from his mouth to find out which way was up. Orienting himself, he realized they were sinking, the weight of the muskie dragging them toward the bottom. Clenching his knife between his teeth, Ryan reached up toward the fish's head with his free hand, searching for its mouth. His lungs were aching now, and he saw small dots of light bursting behind his eyes.

With a final stretch, his exploring fingers sank into the corner of the mutie's mouth—and immediately felt something blocking the opening. Grabbing the corner of the jaw with one hand, Ryan took the knife from his mouth and shoved it between Jak's body and the roof of the fish's mouth. Shoving up with all his remaining strength, he levered the mouth open, but the teen's body didn't float free.

Gritting his teeth, Ryan felt along the bottom of the fish's jaw, finding several places where its teeth had entangled in sodden clothes and pulling them free, aware his fingers were getting cut and slashed from the sharp teeth. At last, however, he loosed Jak from the mutie's mouth, and shoved him up with every last bit of muscle he possessed. The albino youth slowly rose in the water, his white hair haloed around his head, his limbs limp and motionless, his eyes open and rolled back.

Ryan kicked for the surface as hard as he could, aware of his lungs fairly bursting for oxygen. He could now see the lighter surface water, but it seemed very far away, not to mention the strong possibility of one or both of them being attacked by either more of the lizardmen or another of the giant bastard mutant fish at any moment.

His vision growing gray and tunnellike, Ryan felt himself growing light-headed. The surface of the water now seemed to be receding from him, no matter how hard he kicked and swam for it. Jak's motionless form drifted next to him, and Ryan wasn't about to let either of them die without fighting for every last second of life. He scooped at the water above him with his hands, flailing to get to the surface, aware that his starved lungs were about to give in any moment now, and force his mouth to open, letting the brackish lake water pour down his throat…

Before he realized what was happening, his head broke the surface just as his mouth opened to suck in as much air as he could get. A spray of water still hit his mouth, however, making him gasp and cough as he shook the liquid from his face. Jak's body was next to him, although it was starting to sink beneath the waves, and Ryan grabbed him and turned his face up so it was out of the water. Jak's bone-pale features were even whiter than usual, his lips tinged with blue.

Kicking with all his strength, Ryan looked around wildly for the barge, and spotted it coming around to his right. "Hey!" he shouted, forcing his upper body out of the water and waving his free arm to get their attention.

"Stay where you are, we're coming back!" Krysty shouted. Ryan concentrated on keeping Jak's head above water, and keeping himself afloat. He had just reached a perilous equilibrium when he felt something large pass by his back. Twisting his head, Ryan saw the wake of a large fish dissipate as it swam past. He tried to keep it in sight as it moved around, but lost it in the dark water. The waves were getting higher now, and he couldn't help noticing the line of dark storm clouds coming in from what he assumed was the northwest, since they were about to block out the sun.

"Hurry the fuck up, before we become fish food!" he shouted at the barge, which, although listing to one side, still seemed to be moving at a pretty good clip. Unfortunately, he spotted the telltale sign of the mutie fish coming back, its top fin slicing through the water as it came toward its prey. Ryan felt for his knife, but it was gone, lying somewhere at the bottom of the lake now.

Feeling at the back of the collar of Jak's waterlogged jacket, and careful to avoid the razor blades sewn there, Ryan pulled out one of the youth's leaf-bladed throwing knives. Although Jak was incredibly deadly with them at range, in Ryan's hand the weapon felt little better than a toothpick, considering the twenty-foot monster bearing down on them, Still, he held it ready to stab as soon as the fish came within range, planning to aim for its eye. The wake grew larger, enough so that Ryan could now see the bullet-shaped head of the fish coming for him, only a few yards away. The boat was still about twenty yards off, and wouldn't reach him in time. Ryan gripped the taped handle of the knife, tensing to drive it deep into the fish's skull….

Several claps of thunder exploded over the water, and the huge mutie arched as gouts of water burst all around it. Its head came up and out of the lake as it writhed from the heavy bullets slamming into its body and head. Its tail slapped the water one last time, then it sank beneath the waves just as it would have taken a bite out of Ryan or Jak.

Ryan looked up to see one of the prettiest sights in his life—Krysty stretched out along the bowsprit of the barge, aiming Jak's .357 in both hands. She pulled the smoking blaster up as the boat drew nearer to the two men. "You're not getting away from me that easily, lover," she called to him.

"Wouldn't dream of it. Here, help Jak first. He's not breathing."

The barge was close enough now that two other members of the crew were able to reach out and grab the sodden teen, hauling him onto the deck. Krysty disappeared, most likely to see about Jak's condition, and all that was left was to pull Ryan from the cold lake.

A second sailor was reaching down for his hand, and had just caught it when a sudden ripple signaled danger from below. Before Ryan could be pulled out, a lizardman erupted from underneath the boat and lunged for him, wrapping its clawed hands around his waist and pulling him out of the sailor's grip.

"Fireblas—!" Ryan's shout was cut off by the cold lake water rising over his head. He was already tired from the exertion of going after Jak, and this was the last straw.

The lizardman butted at him with its head while it clawed at his back with its fingers, raking painful lines of fire across his skin. Grabbing the mutie's head, Ryan forced it back until he could get his thumbs into its eyes. Once there, he pressed with all his strength, crushing the orbs into jelly.

His attacker opened its mouth in a soundless howl of torture, the bubbles frothing around Ryan's head. It whipped its head back and forth, trying to dislodge the stabbing digits. Feeling the creature's legs kick up in an effort to push him away, Ryan released its head and went for its throat, partly to try to strangle it, and partly to keep its mouthful of teeth from sinking into his torso.

Blind and wounded, the lizardman tried to get away, but Ryan held on remorselessly, feeling the mutie's windpipe bend, then collapse under his crushing hold. His attacker clawed weakly at his face, but Ryan moved his head away from its clutching fingers. The arms scrabbled at him once more, then stopped, floating down to rest at its sides. Ryan gave the creature's pulped throat one last squeeze, just to make sure, then released the body, which drifted off into the dark waters below him.

Looking up, Ryan saw the lake's surface about fifteen feet above him. As he slowly propelled himself toward it, however, it seemed to be a mile away. At last his head broke the surface again, just in time to almost get hit with a line that smacked into the water next to him. Grabbing it with the last of his fading reserves, it was all he could do to hang on as they dragged him to the side of the barge. In his exhausted state, Ryan couldn't help feeling like a 200-pound piece of bait as he was towed to safety, and expected to feel needle-teeth on his legs or stomach any second.

"Easy, now—the man's just been closer to the deep than any of us, and he survived." Saire's voice cut through the commotion as two of the sailors hauled him aboard. Ryan landed hard on the deck, coughing and shaking as the chill air goosepimpled his skin. A rough blanket was tossed at him, and he wrapped himself in its warmth, casting about for his companions.

Jak sat against the outer cabin wall, looking like a drowned rat, his white hair dangling limply around his face, a bloodstained bandage wrapped around his skinny stomach. A small puddle of vomit and lake water pooled beside him, but he was breathing, and nodded his thanks at Ryan as their gazes met.

Next he looked around for the woman who'd just saved his life. "Where's Krysty?"

Chapter Thirty-One

Saire frowned in confusion. "What do you mean? She was right here a moment ago. Mebbe she went below for more supplies."

Ryan pushed himself to his feet, swaying for a moment as a wave of dizziness crashed over him. "No, I just saw her before that mutie tackled me." Stumbling to the cabin door, he threw it open and looked inside, finding the small space empty.

"Krysty!" Ryan's eye was drawn to the starboard side of the boat, where he and Saire had fought for their lives just a few minutes ago. Amid the blood and water sloshing across the deck was a glint of shiny metal.

Ryan stooped to pick up Jak's .357. The entire blaster was covered in muck, and the sight was encrusted with sticky, black matter—as if it had been used to strike someone.

"Jak!" Ryan stalked back to the other side. "Did you tag one of those fuckers with your Magnum?"

"No. Too busy tryin' to shoot." The teen's features wrinkled in a puzzled frown. "Why?"

Ignoring the question, Ryan tossed the weapon to Jak and went back to the starboard railing, examining it more closely. He came up with his answer there—a torn scrap of blue jumpsuit. Leaning over, Ryan's boot hit something in the inches of blood and water on the deck. Feeling around, he came up with a revolver—Krysty's

S&W 640. Snatching it and the scrap of cloth, Ryan clenched it in his fist as the meaning became clear. He stalked back to Saire, who was staring at him in puzzlement, and held the scrap out to him. "They've got Krysty, and we're going after them."

Saire's forehead furrowed. "Go after 'em? Go where? We just saw the bastards for the first time today, and we haven't the faintest fuckin' idea where they might be hidin' now. Besides, if you hadn't noticed, my boat's got a big hole in it, and there's the mother of all storms comin' up, so if we don't get back to shore, ain't none of us gonna be alive to save your woman."

Ryan felt the red rage rise up behind his eyes, and tamped it down with an effort, although a dark part of him wanted nothing more than to lay the barrel of his SIG-Sauer alongside the captain's temple and make him find those bastard lizardmen. But the more rational part of him realized the truth of Saire's words. Without a place to start looking, they could be searching forever before finding where Krysty was being held. Ryan didn't even consider the possibility that she wasn't alive. If they'd wanted her dead, they would have killed her on deck.

"Let's try to get over to the *Banshee*, otherwise we might not make it back anyway." Saire's face was pale, and Ryan noticed the crude bandage wrapped around his middle was stained with dark crimson. But he held the wheel with grim determination, and Ryan got out of the sailors' way while they maneuvered the *Lament* over to its sister ship.

J.B., Mildred and Doc had fared significantly better than their counterparts on the *Lament*. Not only was their boat undamaged by the school of aggressive fish, but they had fought off the aquatic lizardmen's attack without sustaining too much damage. Even better, they had captured two of the creatures alive, one injured, one whole and unwounded. Ryan was all for trying to interrogate the two muties right then and there, but when J.B. pointed out the total lack of a common language, he gritted his teeth and settled down, awaiting his chance to get some information out of them any way he could.

Once the boats were lashed together and heading toward shore ahead of the approaching storm, Mildred began working on stabilizing Saire, even managing to pry him off the captain's wheel to dress his wound. Aided by the rising wind, they managed to reach port just as the first drops of rain pattered down.

Staring at the pair of captives, inspiration seized Ryan. The moment the boat's hull scraped against the dock, he dragged the unwounded lizardman behind him by the rope binding its hands. Donfil More was at the doorway of the fish processing building, his eyes widening in disbelief as the black-haired man stalked toward him.

"Ryan! What is that? What happened?"

The tall man brushed by him, heading for the stairway leading to the elders' room. "Found the bastards attacking your ships. Caught a couple, but they took Krysty. Now we've got to find out where they're holing up. Figure your elders can help with that."

All along the tables, villagers stopped what they were doing to stare at the grim, soaking-wet man dragging the scaly, dark green mutant, which hissed and bared its teeth at them.

"Shut the fuck up." Ryan snapped his fist out and thumped the mutie on the side of its head, which seemed to quiet it down. At the base of the stairs, he stopped when Donfil managed to squeeze in front of him.

"Ryan, you are proceeding without paying the proper respect. The elders will not appreciate this sort of—"

Sticking his face into the taller man's, Ryan's voice dropped to a cold whisper. "Get out of my way. Your people—*you*—came to us asking for help with this problem, and one of mine is missing because of it. Now your people are going to help me, one way or the other. You want these bastards chilled, we'll do it, but you people have to give me something to work with here, too. You hear me?"

He held his stare until Donfil dropped his gaze. "Of course, One-Eye Chills. I'm merely saying that I should go with you, to smooth the way."

"All right, then, lead on." Ryan waved him up the stairs and followed, yanking the mutie along with him. Movement behind him indicated that J.B. and the others had come in as well, and now followed behind him.

Donfil knocked on the door, which cracked open as a clap of thunder shook the building. When she saw who it was, the attendant at the door opened the portal wide. "Donfil More, what brings you here again?"

The skinny Apache nodded at Ryan. "He would ask a favor of the elders."

The attendant considered the request just long enough for Ryan to consider kicking the mutie out of the way and shouldering his way into the room, but then she stepped aside. "Enter, please."

The row of fishmen seemed less alert than when Ryan had first seen them. The one on the far end was even dozing in his chair. Ryan shoved the lizardman out in front of him, hard enough to make it fall to the floor, where it quickly gathered its legs underneath it and tensed to spring until Ryan placed the muzzle of his SIG-Sauer next to its temple. The creature relaxed immediately at the touch of the cold metal.

"It appears it understands what a blaster is," Ryan said.

The elders, prodded into wakefulness by the sudden disturbance, muttered among themselves before one of them spoke up. "What is the meaning of this? Why have you brought this…thing…among us?"

The lizardman growled deep in its throat before Ryan tapped its skull with his blaster. "This is one of the bastards who have been raiding your ships, killing your people. They attacked the ships we went out on, too—just ask Saire, soon as he recovers from the mauling he took fighting them off. Killed a few, but they took one of mine before they left. Now, I can't talk to this thing, but he—" Ryan nodded at the large tank to his right "—can probably read its mind or something, like he put those thoughts in ours earlier today."

The uproar over Ryan's suggestion was much louder this time, with a few of the elders rising from their chairs. Their protests all merged together into an over-lapping cacophony of voices.

"How dare you come in here and demand…"

"Why would you think he would deign to attempt contact…"

"Give us one good reason why we should allow this…"

"Donfil, what is the meaning of bringing these outlanders…"

Ryan gave them their head for a few seconds, then stuck his fingers in his mouth and let out a piercing whistle that cut through the babble of voices. He noticed that while the shrill noise bothered the elders, it actually irritated his prisoner, making it shy away from him as far as it could get before he grabbed its hands again. Pulling his captive along with him, he walked to the glass, where the sixth elder floated, regarding him with those eerie, unblinking eyes.

"I'm only going to say this once. This—" Ryan yanked on the lizardman's bound hands again "—is the only way of finding where the rest of the group is hiding. Once we find them, I'll chill every last one if I have to, especially if they've hurt Krysty. But I need to know where to look, and as I see it, the only person who can answer that question, the only person I need to ask—" Ryan tapped on the glass ever so lightly "—is swimming in there. It isn't your call to make for him. It's his."

The being swam up to the glass and stared at Ryan— no, more like stared through him. That strange light emanated from his body again, bathing Ryan in white phosphorescence. He drifted closer to the glass and raised his flipper-arm, placing the end against the glass. His eyes dipped to the lizardman, then to his arm.

Hauling the captive's hands up, Ryan slapped them against the glass. The mutie started at the sound, but didn't move away. The tall man waited for something to happen, but seconds passed without any kind of reaction from either the fishman or the lizardman. Catching the swimming mutie's eye, Ryan watched as it pointed to his other hand, then placed that flipper on the glass, as well.

"Great." Knowing he had no other choice, Ryan placed his hand against the glass.

Immediately his mind was filled with the elder's presence—not simple word communication, but a tumult of images that flooded over him: a strange birth, aided by machines, in a laboratory; he was aware of it all from the moment he opened his eyes; bright, white lights, whitecoated men, an explosion, the laboratory falling apart around him, escape to the cool, cold water, washing up on shore, saved by the villagers, of Waukee…

Ryan jerked his hand back with a start, sucking in air like he had been suffocating.

"You all right, Ryan?" Mildred asked.

"Yeah, just—took me by surprise, that's all." Turning back to the tank, he gingerly placed his hand on the glass again, concentrating with all of his might.

Let's keep to the here and now, all right?

Another cascade of images sifted through his mind, but this time they were *from* Ryan, the many adventures he'd had throughout his life—people he'd met, others he'd chilled. The strange wastelands he'd seen, from the bone-chilling frozen snowscapes of the far north to the fetid, oppressive swamps near the Gulf, and everywhere in between.

Ryan sensed the creature's eagerness to experience these places and things it had never known. It didn't seem to be affecting him in any way, although a small lump grew in his throat when the telepath saw his first meeting with the Trader, long ago. He also saw enemies he'd crossed both paths and bullets with, including that bald-headed bastard Zimyanin.

He also did his best to keep from blushing when the fishman stumbled across memories of his lovemaking with Krysty. His first instinct was to try to stop those memories, but instead he let them flow, remembering her in the past months and years, and letting his concern for her flow out to the telepath, as well.

At length, the flow of images ceased, and the mutie let out a blinding white light that brought with it an overwhelming feeling of happiness and gratitude.

You're—bored in here…

Ryan wasn't sure how to take the idea that his life might be used for viewing enjoyment by this creature, but if it helped get Krysty back, then he really didn't care one way or the other.

Now, help me find where they've taken her.

He pictured the fight on the barge, and Krysty disappearing, taken by one of the lizardmen over the side and into the dark lake.

The fishman lit up again, and Ryan saw a smile appear on his face. Another image appeared in Ryan's mind: This mutant, swimming again, but not alone—there were others, including females, looking just as strange as he did, but they were all together, swimming in intricate patterns, and doing…other things as well…

Pursing his lips, Ryan watched the scene before him without any reaction or comment, aware that the being before him most likely thought it was repaying him for looking at the intimate thoughts in his mind. At last the show receded, and Ryan refocused on the elder and saw him staring back with that same beatific smile on his face.

He nodded. You understand, Ryan thought.

The fishman nodded back. He concentrated on the lizardman, who immediately stiffened, its black-eyed gaze becoming unfocused as the mutie rummaged through its mind. He recoiled once, but his hand stayed pressed to the glass. The lizardman, however, was not so inclined to cooperate. It thrashed and squirmed, trying to pull its hands away.

Donfil was suddenly beside Ryan, reaching out to keep the scaled, clawed hands against the glass. The lizardman's low growl rose to become a whine, then a shriek of pain, throwing its head back and jerking spasmodically.

The fishman's smile had disappeared, replaced by a stare of grim concentration. Its light increased until the brilliance lit the entire room, so bright that it was almost impossible to look at the mutant. Gritting his teeth, Ryan squinted enough so that he could keep his eye on the lizardman and keep its hands on the glass. A hazy image appeared in his mind, interspersed with other strange images.

A dank room, the walls covered in mold and dripping water—a strange, bas-relief carving of some kind of tentacle-headed figure—maybe some kind of goddess—dark, dripping corridors, the walls cracked and broken—some filled with still water—the outside of the lair, through this creature's eyes as it rises from the water—a large building, half-submerged in the lake, its strange concrete rows on the side now crumbling and falling into the water—feeding on pieces of humanoids—taken from the village—arms and legs—gnawing at the fresh, raw, delicious meat...

Ryan released the lizardman and staggered back, his blaster aimed at the mutie, the only thing keeping him from putting a bullet into the beast's bald skull was the fact that it might go through the mutie's skull and hit the glass behind it. Their victim hadn't moved yet, but was still crouched by the tank. As he stared at it, the lizardman's head slumped to its chest, and it keeled over to collapse on the floor, a thin trickle of black blood leaking from the corner of one sightless, staring eye.

Donfil had also released their captive, and the plaintive look he gave Ryan told the one-eyed man that he had also seen the atrocities the colony had done to their dead comrades in his mind's eye. Breathing hard, he put his hands on his knees and swallowed, then looked up at Ryan again.

"I know...I know where they are."

Chapter Thirty-Two

"So, just exactly what is this place?" Mildred asked.

They had left the elders' room and had retreated to Donfil's quarters, a Spartan set of rooms consisting of a bedroom, small kitchen and outhouse in back. The storm still raged outside, heavy sheets of rain pattering on the roof and lashing at the narrow, shutter-covered windows.

The group had gathered in the candlelit bedroom. Donfil had a hangdog expression on his face as he replied. "Truly the more we learn about these creatures, the more hazardous this task seems. The building they are making their home in is what was once known as the Point Beach Nuclear Power Plant."

"Black dust! You guys expect us to play exterminator for you around an old nuke plant?" J.B. shook his head. "Not my idea of a good time."

"It's not just for them. Don't forget who's in there, as well," Ryan said, his gaze never leaving Donfil.

"Yeah, right. Sorry, Ryan."

"No cause to apologize. I'm not keen on going there myself, except there doesn't seem to be any choice." Ryan fixed his attention back on Donfil. "What can you tell me about the place?"

"It's about sixty or so miles up the coast, like the elder saw, half in, and half out of the water. Obviously the damage along the lakes was severe. It's a miracle the entire structure hasn't fallen into the lake yet."

"Can we reach it by land?"

"The terrain is rough, but passable, particularly with the vehicle you rescued us with." Donfil paused, as if thinking. "No doubt any radioactive material is long gone by now, carried out by the tides from the reactors."

"Yeah, but that shit leaves long, long trails behind."

Doc rubbed his stubbled chin. "I do wonder about the reason for the lizard people's sudden aggressiveness toward your village. It would seem to be a long way to swim for sustenance, when I would expect the lake waters around their home would hold ample food."

Ryan's gaze met Donfil's and the memory of what both of them had seen in the lizardman's memory chilled him. "Whatever the reason, they've developed a taste for something more than fish."

"When we leaving?" asked J.B.

Ryan glanced at the ceiling. "As soon as this blasted storm dies down enough for me to see out the front viewport of our war wag. Krysty's stuck with those mutie bastards, and every minute she's there is one too long." Again his eye met Donfil's gaze, and Ryan chewed his bottom lip as the unbidden thought of those scaly animals tearing her apart like a meal on the hoof rose in his mind. Shaking his head, he banished the thought.

Krysty wouldn't go down that way, he knew. Not without taking some of them with her.

Assuming she's still alive in the first place, his mind chided.

Again Ryan squelched the traitorous thought. If she were dead, he'd know it. He didn't know how, but he would just know. Just like he knew she was still alive right now.

J.B. leaned against the wall, hands behind his head. "Anything else you can tell us about the place?"

Donfil shook his head. "Like most of those types of places, it is regarded as evil by the locals, a symbol of the predark times. I only know of it because we were blown near the location by a storm when I first came down this way. The captain claimed that anyone who went inside of it never came back out. I guess I will see if that's true soon enough."

"Donfil, you don't have to go with us—" Mildred began.

The Apache held up his hand. "Actually, Healing-Hands Woman, I do. Ever since these attacks began, I have felt a draw to the north, a pull to go there and confront whatever I would find. That was the direction I was trying to persuade our group to go when you found us. It seems that the Great Spirit has one more task for me to finish before I can find my peace in this world."

"Fair enough." Ryan crossed the room to the shuttered window and peeked between the slats. "Sounds like the storm's lettin' up a bit. We should be ready to move. If it keeps up, it'll keep anything else inside tonight, and could be the perfect cover to approach the plant by."

Everyone fell silent at that, checking their weapons and equipment. Ryan was particularly attuned to the sounds outside, gauging the wind and rain, waiting for the best time. The others passed the time in their own ways. Doc and Donfil retired to the kitchen to continue their philosophy discussion. Mildred paced the floor until Ryan made her sit down with a single, intense stare.

J.B. and Jak did what most men in the Deathlands did when safe and faced with waiting—they slept.

At last, when night had fallen, and the storm had abated to a steady downpour, he assembled everyone in the bedroom again. "Let's go."

With Ryan leading, the group moved through the empty, rain-slick streets. Flickering candlelight gleamed in the windows of other houses, shut tight against the storm. The air smelled of ozone and metal, and the fat drops had an unpleasant, slick feel to them, as if the downpour consisted more of chemicals than water. Checking his rad counter out of habit, Ryan saw that whatever their composition, the drops weren't radioactive.

Reaching the LAV, they piled in, with Doc and Donfil performing contortions to fit into the rear compartment. When everyone was situated, Ryan fired up the war wag, and they headed out into the night.

Although the wind had died down, the going still wasn't easy. The storm had lessened, but the rain was still heavy, limiting visibility to only a few yards. Ryan also discovered that one of the headlights had shorted out, on the driver's side, naturally. Although he would have rather had J.B. scanning around for potential trouble, he had to rely on the other man's view through the turret-mounted night-vision camera to back up his forward sight.

At best they were able to make about fifteen to twenty miles an hour, Ryan guessed, often having to sidetrack around obstacles even the formidable war wag couldn't traverse. The surrounding land testified to the upheaval caused by those long-ago bombs—jagged, massive ravines carved into the earth, clusters of hills thrown up in the aftermath. The forest was also thicker here, the tall, gnarled trees nourished by the lake.

After three hours of slow, grueling travel, Ryan brought the wag to a halt underneath a huge tree to check the engine and take a quick break. As much as he wanted to press on, he knew that going in with either himself or the wag not operating at top capacity would only hurt their chances. It was almost more important that the wag be running smoothly, as it would play a crucial part in his plan to infiltrate the base.

"You doing all right?" J.B. asked as the others got out to stretch during the brief respite from the pouring rain. A flash of jagged, yellow lightning lit the dark purple sky in the distance, followed a few seconds later by the rolling rumble of thunder.

"Fine. How close you think we are?"

"If the map is even close to our estimated mileage, we're probably within fifteen miles of it—another hour, ninety minutes at the most, depending on what lies between here and there."

"That'll work. By the time we're ready to go, it'll be the deepest part of night—when they're most likely asleep."

The Armorer shoved his fedora back on his head as he regarded Ryan. "Yeah. All we have to do is sneak into a place we know nothing about, which is crawling with psycho lizardmen who'd just as soon tear your head off as look at you, rescue Krysty and get out alive. No problem."

Ryan grinned at his friend's matter-of-fact tone. "That's one of the things I've always liked about you, J.B."

"What's that?"

"Your eternal optimism."

"Oh, I sure as hell bet you're going to do it. I'm just not sure how yet."

"Leave that to me. I've got a few tricks to play on those muties that'll even our odds."

"Care to share?"

"Not just yet," Ryan said. "I'm still working out some of the aspects." That, and he knew that J.B. wasn't going to like a certain part of his scheme, so he wanted to give him as little time to bellyache as possible. "Let's get everyone rounded up and get going."

A low whistle in the night brought everyone back together, and they began the laborious process of packing back into the cramped quarters. Once everyone was wedged back inside, Ryan fired the wag up and kept moving.

The forest thinned out as they kept heading north, giving way to rolling hills and fields covered by tall grass as high as the obport. After nearly sideswiping a four-foot-high anthill, Ryan had to throttle back. It wouldn't help to get the wag hung up on an embankment or stuck in a ravine.

It was closer to two hours later when J.B. signaled Ryan to stop. "I think I've got it in sight. Come take a look."

Squirming out of his seat, Ryan made his way back to the gunner's chair and stared at the monitor. The blocky form of a huge, rectangular building was lit a ghostly green by the night-vision camera. It was completely dark, with no torches, no lights dotting it at all.

Ryan shrugged. "What else could it be? Donfil, can you come up here?"

With muffled grunts and more than a few curses, the shaman poked his head into the already-crowded area.

"Whatever you've called me up here for had better be good."

Ryan pointed at the screen. "Is that it?"

Donfil peered at the screen for several moments. "John Barrymore, is the lake next to this structure?"

J.B. panned the camera over to show the vast expanse of the nearby Great Lake. "If that isn't it, I don't know what is."

Donfil nodded. "We're here."

"Okay, let's get down to the lakeshore, and I'll lay out the plan."

Ryan scooted back to the driver's seat and cautiously found a path between two huge hills that led down to the water. The rain was lighter now, a faint drizzle pattering on the roof. With the front of the wag facing out to the lake, Ryan got everyone out and outlined his plan.

"Black dust, no!" As expected, J.B. objected to the whole idea. "That's your plan? Are you kidding? You're going to go in there and get yourself killed."

"Look, we have the ultimate distraction here in the war wag. If you, Donfil, Doc and Mildred hit them from the lake side, you'll draw them to you. You're attacking their home, and any animal'll come out to fight for where it lives. I doubt these will be any different. Just make sure to keep the hatches locked, and we'll clear the rest of them off when we join back up."

J.B. opened his mouth to protest again, but Ryan held up a hand to stop him. "While you're causing all kinds of ruckus out here, Jak and I will be hitting them from the land side. In the confusion, we should be able to find Krysty and get out, ideally without them even knowing we were there."

"And what if there's more of them than you think? Or they don't come out to see whose tryin' to shoot through their home? Remember what Trader always said: 'splitting your force means splitting your power.'"

"Yeah, but you'll have the wag, which more than makes up for us not being with you, and we're not trying to fight them, but get in, get Krysty and get out. We're stealth this time—the less combat for us, the better. Your job is to make as much noise as possible and let us do ours."

J.B. had folded his arms during Ryan's speech, and for a moment the tall man thought his oldest friend was going to go against him, but at last the Armorer shook his head. "Fuckin' risky, but I'll go along. We'll bring the thunder, make no mistake. Have those scaly bastards swarming out to see what's knocking on their door."

"All right, give us twenty minutes to get into position, then you light up their back door with everything you got. Sync in three, two, one." Ryan and J.B. matched times on their chrons, and the two groups prepared to head out.

Ryan was turning to head into the darkness when he noticed two dark forms beside him instead of the one he expected. "Uh, Donfil, you're with the wag, remember?"

Hefting his Combat Model 686 .357 blaster, Donfil More shook his head. "No, Ryan, tonight my place is with you. I must go inside the lizardmen's lair."

"J.B., can you three handle the wag?"

"Lake's pretty calm, shouldn't be too much trouble. Best get moving—chron's running."

"All right then." Ryan stopped as he saw the six-foot harpoon in the Apache's other hand, but decided not to question his choice of secondary weapon. "You're with us. Quick and quiet, let's go."

Chapter Thirty-Three

Within twenty paces, the lakeshore, wag and Ryan's companions were lost to the night. The light rain was as much hindrance as help now. While it cut down on visibility both for Ryan's group and any enemies they might encounter, it also made it difficult to hear if anyone was nearby.

Ryan set a ground-eating pace for the first five minutes, until they were close enough to make out the dark shape of the building against the night sky. They had hand-cranked lights, taken from the wag, but weren't going to use them until they were inside the building.

As they got closer, the way grew more treacherous. The shattered remains of crumbling buildings lay everywhere, making footing uncertain at best. About to cut over a hillock to scout a path to the rear, Ryan was stopped by a hand on his shoulder. Turning his head enough to look behind him, he saw Jak pointing around the left side of the mound, then tapping his ear, indicating he'd heard something on the other side.

How many? Ryan signed back.

One to three, Jak signaled.

Stay here, I'll look. Although Jak had taken the precaution of tucking most of his stark-white hair underneath the army cap, enough still spilled out from underneath that it might attract attention. Ryan, on the other hand, with his tanned skin and inky-black mane,

blended with the hazy night like a six-foot-tall ghost—
there one moment, gone the next.

Squatting, he crawled up the hill a foot at a time,
always making sure his hand and footholds were secure
before moving again. He was aware of the time ticking
down, but wasn't going to risk alerting those inside with
a careless falling pebble.

It was probably only a minute or two, but it felt like
ten times that long before he crested the hill enough to
poke his head over and see what was going on below. A
splash made him duck back, but the figures before him
were intent on the ground, not anything above them.

A few yards away, three lizardmen were playing some
sort of game with a live rat, chasing it back and forth
between them, much like larger animals would do with
a prey before killing it. The rat, easily eighteen inches
long, and more than a match for anything its size or
smaller, ran through the puddles of water, squealing in
terror as the looming predators toyed with it and made
it run back and forth until it was exhausted. Everywhere
it turned, there was no escape—a clawed foot or hand
would come down to block its path, sending it back to
the other two muties.

Ryan could almost have felt sorry for the tortured
rodent, but this night he was glad for the distraction.
Ducking behind the hill, he waved Jak and Donfil to join
him at the top. Once they were both there, he signaled
who would take which target. When they had all gotten
the message, Ryan drew his hand blaster, thumbed off
the safety, and stuck his head back up to see when they
would make their move.

A frightened shriek caught his attention just as he
realized he couldn't see two of them. Rustling in the
grass on the other side of the hill made him realize what

had happened—the rat had to have found a hole in the circle of lizardmen and made a beeline straight for the hill they were lying on.

He brought up his blaster just as the wet grass in front of him parted, and the nightmarish head of one of the muties appeared. Scanning the nearby ground for its prize, it had just enough time to register a much more dangerous presence before Ryan put a bullet into the top of its skull. Its brain turned to mush from the 9 mm bullet's passage, the lizardman fell on its face and slid back down the hill in a soggy, lifeless heap.

At the same time Ryan fired, Donfil rose from cover and launched his harpoon at the second lizardman, who was just starting to climb the wet slope. The metal shaft impaled the mutie through its collarbone, slicing deep into the vital organs to kill it where it stood. The creature reached up with a tentative hand to feel the long wooden shaft protruding from its shoulder, exhaled its last breath in a gout of blood and saliva before falling to its knees, then over on its back.

The third one was quick enough to see his companions killed, and turned to run back to the safety of the tall grass around the clearing, only a few yards away. He had just taken his first full step when Jak let fly with one of his throwing knives.

Ryan was passably good with the blades himself, but he had to admit that the albino youth's mastery of them bordered on the supernatural. While most men used them as a distraction, Jak performed incredible feats with his blades, such as the show he had put on in Toma. This throw—at a dark target fifteen yards away, in rainy darkness—was another.

The lizardman dropped as if poleaxed, skidding on his face in the muck and water for another couple yards before stopping. A gleam of wet metal poking up from the back of the lizardman's neck showed where Jak had hit, severing the spinal cord and causing instant death.

"Clear the area!" Ryan whispered, already on his feet and sliding down the far side of the hill, his blaster tracking the slightest twitch of movement from the three bodies. Jak skidded down the side as well, with Donfil following more carefully. Prowling through the clearing revealed no obvious sign of anyone else nearby, although Ryan never trusted first impressions. The only way to be sure was to either sweep and clear the entire area, or be standing over the bodies of anything that had been there.

Sure enough, he had just taken another step into the clearing when a dark form broke from cover and dashed through the puddles toward the building. Ryan snap aimed and fired, but the bullet went wide as the fourth lizardman kept going, ducking out of sight into the grass. Ryan ran to the far side of the clearing to chase it, flanked by Donfil, harpoon in hand again, who climbed on top of a small hill, maybe three feet high, on the other side.

There wasn't enough room on it for both of them, leaving Ryan standing on his tiptoes, trying to see any movement through the tall grass. "See him?"

"Shh!" warned the Apache. Donfil turned his head to listen for a moment, then cocked his arm and let fly, the harpoon arcing into the night and vanishing out of sight. A few seconds later, there was a frantic rustling and a loud grunt.

"Come on!" Donfil jumped from the hillock and disappeared into the grass, with Ryan close behind. He sensed rather than saw Jak bringing up the rear, and knew they were safe from ambush.

At least thirty yards from the clearing, Ryan and Donfil came upon a large swath of crushed grass. In the middle of it was the last lizardman, lying on its back, both hands wrapped around the steel and wood shaft of the harpoon sticking through its stomach. Black blood pulsed from the mortal wound with each agonized breath it took, and its inhuman eyes cast around at the three men standing above it in a mute appeal for mercy.

Without a word, Ryan drew his panga and swung it with all his strength, severing the mutie's head from its shoulders. Donfil wrenched the harpoon from the corpse and cleaned the head and shaft on the wet grass.

"Hell of a shot, that was."

The Apache shrugged and smiled. "Much like spotting muskie on lake, only you have to lead the two-legs a bit more."

Ryan checked his chron, seeing they had nine minutes left before J.B. and the others began their attack. "Come on, we still have to find a way into this place."

"They came out, so must be way in nearby," Jak opined.

Donfil shook his head. "Assuming they didn't come from the lake itself onto shore."

"Button it." Ryan stepped cautiously through the grass, trying to gauge where it stopped and the building began. A few more paces brought him to the edge, with the gargantuan structure looming above him, its shape lit by a sudden flash of lightning.

"Okay, where the hell is it?" In the flash of light, Ryan saw an unbroken wall of crumbling concrete, with no door, window, or other access point. Only a large pool of occasionally bubbling water at the base of the wall lay before him. With a sinking feeling, Ryan realized how they were going to have to get inside.

"Anyone afraid of the dark or going underwater, speak up now."

Jak turned his head and spit. "Got no problem."

Donfil looked less sure, but nodded. "My place is at your side, One-Eye Chills."

Ryan nodded once. "Okay. Me, then Jak, then Donfil to the wall. I'll go in first, make sure nothing's waiting to fuck us up on the other side, then come get you."

"I have a better idea." Donfil unwrapped several lengths of braided cord from around his waist. "We use this as a lifeline on the boats. Tie it to yourself and go in. Two tugs means follow, three tugs means trouble, and for us to bring you back."

Ryan eyed the line dubiously, then glanced back at the black pool he was about to head into. "Couldn't hurt. At the least you'll know about how far you have to go. Make sure you stand still when I go in. When I give the signal, swim toward the light."

He tied the strong cord around his waist, making sure it was secure but not binding him, then took a deep breath and waded into the pool. The cold, dark water enveloped his ankles, then his knees, and rose halfway to his hips before he reached the wall. Moving carefully to where the bubbles were coming up, he felt around carefully near the base of the wall with his boot. As he'd suspected, there was open space underneath it, a narrow corridor the muties used to exit the building.

Ryan made sure his weapons were secure, then his equipment, including the small, waterproof flashlight from the wag. Although he ached to use it, he knew that the light would just make him a brightly illuminated target. If they wanted to keep the element of surprise, he had to go in blind.

Just before he went under, he checked his chron once more. The timer had just hit the two-minute mark. Inhaling deeply once, twice, three times to fill his lungs with air, Ryan closed his eyes and descended into the blackness.

The chilly water needled his face, and he involuntarily let out a small gasp as the cold penetrated his skin. Keeping one hand on the surface of the broken wall above him, Ryan edged forward. His plan was simple—keeping the line taut behind him, he would move forward, using the ceiling as his guide, until it ended, and he could stick his head above water. That was the idea, at least, depending on how long this crude underwater passage extended.

Almost with his very first step, Ryan ran into trouble. The ground underfoot was rough and broken, making each step difficult. He took one step forward, then another, then his foot almost slid off what felt like a large, slanted slab of concrete into empty space.

The bottom was deeper than he thought. Improvising quickly, Ryan attempted to relax enough to let his legs float up, until he was lying parallel with the ceiling above him. He'd made sure to stay oriented in the direction he wanted to go, the only difference now was that he faced the ceiling. Reaching out, he slowly began crawling forward, using the thick concrete as his guide.

The lack of sensory input quickly grew maddening. With only the icy water around him, it wasn't just as if he was moving through darkness, but moving through a complete absence of light. Since he only had the rough stone as a marker, Ryan had no idea if he was heading deeper underwater, or if he was even still going in the right direction. The familiar burn of oxygen deprivation had begun in his lungs, as well. He hadn't expected the wall to be this thick, but every time he reached out with numbed fingers, the tips met more unyielding concrete ahead.

The ache in his chest was growing more painful with each second, but Ryan kept pulling himself forward, knowing that if he didn't find air in the next thirty seconds, he would be dead, since he was now too far in to return in time. Reach forward, more concrete. Pull himself along and reach out again—

His hand met with nothing this time, scraping his forearm on the edge of the wall. Resisting his first instinct to push forward and shove his face up into the life-giving air that had to be nearby, Ryan pulled himself up slowly, not wanting a single bursting bubble or drop of falling water to give himself away. Clinging to the side, he raised himself until his face broke the surface.

As cold as the water was, the air was colder still, stinging his cheeks and nose and making his lips shake. Ryan clenched his jaw to prevent his teeth from chattering, sucking in a breath of dank, fetid air that tasted wonderful.

He had no idea where dry land was, or if anyone was in here with him. For a moment, he stayed right where he was, letting rivulets of water flow off his hair, straining to hear the slightest noise in the room. He remained frozen for at least an entire minute, listening, waiting. Only when he was sure the place was deserted did he start moving along the wall to try to find someplace to get out of the water.

He'd gone a few yards when he reached a corner, with the new wall extending into the room. Following this one brought Ryan to broken chunks of rubble under his feet after what seemed like a hundred years, but was probably no more than twenty seconds. Crawling gratefully out of the pool, he took a moment to catch his breath. His muscles trembled with a combination of the cold and the energy spent in getting here, and only pure will on his part stilled his body. Reaching for his flashlight, Ryan unfolding the tiny crank on the side and turned it between stiff fingers. After a few dozen turns, he shielded his eyes before turning it on so he wouldn't blind himself.

The light shone out like a beacon of white, its brilliance making his eyes water after the impenetrable darkness. Ryan was reaching for his SIG-Sauer when he noticed what the flash was illuminating.

The scaly, clawed foot of a lizardman, standing right next to him.

Chapter Thirty-Four

Lurching back, Ryan tried to draw his blaster even as he raised the light to shine its beam directly into the mutie's face. Caught by surprise, the lizardman growled and threw its arm over its eyes as it reached down to grab Ryan by the back of his shirt with its free hand.

He'd only have a second to aim. Ryan tried to line up the metal sights on the creature's squat body even as he was being lifted into the air. Swaying wildly, he couldn't steady himself long enough to draw a bead before he was flung through the air.

Ryan hit the pool with a giant splash. Instinctively he held tight to both the flashlight and his blaster, aware he'd be dead if he lost either one. Unfortunately, his full hands made swimming back to the surface more difficult than expected. Ryan ended up jamming the light in his pants pocket before he could claw his way back to the surface.

His head broke the surface just in time to hear a splash in the water near the shore. He turned to see the lizardman rushing toward him, all claws and teeth, ready to tear into his flesh. Ryan brought his blaster around again, but was hit in the side before he could line up a shot, the shoulder blow almost paralyzing his already cold, stiff muscles. And as fast as it had appeared, the mutie was gone, vanishing into the darkness.

Kicking his legs and treading water with his free

arm to stay afloat, Ryan turned a slow circle, trying to see where the dry land was. The flashlight in his pants didn't give off enough light to show him which direction to go.

The line! Ryan cast around for the line at his back, seeing which way it trailed off, since that would be the direction of the entrance. It was tangled at his back, but seemed to be curled around his waist and snaking off into the distance ahead of him, which meant—

Ryan felt a tremendous jerk on the line that almost pulled him under the water. Turning, he starting splashing in the opposite direction, but was brought up short by the line tightening around his waist, dragging him under the surface. His eyes widening, Ryan realized what was happening.

That scaly bastard's fishing—and I'm his catch!

Ryan tried to resist the steady pull, but soon realized that the lizardman was braced against something, and he was going under no matter what. He thought about pulling his panga and cutting himself free, but that would leave Jak and Donfil without a way in—and more vital, all of them without a safe way out. There was only one way to go. Sucking in a last lungful of air, Ryan plunged below the surface.

Letting himself be pulled deeper, he yanked the flashlight out and shone it ahead of him, following the taut rope down. As he descended, he felt pressure building in his ears and swallowed to relieve it. A dark, humanoid form was now visible a few yards below, its feet gripping a large, jagged chunk of stone. Ryan held his blaster behind his back and kicked with his legs, trying to give the illusion he was struggling to escape. The lizardman's face split into a needle-toothed snarl as it saw its prey drawing closer. He was only a few yards away—one more pull and he would be caught in the monster's claws for sure.

The mutie yanked on the rope one more time, its free hand outstretched to grab Ryan's futilely kicking leg. Ryan let his foot slow a bit, just enough for the clawed fingers to grab him. He had to time it just right...

The lizardman pulled him down, its mouth open to take a huge bite out of his torso. As he was dragged toward the gaping jaws, Ryan swung up his SIG-Sauer and, placing it squarely against the mutie's head, squeezed the trigger.

With what sounded like a muted thunderclap, the blaster fired. Even underwater, at point-blank range the bullet had enough power to penetrate the scaly skull and burrow deep into the brain of Ryan's captor. Its hand tightened once on his foot, then let go as the body relaxed and floated in place, its feet still gripping the rocky floor.

Ryan's lungs pulsed with pain now, and he jammed his blaster into his pocket and kicked hard for the surface, the light bobbing crazily in his hand as he ascended. Breaking the surface with a gasp, he sucked in air again, just in time to see a familiar white-haired head appear at the underwater entryway.

"What...the hell...took you...so long?"

Jak paddled over, his soaked hair forming a helmet around his head. "Waited till you pulled rope twice, then came in. Not have light follow—thanks lot—had come in blind."

Just then the limp body of the lizardman bobbed to the surface, making Jak start and scoot away from it, a throwing knife appearing in one hand as if by magic.

"Yeah, I kind of had my own problems." Ryan didn't give the corpse a second glance as he shone his light around to find dry land. Once he had it in sight, he started moving toward it. "Where's Donfil?"

"Right." Ryan felt his rope tighten, then slacken before tightening again. "Donfil be along."

Reaching the shore, Ryan crawled up on his elbows and knees. The rough ground was empty of any other muties, although their tracks crisscrossed everywhere in the mud.

"Hey, hear that?" Jak said, cupping a hand to his ear.

Straining to hear above his dripping hair and clothes, Ryan made out a faint, steady noise—the dull roar of a heavy automatic cannon. "J.B.'s started his assault. Soon as Donfil gets here, we move out." Untying the rope from his waist, he found a suitable rock and tied it around that, placing it near the wall so it wouldn't attract attention.

A splash behind them alerted both to the shaman's presence in the entry cave. Donfil's lean face popped up as the shaman sucked in a deep breath, his iron-gray hair plastered to his head as he paddled awkwardly toward shore. Jak helped him clamber onto dry land, where he immediately drew his blaster and cleared the barrel.

SIG-Sauer drawn again, Ryan stood at a dark, doorless opening leading deeper into the structure, shining his light down the angled corridor. The floor had once consisted of smooth linoleum, but was now a cracked, uneven mess, with muddy lizardman tracks everywhere. The ceiling was an exposed mess of twisted metal rods, dangling wires, pipes, and tubes, reminding Ryan of the ceiling in the Fort McCoy hallway. This place contained its own hazards, however, just as deadly as those thrice-damned pig-rats.

"You two ready?" he whispered when Jak and Donfil

joined him at the entryway. The short boy and tall man nodded. "All right, stay near the walls, and check every corner before rounding it. Also watch above—wouldn't put it past these bastards to hide in the ceiling."

"Where going?" Jak asked.

"Head to the middle of the building. Most likely that's where their nest is—and where we'll find Krysty," Ryan said. "If we get separated before we find her, you two get back to the entrance and get out. If we find her and get separated on the way out, same rule applies."

With that, Ryan crept into the passageway, stepping carefully to keep his footing on the slick surface. The corridor extended for about ten yards, ending in a T-intersection, its floor covered in a puddle of black water. Before he took another step, Ryan checked his rad counter, which was at the top of the safe green range, edging into red. He had no doubt it would probably go higher the farther in they went. "All right, stay sharp— let's get in, get Krysty and get out."

His back against the wall, Ryan began making his way down the hall. About halfway down, his foot slipped and he fell on his butt, sliding down the sloping floor to land in a splash at the bottom. The accident saved his life. As Ryan shook water out of his eyes, he saw two long objects blur over his head—crude spears, thrown by the lizardmen who had been waiting to ambush whoever came in from the entrance.

Raising his SIG-Sauer, Ryan tracked the path of one spear back to its owner and triggered the blaster, sending two rounds into its chest. The lizardman splashed on its face in the ankle-deep water, but was replaced by another one rushing forward, spear braced to skewer Ryan. Adjusting his aim, he sent two bullets at its head, one of them punching the mutie's left eye out and instantly terminating all higher brain functions. It slid to a stop only a step away from him, the spear splashing into the water.

Ryan immediately whirled to locate the other attackers, but his vision was blocked by a skinny form in dark blue broadcloth. Donfil had slid down the corridor as well, and now let fly with his harpoon, the barbed metal head finding its target with a dull thunk as it pierced skin and flesh. His target let out a low wail as it collapsed against the wall, unable to move.

The second one was, however, also charging the Apache at full speed. Donfil raised his .357, aiming at the lizardman's broad chest.

A snow-white blur appeared at the shaman's shoulder, pushing his blaster aside. Jak took two steps toward the mutie, until it seemed the spear held in its hands had nowhere else to go except into his chest. However, the albino youth dodged the stone point by leaping into the air above the shaft. At the apex of his jump, his steel-toed combat boot pistoned out, its tip connecting with the lizardman's temple. The sharp crack of breaking bone echoed over the splashing footsteps, and the creature was down, its face smashed into the wall where it had fallen in midstep, still clutching its spear. Landing with hardly a splash, Jak toed the lizardman's limp body, making sure it was dead.

Donfil had just managed to get his gun back under control. "Thank you, Eyes of Wolf."

The teen nodded at the shaman's blaster. "Too much noise. Bring mutie bastards running. Let's go."

"Right." Approaching the mortally wounded lizardman, Donfil raised the butt of his blaster and slammed it on the mutie's head, knocking the creature unconscious before pulling his harpoon out. "Yes, but which way?"

The Apache shone his light down the leftmost corridor. Ryan had already risen and checked the right.

"This way looks blocked off. I see some open doors, but the hall ends in a big wall of rock. Let's go your way."

Donfil frowned. "You don't think Krysty is nearby?"

Ryan's smile was tight. "If she'd been held this close to the entrance, she would have escaped already. Probably would have found her before we came in. Come on." Slogging through the water, he pushed forward, sweeping from side to side with his light, blaster ready to fire at the slightest glimpse of scaled skin or huge, black eyes.

This hall was lined with more metal doors, most of them rusted and hanging from one hinge, the glass in their windows long gone. Ryan, Jak and Donfil cleared each one they came to it, making sure no mutie surprises lurked in the dark recesses. They kept their lights pointed at the floor immediately in front of them to avoid alerting anyone ahead to their position. The building creaked and groaned as they went, and every time it did, Ryan half expected the ceiling to come down on their heads. The staccato machine-gun fire couldn't be heard anymore, but he assumed that was because they were deeper underground now.

The passage ended in a right turn, and Ryan caught the flicker of orange light coming from somewhere around the corner. Dousing his light, he motioned for the other two to do the same. He edged to the corner, sliding his feet through the water so he wouldn't warn anyone nearby with an errant splash. Right at the edge of the wall, Ryan carefully stuck his head out for a look.

Two lizardmen stood in front of a pair of closed double doors with large, frosted windows set into them. The wavering orange light came from the room beyond them. These two were dressed much differently than the other muties they had encountered so far—for one thing, they were actually wearing clothes. Simple squares of cloth covered their waists, and their necks and wrists were decorated with twists of copper wire from which strange ornaments dangled—green boards that Ryan knew to be from the insides of computers, the keys from keyboards woven into a necklace and hanging from one's protruding snout. Their weapons were better, too—straight shafts of polished metal, with gleaming steel spearheads attached, not crude stone. They were obviously guarding whatever lay in the next room.

One of them was looking over its shoulder through the window, but the other one happened to be staring right at the corner of the hallway, and immediately spotted Ryan the moment he appeared. With a startled snort, he nudged his companion and stepped forward, lowering his spear.

Stepping from cover, Ryan braced his blaster and fired twice. His first bullet entered the approaching guard's open mouth, chipping off its front teeth before puncturing the soft palate at the back of the throat and spiraling into its brain. The guard took one more step before the lack of neural commands caught up with its legs, and it began to fall.

Before that was done, the second bullet caught the second guard as it was turning to see what the commotion was about. The slug penetrated its vestigial ear canal, shattering the tympani and tunneling through the beast's brain before exiting out the other side, taking a fist-size chunk of bone and brains with it. Emitting a startled grunt—the last noise it would ever make—the second guard slumped against the corner of the hall, stuck between the wall and the door, which sagged open slightly under the added weight.

Springing forward, Ryan caught the first guard's body before it could splash heavily into the water, sticking out his leg so the spear shaft bounced off it and slid into the water. "Psst!" he hissed to Jak and Donfil, who rounded the corner and grabbed the second body. They hauled the corpses to the nearest open room and dumped them just inside the door, hoping a casual look around might miss them.

The moment they hit the floor, Ryan headed back to the double doors. Once the other two had caught up with him, Ryan signaled the plan. He'd go up the middle, Jak to the right, Donfil going left. Ryan tapped the barrels of their revolvers and nodded, making sure they got the message to blow away anything in their way. From inside, they heard muffled sounds—wet, meaty slaps and an incoherent cry that might have been of pain or pleasure. Ryan's face tightened as he thought of the ways they might be violating Krysty. He pushed the sudden, noxious catalog of atrocious thoughts out of his mind and raised his SIG-Sauer again.

Poised at the door, he counted down with his fingers. Three…two…one…go!

Shoving the door open, Ryan burst into the room to witness a scene of shocking carnage.

The first thing that caught his attention was the huge, bas-relief figure on the far wall, a crude, humanoid figure sculpted out of mud, with scales covering her body. She had large breasts, outstretched arms ending in claw-tipped fingers, and hair consisting of a dozen waving snake bodies, their mouths open and dripping venom.

But what was much more important to him was the tableau underneath the giant effigy.

Four lizardmen, each dressed in garish accoutrements similar to, but more ornate than what the guards outside wore, were sprawled around a dais in front of the statue, their splayed limbs and bleeding heads indicating that they had died suddenly and violently.

Krysty stood on the raised platform, still in her damp jumpsuit, broken ropes dangling from her wrists. She clutched the head of a kneeling mutie. As Ryan was checking his aim, she twisted its head clean around, the snap of cracking vertebrae heard throughout the room. The lizardman's body trembled once, and fell to the floor when she let it go.

"Krysty!" Ryan ran to her just as she started to topple over, catching her in his arms.

"Ryan…knew you'd come. Had to use…power of Gaia…to free myself."

He hugged her tightly, his gaze going to Jak and Donfil, both of whom had cleared the room without firing a shot, and who nodded back at him. "I've got you, you're safe now. Come on, we're getting out of here."

She pushed back to look at him. "Wait! We can't go. Not yet. They're planning to destroy the ville. We have to stop them!"

Chapter Thirty-Five

"Time go, Ryan," Jak said from a pair of doors on the other side of the room, where he was peeking through the windows. "Someone come and be pissed seein' bodies here."

"Just a sec," Ryan said, turning back to Krysty. "What are you saying?"

"They're planning...to attack the ville. All at once... leaders whipping the rest into a frenzy...at least a hundred of them. They'll massacre everyone."

One hundred minus six, Ryan thought, but frowned as he considered the problem. "Okay, but how are we supposed to stop them?"

Krysty had regained enough of her strength to stand, although she still held on to Ryan's arm. "As they were taking me through...the passages I saw a sign next to a room...just down the stairs there. It contains radioactive material. We open it...flood the entire building. Kill them all. Take only a few minutes."

"Doesn't sound like it leaves us a gnat's chance in hell of making it out of here ourselves."

"No, we can rig it to open slowly." Krysty grabbed the remnants of rope that had bound her and thrust them at Ryan. "It's our best shot, otherwise we have to fight them out there again." She faced him, all bedraggled hair, filthy clothes and flashing eyes. "We're not going to leave those people out there to these things' savagery. By

Gaia, the things I've seen down here—" She swayed for a moment, but brushed off Ryan's hand. "You stopped the cannies, now I'm putting my foot down—this ends here. What was it you said to Mildred? 'You can either help, or get out of the way.' Now strip them of those clothes or get the hell out of my way!"

Krysty turned to begin stripping the nearest corpse. Ryan pushed the body of one of them over with his foot, finding her Smith & Wesson blaster tucked into the belt of one of the priests. Grabbing it, he straightened and stared at her for a long moment, watching her, coiled and efficient, as she stripped the body and moved to the next one. A wave of love swept over him at that second. "Krysty?"

She was busy stripping another of its gaudy tabard. "Yeah?"

"You're gonna need this." He tossed her the weapon, which she plucked out of the air with one hand.

"Thanks, lover."

Donfil came over while Ryan was stripping the last two bodies. "Exit corridor is clear. Why are we not leaving?"

"Krysty says the nest plans to attack the ville in force. She wants to flood the building with radioactive material to chill them once and for all."

"Is that possible?"

"She thinks so, and doesn't seem inclined to leave until we do this, so yeah, we're going to try. Better than trying a straight-up fight in the ville itself."

"All right, I'm with you."

"Good, then take this." Ryan shoved two sets of rough clothes at him. "Krysty, we have to move, now!"

"Done, come on." Arms full, she trotted to the set

of doors on the other side of the room. "Are we clear, Jak?"

"So far. What plan?"

"Just follow me." She peeked out the glass and frowned. "Funny, there should be a lot more muties out here."

"J.B., Mildred, and Doc are making a diversion on the lake right now, during which we're supposed to be getting you out of here."

"Good, easier for us." She pushed through the doors and turned left. Ryan was right behind her, followed by Donfil, then Jak. Krysty crept about ten yards down the hallway, then turned right again, leading them to a vertical passageway with a ladder leading down. "This way. It's right off this corridor."

She dumped the armload of clothes down the shaft first, causing a surprised grunt from below. Grabbing the light from Ryan, Krysty shone it down just in time to catch a lizardman's surprised face appear in the circle of light, throwing its hand up to shield its sensitive eyes.

"Shit!" Still holding the light, Krysty jumped down through the hole, not touching the ladder as she fell. There was a quick scrabbling from below, then a loud thwack, and a muffled mewling.

"Damn," Ryan muttered as he swung onto the ladder and descended, his feet and fingers sending showers of wet rust down as he gripped each rung. Above, he heard someone else climb on, but he only had an eye for what he found when he stepped off the ladder.

Breathing hard, Krysty stood over a fallen lizardman, its hideously distended jaw hanging off its face. As Donfil hit the bottom, he shone his light over, revealing the wet blood on the heel of her cowboy boots, and it all became clear.

"Finish it." Ryan was already scanning the small, square chamber for the door Krysty had claimed was here, catching the sharp snap of the lizardman's neck breaking as he looked around. Small corridors led away in two directions, but he paid no attention to them after making sure they were empty.

"Ryan?" Donfil pointed to a shadowed alcove containing a heavy steel door with the familiar three black, rounded triangles arrayed around a small black circle against a bright yellow background on it. A large, red-and-white sign, dotted with rust, hung on the wall next to it. Warning! Nuclear Containment Unit! Radioactive Materials Inside!

The sign went on to say that the outer entry door to the containment unit had to be sealed and locked before the inner door was opened. All personnel had to be wearing level 4 hazmat protection to enter, and personnel had to submit to a chemical bath immediately upon exit.

"That's it." Krysty trotted to the door and reached for the large wheel in the middle. "Come on, let's get this over with."

Ryan placed his hand gently over hers. "Hold on a moment. Let's get a look inside first." While he calmed her, he snuck a look at his rad counter, finding that it had gone down to the midpoint of the green range. "Shine that light in this porthole first. Let's make sure that inner door is sealed before doing anything we might regret later."

Krysty's fingers tensed on the metal, and for a moment he thought she might resist him, but she leaned into him and sighed. "You're right, lover. Sorry. I just want to get this done and get the hell out."

"You and me both." He wrapped an arm around her

while taking the light from her other hand and shining it through the thick, cloudy window. "Fireblast! Can't see much in there. Jak, get over here."

The albino teen stalked over, catching the flashlight as he approached the door. "See if you can make out whether the inner door is closed."

Standing on his tiptoes, the skinny teen could just barely get his eyes above the bottom sill of the window. "Looks like—yeah, shut."

"Okay, stand back." Jak got out of the way as Ryan gripped the wheel firmly and applied pressure, slowly at first, then more and more, until the veins stood out on his arms. "Donfil, give me a hand."

The shaman broke off from watching the rightmost corridor to walk to the other side of the door and grasp the lower part of the wheel firmly.

"On three—one...two...three, now!" Both men strained at the wheel with all their strength. For a moment nothing happened, then, with a high-pitched shriek of metal, the wheel budged an inch, then another. One more mighty heave, and it rotated a quarter-turn, then another, then Ryan was able to turn it by himself, although still with an effort.

"All right—let's crack this and see what we can see. If my rad counter touches red, we get back out, all right?" When everyone had nodded in agreement, Ryan pushed the door inward.

A wave of stale air whooshed out over them, carrying the smell of metal and dust. Ryan checked his counter, but it had only risen to high green, just below red.

"So far, so good. Let's go." Stepping into the room, the first thing Ryan saw was a slumped skeleton next to the inner door, its bony fingers still clutching a small-caliber blaster close to its head. A faded, dark rust-colored stain on the wall above its holed skull left no doubt what had transpired here more than a hundred years ago.

"Pop inside door and get hell out, right?" Jak asked, still hovering near the first doorway.

"I do not think it will be that easy, Eyes of Wolf," Donfil said, pointing to a sign next to the inner door: Warning! Nuclear Containment Unit! Radioactive Materials Inside! Outer door *must* be closed before inner door can be opened!

"Does that mean what I think it means?" Krysty breathed as she stared at it.

"Yeah." Ryan's shoulders slumped. "If we're going to do this, somebody's got to stay inside to open the outer door once this room's flooded with radioactive material."

Chapter Thirty-Six

"No, no, there must be another way." Krysty went to the smooth metal wheel of the door and pulled on it before anyone could stop her. Unlike the other mechanism, this one looked new, and even shifted a fraction under her hands before stopping hard. "Come on—help me. If all of us try, we can get it open."

Ryan, Jak and Donfil exchanged glances, and Ryan walked over to Krysty, gently taking her hands, which clenched into tight fists, from the wheel. "Krysty, you know that isn't going to help."

"It has to! We can't just leave someone in here to sacrifice themselves—"

"I will stay."

Ryan, along with Jak and Krysty, turned to look at Donfil, who was stood straight and tall, his shoulders back, the top of his head almost brushing the ceiling, every inch the proud Mescalero Apache. "Donfil, you don't have to—"

"No, One-Eye Chills, I do. I would certainly not ask any of you to do this for our ville. You have done enough already. I am sure of my purpose now. This is where the Great Spirit has been guiding me—only when I stepped inside this building did I begin to feel a moment of peace. And now, upon seeing what must be done, I understand that this is where I am meant to be."

Krysty started to speak, but Donfil cut her off. "Fire-

Hair Woman, you and the others must leave. Doubtless the lizardmen will be coming soon, and you do not wish to be caught between this—" he smacked the inner door with his palm "—and their anger." He walked to the inner door, his steps stately and dignified. "Go now, my friends. I only ask that you let the ville know what has happened here."

Ryan stared at the shaman, then at his friends, knowing there was nothing left to say. It was Donfil's choice, and as far as Ryan was concerned, it was the right one. It was the only way they could do what needed to be done. There was only one thing left.

Krysty walked over to the skinny shaman and hugged him hard. "Farewell, Man-Whose-Eyes-See-More."

Donfil regarded her with grave eyes. "Farewell, Fire-Hair Woman. Until we meet in the next life." Krysty turned and walked out without looking back.

Jak was next, staring up at the towering Apache, his slight stature incongruous next to the tall man. He nodded goodbye. "Chill lots, Donfil."

"I intend to, Eyes of Wolf. If you see any out there, may you have happy hunting as well."

"Know it." The albino teen ducked out of the doorway, leaving Ryan and Donfil in the thick-walled chamber.

"You know what to do?" An unnecessary question, but suddenly Ryan didn't want to leave the other man to his fate so quickly. He'd seen what the rad sickness could do. Ryan had no idea what lie beyond that windowless inner door, but he hoped Donfil's death would be quick.

Donfil nodded. "All I need you to do is close that door behind you. I will take care of the rest."

The two men faced each other for a moment, then Ryan extended his hand, which Donfil grasped and shook, his grip strong. The shaman grinned, showing his strong teeth. "It is a good day to die."

"We'll let the ville know what went down here." Ryan swallowed through an uncharacteristically thick throat. "They'll be singing your praises for years."

"Only if we stop the muties here." Donfil nodded at the outer door. "Time to go, One-Eye Chills. Until we meet again."

"Yeah." Ryan walked to the door, unable to stop himself from looking back once more. Donfil stood beside the door, one hand resting on the wheel to open it. His lips moved, and words came out, the chant soft at first, but growing louder: "Great Spirit, make me like a strong bear, Great Spirit, make me like a strong bear, This I pray…Make me strong…"

"Farewell, Donfil More." Stepping outside, Ryan pulled the heavy door shut after him, spinning the wheel hard until it snicked into place. He gave it one more twist to make sure it was sealed, then turned to the others. "Time to go."

Leading the way back to the ladder to the main level, Ryan was about to put his hand on a rung and haul himself up when a slight scrape from above caught his attention. He jerked back just as a spearhead jabbed down through the space where his head had been a moment earlier.

His blaster blurring into his hand, Ryan triggered three shots at the dark opening. Hearing a gurgle, he stepped back as a dark form plummeted through the hole to slam onto the metal floor, the dying lizardman's lifeblood geysering from his perforated throat. A quick glance confirmed what Donfil had suspected would happen—the muties had returned in force.

"Can't go that way." He grunted, looking at the right

and left passageways. "Can't tell which way is which in this place."

"One good as another right now," Jak said, pointing to the left. "Take that one."

"Why?" Krysty asked.

"Heads away from where came in. Gotta come out somewhere."

Ryan frowned. "Or dead-end and trap us in here."

"Got better idea, I'm waitin'," Jak challenged.

"All right. Give them a blast from that cannon of yours. Something to think about while we go."

Bracing his right hand with his left wrist, Jak pointed the .357 at the hole, through which furtive scuttling could be heard. When Ryan and Krysty had covered their ears, he squeezed the trigger twice, the Magnum weapon's barrel exploding with flame in the narrow passageway as the heavy pistol bucked in his hands. As the concussions died away, they heard an agonized howl that was suddenly cut off by a meaty thud.

"One less to worry about. C'mon!" Ryan waved Krysty down the narrow corridor, then Jak, taking the rear himself. He waited until a clawed foot cautiously appeared at the top of the ladder, took aim, and squeezed off a shot, hitting it near the ankle, and causing the maimed limb to vanish out of sight. With a last glance at the thick metal door, Ryan ducked into the hall, hurrying to catch up with the bobbing light ahead.

This tunnel was cramped and musty, with the dust on the floor blending with the water vapor to form a thin, slippery layer on the tiles. Ryan kept one hand on the wall as he trotted down the corridor. He caught up with Krysty and Jak just as they rounded a corner and stopped only a couple steps beyond, nearly causing him to bump into them in his haste.

"What the hell—"

"Shh!" Krysty's urgent whisper cut him off. When Ryan craned his head over hers to see what was making them so quiet, he suddenly understood.

Ahead was a large chamber that might have been a power generating room at one time, but was now a huge indoor lake. Water had submerged the entire floor, the grated stairs in front of them disappearing under the waterline. The opposite wall of the room was at least thirty yards away. The odor, redolent of fuel, lubricant and mold, was so strong it made Ryan breathe through his mouth. The shells of half-submerged machines, perhaps generators of some kind, rose out of the water in rows, covered in dark orange rust and slime. Around them, the water flowed strangely, forming strange eddies and whirlpools on its oil-slicked surface, as if something underneath was lazily moving around the perimeter. The entire room was ringed by a metal walkway with a railing on one side. It reached almost to the other side, but had been broken off near an identical doorway on the far wall several feet above the water, leaving a gap between them and the exit.

"Head out there?" Krysty asked, wrinkling her nose at the stink.

Ryan ducked back and played his light along the walls, searching for any kind of alternate way out. "Looks like. At least there's no one here." He glanced around the room, sensing something that made the hair on the back of his neck stand up. "No blasting, however." He'd caught the acrid stink of fuel fumes. Hearing a far-off thump shake the floor under his feet, the decision was made. "Get out there."

Jak had already edged out onto the catwalk, testing

it with tentative steps. The struts underneath trembled a bit, but held firm. "Looks all right."

"Head out a few more yards first." A splash from below caught Ryan's attention, and he shone his light at where the sound had come from, but saw nothing except an eddy of black water. He turned back to Krysty. "Give him a few more steps, then you go. I'll follow in a bit."

"No more heroics, lover." She leaned up and kissed him hard. "Already saved your hide once today, and I don't want to have to come back for you again."

"Hey, who saved who in here?"

"I'd already freed myself and killed the lizardmen, remember? You were a few seconds late. Now hurry up— I've had enough of this hellhole to last a lifetime."

"You and me both. Go! I'll be right behind you."

Krysty stepped onto the walkway, which settled a bit more under her weight. Sticking close to the wall, she began her trek around the room. Jak had already rounded the far corner and was heading toward the door, picking up speed to leap the gap between him and freedom.

Ryan checked the hallway behind them one more time, hearing the slap of many bare feet against the metal floor. Glancing over his shoulder, he saw Krysty carefully easing around the near corner. Across the room, Jak was framed in the doorway, waving them on.

Drawing his panga, Ryan set his flashlight on the floor and crept noiselessly back to the corner where the hallway turned and waited, blade poised to slash. The point of a spear suddenly thrust around the corner, the tip missing Ryan's waist by a fingerwidth. Grabbing the weapon behind the head, he yanked it forward, pulling a startled lizardman around the corner. The mutie looked up just in time to see the eighteen-inch blade slice down at its head. Ryan buried the edge a good inch into its skull, parting the skin and spraying black blood into the air. Wrenching his knife free, he shoved the dying creature back into his fellows and ran for the large room, snatching his light off the floor at the entrance as he passed. Rounding the corner, he hit the catwalk and slowed to a cautious walk, feeling the grated surface flex and shift with each step. Krysty was almost at the doorway now, tensing to make the leap across.

He had just turned the first corner when a chorus of furious howls erupted from the passage behind him, and Ryan looked back to see a cluster of raging lizard-men erupt from the dark passageway and stream across the walkway on both sides of the room. Others stayed near the entrance, but lobbed harpoons at him—a few coming too close for comfort.

Ryan took off just ahead of the advancing horde, pounding down the catwalk with huge jumps, feeling it creak and strain with each step. It only had to stay up for a few more seconds, he thought.

He was about halfway across when he heard an ominous snap, and felt the section of walkway he was on tilt dangerously toward the water. Only a leap away from the next part, Ryan crouched to spring forward just as the first of the oncoming lizardmen hit his section of walkway. Its added weight was the last straw, and with a shriek of overstressed metal, the path gave way, pitching both Ryan and the mutie into the dank waters below.

Chapter Thirty-Seven

Falling headfirst, Ryan plunged through the thick, top layer of sludge into the dark water below. The cold hit his ribs like a punch, taking his breath away and leaving him spluttering and gasping as he fought his way to the surface.

He had just gotten there when a clawed hand clamped onto the top of his skull and pushed him back down right as he drew a breath. Ryan went under again, and in the light, through the clouds of bubbles caused by his thrashing, he saw something that made his blood run even colder.

Several of the giant muskies swam around the protected pool, doing lazy figure eights among the useless hulks of the giant power generators. But what startled him even more was the long, tubelike appendages, half as thick as his waist, attached to the sides of several. At first, he thought they might be some sort of vestigial appendages, but as one fish swam past, he saw a large eye regard him coldly, and he realized what they were.

Lampreys! He knew about the cold-blooded parasites. Once, during his travels with Trader, Ryan had seen a large school of them attacking a huge whale in the water, sucking the blood and life out of the huge animal until it beached itself to slowly die, at which point the lampreys, each as thick around as he was, dropped off and squirmed back into the water. Curious, Ryan had gone down on the beach and taken a closer look at the carcass, seeing the holes bored into its hide, some as large as his head. He had never forgotten how those small animals had brought down something much larger, just by clamping on and sucking it dry.

In his crazily bobbing light, he saw several of the un-attached bloodsuckers weaving through the water toward him and his attacker. Grabbing the lizardman's hand, Ryan wrenched it off his head and bent the limb back, forcing it around the mutie's back and up between its shoulder blades into a hammerlock. He forced the creature to turn just as the first lamprey reached them.

Ryan saw its circular mouth, filled with rows of sharp teeth, along with the rasping tongue that flicked back and forth, as if tasting the water. He shoved the lizardman into its path, and the lamprey struck at the movement, its mouth attaching to the mutie's chest, causing him to gurgle in pain. Unlike the lampreys in the ocean, this one whipped its body around its victim, nearly catching Ryan in a thick coil. The lizardman tried to pry off the greedily sucking head, but he was already weakening from the sudden loss of blood. When another one swam up and fastened high on his inner thigh, the mutie's eyes rolled back in its head, and its blows grew weaker as it beat listlessly against the large parasites.

Pushing his bait away, Ryan clawed his way to the surface, feeling something brush by him, but unsure whether it was a muskie or a lamprey. Not sticking around to find out, he swam toward the nearest generator casing, spotting a row of thick bolts he hoped to use to climb onto the rounded, slick metal.

Once there, he grabbed the nearest one, uncaring of the cuts it inflicted on his already battered hands, and hauled himself up, scrabbling for every inch of progress.

He managed to get his boots onto one of them, only to
have the bolt snap off under the pressure, nearly sending
him back into the pool. Glancing down, he saw one of
the lampreys approaching, saw its open, pulsing mouth,
as big around as his clenched fist, saw it gather itself
and rear up out of the water at him, those teeth ready to
slice through his pants and fasten onto his thigh, where
that saber-sawed tongue would go to work rasping away
the skin and flesh to suck his blood out....

"Fuck you!" Ryan lashed out with his foot, the combat
boot catching the lamprey in the head and sending it
splashing back into the filthy water. He reached up and
hooked his fingers onto the row of bolts at the top of
the housing, pulling himself up with one final heave.

The last of the sludgy water dripped from his ears,
and he heard the hoots and screams of the lizardmen on
the railings as they saw him emerge. Amid the chaos,
he thought he heard Krysty or Jak yell something, but
he couldn't be sure. One or two spears whizzed by, but
the furious muties hadn't taken the time to aim properly,
the missiles clattering on the tank or splashing into the
water. However, they'd figure out how to get at him
soon enough, whether by taking their chances through
the lamprey-infested waters, or possibly leaping at him
from the catwalks.

As if reading his mind, one of the lizardmen jumped
up to the top of the railing and pushed off, soaring out
into the air toward him. Ryan tensed for a moment until
he realized the mutie was going to fall several feet short.
The lizardman arced into the water with hardly a splash.
Ryan peeked over the side to see where he had gone, and
nearly got his face bitten off when the humanoid burst
out of the water in front of him a moment later, leaping

into the air to land on the edge of the large cylinder in a graceful crouch.

Rearing back, Ryan stumbled, slipping on the curved surface and falling hard on his rear. He started to slide off one side, and only a desperate lunge for the far row of bolts prevented him from taking another dip in the lake. The lizardman stood and stepped forward on sure feet, unbothered by the slick surface. Ryan rose as well, one hand going to his panga to finish his adversary off with a couple of well-placed chops. To his right, he saw Krysty taking aim with her Smith & Wesson, and shouted, "No blasters!" Ignoring her puzzled frown, he tugged the blade free of its scabbard. Or tried to. Looking down, he saw the panga blade stuck halfway out of the wet sheath. "Shit!" Before he could yank it out, the lizardman was on him.

It barreled into his body, muscular arms wrapping around him and lifting him off the housing in a spine-cracking bear hug. Ryan matched its peculiar, hissing roar with a loud one of his own as he raised his arms and brought his cupped hands down on the mutie's ear holes. It staggered, but didn't release him, so he did it again. This time his attacker dropped him, but immediately launched itself at him again, intent on tackling him and driving him into the metal housing. Ryan tried to keep his balance, but slipped again on the wet metal and fell, the impact jarring his spine and making his teeth click together.

The lizardman came at him again, clawed hands seeking his face. Ryan blocked one questing arm with his own, levering it away from his eye. With his left hand, he grabbed the mutie's other wrist and pushed it to the side. The lizardman thrust its face forward, trying to sink its teeth into Ryan's nose. He avoided the snapping fangs by turning his face to one side, then brought his own head up, cracking the lizardman in the jaw with his forehead. The blow caught it by surprise, and Ryan did it again, this time catching his opponent in its vestigial nose, and making it rear up, bellowing with pain and anger.

Ryan followed up his advantage by twisting his hips to one side, half throwing the mutie off. It tried to recover, but he was faster, clubbing it in the side of the head with his fist, and knocking it over. Scrambling out from under it, he jumped to his feet and tried to draw the panga again, which refused to budge from its scabbard.

Seeing the mutie about to get to its feet, Ryan stepped forward and kicked its foot out with all his remaining strength. It crashed down, and he drew back his foot and lashed out again, catching it where the temple would have been on a human. The steel-capped combat boot impacted the creature's skull with the force of a brick dropped on an egg, shattering the temporal bone and sending fragments into the brain. The lizardman fell over, twitching, its eyes rolling back in its head.

Ryan took a deep breath, wincing as the movement caused a flare of pain in his aching ribs. Looking up from the dead body, his eye widened as he saw two more of the ugly muties climb onto the tank and start toward him. Ryan looked toward the doorway, and the generator he would have to swim to in order to get to it. A quick glance around confirmed his increasing peril, with more lizardmen crowding onto the catwalks, and several jumping into the water, heedless of the lampreys and muskies in their single-minded determination to get at him. The occasional spear or harpoon still whizzed by, but they were more cautious about hitting their brethren, so the throws weren't as furious as they'd been earlier. Still, in the few seconds he stood there, four harpoons sailed through the air at him, one close enough to graze the back of his leg before skittering off into the water.

Gripping the bottom of his scabbard with one hand, Ryan wrenched at his panga one last time, twisting it as he did so. This time the eighteen inches of honed steel slid free as if it had been greased, and he smiled.

Whirling, he drove the blade into the shoulder of the lizardman that had been trying to sneak up on him from the side of the generator. The mutie howled in agony, and Ryan planted a foot in its face and shoved it off the side, following it down into the water and driving the injured creature under the surface with a huge splash as he stepped on it, using its body as a crude launching platform to get a another foot of distance toward the last generator.

The second he hit the water, Ryan clamped his knife in his teeth and swam as hard as he could. The injured lizardman tried to grab him, but it was attacked by a pair of lampreys and was too busy fighting for its own life. He heard more splashing around him as other muties hit the water, but he was almost to the housing. Reaching it with one last lunge, he climbed up. Three-quarters out of the water, he felt claws on his leg, and, holding on to a bolt with one hand, he took the panga out of his mouth and swept it down and behind him, feeling the familiar shock up his arm as the blade bit into muscle and bone. The grip weakened, and he wriggled out of it as he pulled himself onto the metal.

"Ryan!" He lifted his head to see Krysty in the doorway, only a few yards away, but it might as well have been a mile. Lizardmen were clustered on either side of the doorway, one making a leap for the opening, only to be repelled by Krysty with a front kick to the face, sending it splashing into the water below. On the other side, they gained a bit of a respite when the entire section pulled away from the wall and hit the water, spilling the scaly berserkers off in every direction. "We have to shoot them!"

"No! Don't! You'll kill us all!" Seeing the empty, twisted catwalk lying in the water, but also still connected to the next section gave Ryan an idea. He leaped forward, sailing through the air and landing on the shoulders of one of the lizardmen in the water, snapping his collarbone and sending him down into the murky depths. Falling forward, Ryan reached out and managed to snag the railing of the walkway, hauling himself up onto it before any of the nearby muties could grab him. He climbed up the slanted metal grating, using his free hand to hold on to the railing like a ladder, and keeping his panga ready in case any of the lizardmen tried to be a hero.

Halfway up, he was as close to the doorway as he was going to get, which meant he was still several feet away. Then Jak reappeared next to Krysty, carrying a length of chain. "Catch!"

The albino teen tossed the links at him, and Ryan had just enough time to sheath his panga before catching the chain. He wrapped the steel around his left hand and shouted. "Pull!"

Krysty and Jak both disappeared from sight, and Ryan practically flew through the air toward the doorway. As he rose, he caught sight of a blurred shape flying through the air at him, arms outstretched to tear his face off.

Ryan brought his right hand up and slammed the butt of his blaster into the mutie's skull as it crashed into him, grabbing him in spite of the damage it had just taken. He hammered the blaster into its head three more times, until its grip weakened, and it fell into the lake. Ryan spun wildly in midair, then he was at the lip of the doorway, hitting it with his aching ribs and sending new needles of pain through his chest. Still gripping the SIG-Sauer, he hauled himself through as more spears clattered against the wall around him.

Scrambling into the dark hall, he was met by Krysty and Jak, but shrugged them off. "Get back!" he shouted as a dark shape appeared in the doorway. The lizardman licked its lipless mouth as it stepped forward, ready to lay into the invaders.

Ryan pointed his blaster at the scaly form and squeezed the trigger three times. The trio of bullets plowed through the mutie's chest, not stopping it, but mortally wounding it enough so it wouldn't be a threat to him. The dying lizardman fell to its knees, a frown crossing its face as it heard a strange roar around it.

Ryan scrambled back from the bloom of red-gold flame that had appeared around his hand and wrist as the fire from the muzzle of his blaster ignited the thick fumes in the corridor and spread back to the huge room behind the wounded lizardman, wreathing it in flames. Spotting a doorway a few feet away, he lunged for it, getting inside as the whoosh increased to a deafening roar. Scrabbling for the door, he pushed it shut just as a blinding inferno erupted in the hallway, the corridor channeling the blast up and down its entire length, and sending little tongues of fire spurting under the doorway. Ryan, Krysty and Jak scurried to the corner farthest away from the door, crouched on the floor and breathed long and shallowly, trying to draw what little oxygen remained out of the atmosphere. They couldn't hear anything beside the sudden roar of the flame, but they didn't need to hear anything to know what was happening to the group of lizardmen in the giant room.

"Fireblast, Krysty, what're you doing?" Ryan wheezed as Krysty starting patting at his chest and shoulders.

"Hold still, you stupe! You're on fire!" Krysty smothered the flames licking at his sleeve and leg, then checked the rest of him for any injuries.

Exhausted, all Ryan could do was slump back again the wall, panting and holding his side with each breath. "*That* is why I told you not to shoot in the big room."

Chapter Thirty-Eight

Ryan stood near the bowsprit of the *Lament*, one hand on the foremast, the other around Krysty, who stood close to him, keeping her footing with ease as the barge cut through the glass-smooth lake.

The storm system that had lashed the area for the past two days had finally moved on, and the sky was its usual mix of lemon yellow clouds and lavender again, with a hot golden sun beating down on them. The east wind was brisk, however, and dissipated most of the rising morning heat.

The rest of their group was scattered around the small ship, J.B. and Mildred lounged on one side of the cabin, hand-in-hand as they moved with the ebb and flow of the boat. Behind them, Jak stood on the cabin roof, shading his eyes as he scanned the horizon, unaffected by his brush with death just a few days earlier. Doc stood near the wheel, observing the first mate at the wheel, and for once not his usual garrulous self. Although the weather couldn't have been better, none of them felt like talking much.

Escaping the nuclear power plant had been easy after their close call in the generator room. Once the fire had died down in the hallway, Ryan, Krysty and Jak had gone down it and found a half-submerged room with a window that looked out onto a narrow strip of beach. They'd smashed the glass and jumped out. Spotting a light on the lake, they'd signaled it with their last hand light, and saw the welcome sight of the LAV-150 rumbling out of the water, smoke drifting from every gun on it, and the top and sides slick with gore.

J.B. had summarized the effects of the diversion with his usual terseness. "Got into position, started the cannon up, and they boiled out like we'd poked an ant-hill with a stick. Bastards were all over us. I rotated the turret once, firing the whole time, blew a dozen of them clean off the top. They tried stabbing through the ob ports, but a couple of shots put an end to that. Eventually we killed them all, and were about to head back to the waypoint when Mildred spotted your light."

Ryan had filled them in on what had happened inside, including Donfil More's sacrifice. He didn't say what he was thinking—that the Apache's selflessness may have been unnecessary, given how many of the lizardmen they'd chilled in the fire. Still, it might have made all the difference, since there'd been more muties in the building than just the ones they had killed.

They'd immediately headed back to the ville. The LAV had quit on them about halfway there, pushed beyond even its remarkable limits over the past few days. They'd spent the next day and a half walking, reaching the ville at midafternoon of the second day they'd been gone.

The villagers had assumed they'd been killed, and their survival was met with a mix of shock, disbelief and even a bit of suspicion. Ryan had bulled his way into the elders' room and told them what went down, which was confirmed by the sixth elder. There was a period of mourning for Donfil by the entire ville, with a strange service held on the dock to commemorate his bravery and courage the next day.

So it was quite a shock when one of the fishing boats pulled into port with a smiling Donfil More standing in the prow.

He had completed his task in the old plant and exited the room via an escape hatch that had dumped him into the lake. It had taken his hastily constructed raft— two trees lashed tighter with some vines—two days to come within range of the fishing boats, and rescue. Mildred had examined Donfil and announced that he had gotten a dose of radiation, but he wasn't in any serious danger.

After much rejoicing and words of gratitude, the companions retreated to their billet to recuperate. Donfil retreated to his.

Two days later, Donfil and the companions stood on the dock. "Farewell, friend. May the Great Spirit keep you safe and have your back," Ryan said.

"Farewell, dear friend. Our debt to you can never be repaid."

With a final wave, the companions boarded the *Lament*.

Saire had also promised to drop them off near the blackened, blasted ruins of what had once been the city of Chicago, although he couldn't figure out why they'd want to be in such a hell-blasted place. "Shoot, I'll take you anywhere on the Lakes you might want to go—the forest of Michgan, or up north to Canada, if you like, just say the word."

But Ryan and his group had been implacable, so six hours later, the *Lament* dropped them off in a small cove that J.B. said would be the best place to go ashore. The captain accompanied them personally in the dinghy, riding with the second group, consisting of Ryan, Krysty and Doc.

Just before they splashed ashore, he'd taken Ryan's hand in a firm grasp. "Just remember, if you're ever in the area again, come by and see us. Be glad to have any of you on board my boat again." They'd waded ashore, and Saire's men had pushed off again, rowing back to the barge. The sails had risen, and soon the trim craft was heading back up the lake.

Ryan and company watched until the fishermen were just a speck on the horizon before turning to head inland. J.B. estimated they could make the concealed redoubt before nightfall, and set a hard but not grueling pace. The baked plain stretched out all around them, with only a scattered ruin of an unidentifiable structure breaking up the landscape.

True to the Armorer's word, they reached the hidden door as the sun was starting to slip below the horizon. Ryan entered the standard code and the door ground ponderously open.

Doc's face was expectant as the door opened, and Ryan caught it falling as the barren corridor was revealed. "There was nothing in here the last time we came by, what made you think anything might have changed?"

The old man turned sad eyes on him. "Oh, Ryan, you have no idea what hopes I have every time we come to one of these doors, that each one might hold the secrets of, if not escaping this hellish world, then of somehow making it better for those who are forced to dwell in it every day of their nasty, brutish and short lives."

Ryan stared at him, unsure as to whether he was serious, or slipping into one of his spells again. "Well, maybe the next place'll have just that. Come on, Doc, it's time to go."

They threaded their way through the labyrinth of corridors until they reached the familiar mat-trans room. Ryan waited until everyone was comfortable on the floor before closing the door and sitting down as he waited for the comps to cycle a jump that would spirit them to who knew where.

* * * * *